Rock N Roll is Dead

Edited by Marc Ciccarone

Rock N Roll is Dead

ISBN: 978-0984540846

Cover artwork by Andrej Bartulovic

Printed in the United States of America

Table of Contents

End of the Line

G. Winston Hyatt

Inspired by Dio's *The Last in Line*

We set fires and took beatings. Our T-shirts were black, our cigarette packs red. We sprayed pentagrams in abandoned halls, we broke bottles in parking lots, we looked at the world through blood webbed eyes, we wanted to die because we did not know how to live. We kicked around in dirty hi-tops and combat boots. We were loudmouth rednecks, suburban assholes, druggie sluts, back-stabbing thugs. We were quiet girls with blasting headphones; we were gentle boys longing for war. We wore leather jackets and trench coats, we got blamed for things we did not do, we got away with things we regretted. We huffed glue. We totaled cars. We spilled paint. We drew skulls in textbooks. We fingered in coat closets and gave head in graveyards. We promised to pull out. We said we were older. We lied. We built pipe-bombs and shot squirrels. We were easy targets. We didn't give a shit. We took it seriously.

We fell in love again and again. We burned bridges, we smashed windows. We hung up when they answered. We didn't trust anyone. We liked to piss them off. We always made something happen. We were handcuffed and bloody. We were always waiting—for a ride, the bell, our bail, for the insurance to run out, for a reason. We had sore necks and ringing ears. We learned our modes and scales. We puked on the floor, our friends' shoes, in our laps, in our hands. We passed out on the steps. We didn't apologize. We cursed God, family, one another, but mostly ourselves. We had it all figured out. We didn't know any better. We did not ask to be understood. We wanted to be left alone. We needed an audience. We were selfish, we gave too much away.

We dreamed. We had nightmares too strange to explain. We filled our heads with the horrors of our choosing. We rejoiced. We had electric minds; we hunted dragons and wandered forests. We never knew when to run. We took the wrong path. We got lost, got home late. Some of us never came home again.

Our tattoos faded. Our records were permanent. Our bands broke up.

Our heroes died. We cut our hair, we kept our distance, we learned from our mistakes. We woke up on time; we paid our bills. We finished things. We owned things. We took spouses, we became parents. We weren't left to ourselves.

We don't sleep well. We want to close the bar, to throw a punch, to fuck a stranger, to push it too far, to wake up hurting, shamed, and forced to confront the latest way we're ruining our lives. We worry we will actually do it. We worry we never will again. We know what's out there, we toss and turn, we pace the room, the street, our conscience, we wonder. We look at the ones we love. We hope they'll have an easier time of it, but we know they won't. We lost teeth, hair, friends, chances. We are lucky to be alive. We are needed. We are thankful. We are still afraid.

We'll always have the music.

Faking It

KV Taylor

Inspired by The Beach Boys' *Caroline, No*

Elsie never knew getting fired could be so lovely. She hated the surreal, fluorescent-lit cube farm, hated the glare of the computer screen, hated the papery, insincere voices of her co-workers. Not only had the pink slip been her ticket out of that cardboard country, but it had come with a consolation prize: six weeks' severance. It wasn't bad, and maybe she could get her old job back at the bookstore.

Her happiness would've been overwhelming, if she hadn't dreaded disappointing Gwen. And Gwen was *very* disappointed—sitting at the kitchen table still in her high heels, long legs crossed at the knee, that look of disgust creeping across her face, inch by agonizing inch. She was so frighteningly pretty; pretty like a mean girl in high school. Otherworldly, icy eyes looking down her nose, all golden and shiny, a demanding fairy princess in a drab world. It still made Elsie's insides warm just to look at her. She could hardly believe Gwen was hers, most of the time.

"Why?" was all Gwen said.

"Cutbacks. They said they'd give me a good reference, and I have the six weeks—"

Gwen sniffed. "Well, I guess we won't be getting that new flooring in the dining room any time soon."

Elsie's knees went weak.

She must've seen, because Gwen's expression softened.

"Forget it. I'm just stressed. Tax season. Shit's gone wild at the office."

Elsie nodded. No point waiting around for a little solace, so she left Gwen with her TV dinner and poured herself a drink from the wet bar in the living room. Scotch made the stomach aches a little less intense.

She busied herself like she had done in that soul-sucking office for the last few years, keeping company with the people in her head. Not real people; she wasn't crazy or anything, just characters in stories she made up to take her out of that place.

Her favorite was Marianne, the wanna-be rock star, because she was mean and honest about everything. Just like Elsie couldn't be. Maybe they could make fun of the prime-time lineup until Gwen forgave her enough to come around.

***

After a few months, Gwen began to suspect Elsie was faking it.

She was also beginning to suspect there was something about her that attracted irresponsible women. Was it too much to ask that Elsie look for a job that didn't involve a cash register? And God, the woman she'd left for her had been even worse, with her weird, black magic pseudo-voodoo crap, burning twenty-dollar black candles every night and working in a dive bar to forward her delusions of stardom. Sweet little Elsie looked like a step up, but apparently sweetness came with a hell of a price tag.

Gwen rolled these things over in her mind all day until she came home and looked at Elsie, saw how pale she'd grown, saw her curled up in a ball with those mysterious stomach pains, and melted a little. Sometimes it made her eyes burn, which was goddamn infuriating. Crying left her with a headache and puffy eyes.

She couldn't be faking it, Gwen would think then. She does look sick. She's too angelic to fake it.

Then she'd see the half-empty bottle of Scotch, or catch Elsie talking to herself, and change her mind again.

Gwen sat down on the far end of the couch. "You look for a job today?"

Elsie shook her head, and her brilliant red hair flashed in the fading evening sunlight through the windows. Gwen had a nearly uncontrollable urge to move closer and touch it, feel it running between her fingers. It was shining and soft and always smelled like white flowers.

"I'm not feeling so good," Elsie said. "My stomach hurts."

"I doubt the Scotch helps, honey."

"Dulls the pain. Anyhow, I can't go to the doctor."

A tirade against the government-sanctioned discrimination of the insurance industry built up, until Gwen felt like her head was full of a high-pressure storm front. "Well, you could if you got a job. We wouldn't have to worry."

Elsie looked at her through her bangs. She was silent for a minute, then said, "I know."

Gwen took a deep breath. "I'm not trying to be mean."

Elsie nodded.

"I love you. I want you to get better. You don't know how hard it is for me when you're like this."

Elsie's eyes widened, eyebrows crawling slowly upward. Gwen took this as a hopeful sign.

"We haven't gone out to dinner or had a conversation or made love in weeks," Gwen said, surprising herself. Jesus, was she...lonely? "I miss you."

"I'm sorry. Do you want to—" Elsie hesitated, then whispered, "go upstairs?"

Gwen let her eyes drop. Elsie was thinner than she used to be, but she'd always been a little flat-chested and leggy. She still had those long, elegant lines to her, if only just barely. And she had such a pretty smile when she bothered anymore.

A warm feeling spread out from her middle, that same melting one she got seeing Elsie curled up, looking quiet and innocent.

Okay, not exactly the same. But close enough.

***

Elsie talked to Marianne in her head the whole time they were in bed. It wasn't that she wasn't interested—she was, she loved Gwen, she loved her so much that all she wanted was to make her happy. But her insides hurt, and it wasn't just her stomach anymore. It had spread to her chest, and sometimes when she least expected it she'd get a sensation like something was twitching in there. Not her heart or anything, but like her chest muscles were having spasms, then curling into tiny protective knots inside her. And her stomach wasn't any better.

It didn't interfere too much when she was working on Gwen, but it was too hard to concentrate on getting off herself when she felt like that. So, she moved her hips a little and made a small sound now and then—she'd never been very loud, anyhow—and listened to Marianne make fun in her head.

Marianne never would've put up with this kind of bullshit. What a fucking joke (*haha, literally! "Fucking," get it?*), laying there in the bed pretending Gwen's tongue still did it for her. If it were up to her, she'd tell her to get stuffed and make her beg for it next time.

For fun?

Oh yeah, of course. That's fun, bringing Princess Pretend to her knees. No harm in it, just for kicks.

Elsie thought that was funny—maybe not in real life, but in her head, anyhow.

And when it was time, she pretended to come. Marianne thought she was bad at it, but that just made Elsie want to laugh out loud.

If Gwen noticed that the wetness between Elsie's legs was nothing but her own spit, she never said a word. She just curled up, smiled, talked about nothing for fifteen minutes, then got up to take a shower.

Take, take, take, thought Marianne, with a little snort. *She doesn't care what you want, she just gives you what she wants. A queen to your peasant.*

Elsie rolled over and tried to go to sleep, letting Marianne talk the pain in her stomach away.

***

Marianne thought this whole set-up was bullshit—but Marianne thought everything was bullshit. She wanted to swear at the urgent care doctor and call him a lying douchebag right to his face. Elsie agreed. She agreed with Marianne more and more instead of just finding her funny, even though she knew she shouldn't. This time, though, she felt justified.

"I can't find anything wrong with you, not in all the tests we sent out," the doctor repeated.

Awesome, Marianne thought. *We're paying for this? Dickweed.*

Elsie shook her head. "But it hurts." It wasn't just her stomach or the twitching in her chest for the last few months—that was why Gwen had finally screamed at her to just go. It was in her arms and legs now too and just starting to creep into her hands and feet. Like her whole body was being taken over by the sickness, and the sickness was some kind of creeping oily ooze that froze up the minute it seeped into the spot it wanted. It made her weak and stiff, and the more it hurt, the less she could fight it.

She let Marianne make the decisions for her most of the time. That seemed a lot easier.

"Have you considered," he trailed off there, chewed at his lower lip as if he was going to say something painful. Then, "Psychiatric evaluation?"

"I don't have insurance." She said it flatly, because she didn't know how else to say it. It wasn't as if her brain could hurt her stomach, chest, and various extremities. There was something in her, and it was his job to wave his magical doctor wand and get it out. "I came here so you could fix it."

He looked down, started scribbling on his pad. "I'll write you a scrip for some more powerful H2 blockers, but I'd like to speak with your husband—"

"Partner."

He looked up again. "Oh."

Not wife. Which was bullshit, too, by the way.

Heh. Sometimes she wasn't sure if it was Marianne or not anymore when she got really carried away like that. But it passed the time and kept her from being angry. She didn't think her body could handle angry anymore, so it was good to let Marianne get it out for her.

"I'll talk to her," she said.

"Whatever you like," he agreed in one of those voices that suggested he'd agree to anything if it got her out of his office. Papery and insincere, like the voices around the water cooler a long time ago in a far away land.

In the car on the way home, she had to pull over. She curled up in a tight ball with her head in the passenger seat and cried, her stomach and chest spasming so badly she couldn't breathe.

She wished she could just die here, locked inside her hot car like a forgotten animal, but Marianne laughed and told her that would be weak. What she needed to do was go tell Gwen that doctor was full of shit, and Miss Fairy Princess could stick her attitude straight up her ass. And while she was at it, she could pay the mortgage on that ugly-ass castle of hers on her own, if it was so much more important than The Love of Her Life's health.

Elsie listened to her talk and nodded in helpless agreement until the pain subsided. And then she went home.

***

Gwen stared at the light blinking on the phone, knowing what it meant. A new trickle of messages from various creditors, with their "I-pay-my-bills" smugness. And then she looked to Elsie and her shining hair, like living flame in the glare of the Tiffany glass chandelier, telling her what she'd known all along.

"I knew you were faking it."

"No. There's something wrong, I swear—"

"I'm working overtime and you're sitting on the couch sucking on that bottle all day. Talking to yourself and hoping if you fuck me once a month, I'll just let you live this way forever. You're out of your mind."

Elsie's mouth fell open. "How can you—"

"We just paid for that doctor on our last inch of credit, which is about to go extinct because of you, and he said you're fine. How the hell do you think that makes me feel? Almost six months of having to live with you being sick and it was all a lie?"

Elsie shook her head, eyes growing wider. Her lips started moving, but silently.

Gwen wouldn't have stopped if she'd started screaming back anyhow. She was so beyond over this shit—it felt too good to finally let it go. "So, you stopped eating to make it look real, but now I don't even want to fuck you anymore. You look like a goddamn zombie, all sunken in like that." She wrinkled up her nose and looked down it at the same time. "If it wasn't for your hair, I wouldn't even believe you were the same woman."

Okay. Maybe a little over the top, but Gwen felt a backdraft of righteous fury; she was right and she knew it. Jesus, it almost made her dizzy it felt so good.

Elsie continued to stare, and Gwen continued to fume. Until Elsie finally said, "Just my hair, huh?"

God, was she finally getting it?

"Well, I'll have to fix that, you selfish little bitch." Gwen's breath caught in her chest. *You selfish little bitch?* Elsie never used that word, but it sounded familiar, somehow. "What did you just say?"

Elsie's eyes had come to life though, no longer the dead, dark holes in her wasted face. They blazed behind a fringe of displaced bangs.

"You called *me* selfish?" Gwen tried again.

Elsie turned around and stalked out of the room.

Gwen watched her go, her heart thudding in her throat with sickening quickness. And she didn't know why, exactly. She just felt very, very—

Wrong.

And then she turned around, grabbed her Coach bag from the table, and went out the kitchen door. Careful to slam it behind her so Elsie, who had obviously lost her fucking mind, would be sure to hear.

***

Marianne had a laugh that was more of a cackle. She was so amused that Elsie had said exactly what she'd been thinking to that bitchfest of a girlfriend that she hadn't stopped laughing since.

Elsie laughed too, but she wasn't sure why. The pain was all the way in her fingers and toes and up into the crown of her head and matching up her feelings with Marianne's was the only thing that made it hurt a little less.

She snipped off the last lock and ran aching hands through her hair.

She wished she had some black dye. But she didn't, so the cropped and chunky look would have to do it.

Yeah, that'll show her. Hey, you should do it up some more—jump out a window and break your leg or something. We'll give her something wrong with you.

Not one of Marianne's best ideas. Elsie shook her head at herself in the mirror, then winced when it made a sharp pain flare in her head.

Bet you'll forget all about the headache if you break your leg! Ha!

Sounded like the kind of joke her dad used to crack. Silly dad humor.

Oh, don't be a fucking wet blanket. Come on, this is your Declaration of Independence. It's gotta be a show. Star quality performance.

Elsie laughed and mussed up her hair again. It felt so nice, like she could breathe without all that heaviness holding her down. *Or you got a rope around here? What if she found you hanging from the ceiling, huh? That'd fuck her up.*

Elsie laughed again.

But then stopped.

No. She didn't think that would fuck Gwen up. Not one little bit.

She didn't think anything she could do now would fuck Gwen up. Not more than cutting her hair off, anyhow.

***

Dead silence in the house, and Gwen's buzz was wearing off, so it made her skin crawl. She probably shouldn't have gone to a bar on a weeknight, but it was Elsie's fault for being a goddamn liar. She tripped through the kitchen and living room, then up the stairs. No lights, which meant Elsie was in bed. But when she swung around the corner into their bedroom—

No Elsie.

Maybe the lying brat was going to sleep in a spare room from now on. Perfect. As soon as Gwen could get rid of her, she would. What the hell was she, anyhow, a bank? A soup kitchen? A home for the unemployed and useless?

She'd thought these things roughly ten thousand times as she'd chugged through five or six martinis. But they still felt great rolling around in her brain.

And Jesus, she had to piss.

She stepped into the bathroom and noticed one little black votive burning on the sink—fucking things always made her think of black magic ex. Normally that was irritating, but just now it was almost comforting.

The faint light reflected in the mirror but still didn't reach the darkest corners; it was almost dead, down to the very end of its wick. Great; not only was she useless, but now Elsie was willfully endangering their home. The home they were probably going to lose if—

When she turned, her train of thought slammed into an immovable wall.

Because there, in the flickering light of one candle in the mirror, was a tub full of dark water. Far, far too dark water.

And an ivory-pale Elsie, skeletal and naked and nearly bald. Half sitting, half floating. Eyes almost closed, but not quite. The blackish (*reddish? Oh God, reddish*) water reflected her ghastly face with a kind of quivering mockery.

Her lips moved just slightly.

Gwen screamed at the top of her lungs.

***

The sun beat down on her manicured blonde hair, and Gwen flipped a few curls over her shoulder. That was the last hospital visit she'd be making. Elsie was her parents' problem now.

Gwen probably hadn't done her a favor by calling 911 just in time. Poor, poor Elsie; those slashes on her arms would tell everyone she met what she'd tried to do to herself. Not to mention what she'd done to—

"Gwen."

She looked up when she heard her name. A punk-ass looking woman leaned against a red-brick storefront, smiling around a fat cigarette. Wild dark hair and a glint in her eye, dressed all in ratty black attire and heavy metal accessories, as usual.

Black magic ex. Gwen smirked. "Long time, honey."

"Heard about your girlfriend. That sucks. Total bullshit." The sad face wasn't even that hard to manufacture. "It was hard to watch it happen," Gwen said. Not that it had ever mattered to Elsie, what it was doing to her. "But there was nothing anyone could do. God knows I tried."

But when she'd looked at Elsie in that hospital bed, her hair all hacked and her face wasted away, that old warm feeling hadn't come to her. That wasn't her Elsie.

Poor, poor Elsie; but what about poor, poor Gwen?

"So let me guess," Marianne said. "You're not even sad?"

"Of course, I am." Sad wasn't the word exactly, but it was close enough.

Marianne smiled again, that wicked smile that had attracted Gwen in the first place. She said, "Guess I need to be more direct next time."

Gwen raised her eyebrows. "You think you'll get another chance with me just because my last girlfriend went insane?"

Marianne took a long drag on her cigarette (one would think a singer, even one in a crap band like Marianne's, would try and take care of her voice), then said, "Gwen, you probably drove her insane by being a selfish little bitch. Just like you did to me."

Gwen rolled her eyes. Marianne wasn't worth arguing with, though. Hot as hell with that attitude, but not hot enough to be that full of herself.

Marianne blew her smoke in Gwen's direction.

And Gwen started walking again.

Halfway down the block, she got a sudden, sharp pain in her stomach. She stopped walking and clutched at it.

Had she forgotten lunch? Jesus, what a stupid—

You don't think it's going to be that easy, I hope, Marianne said.

But when Gwen turned to mock her for following her like a lost puppy dog, Marianne wasn't there.

Thermogenic

G. Winston Hyatt

Inspired by Throbbing Gristle's *Hamburger Lady*

"Of course, I'm still attracted to you," Brian said, pulling the bed sheet up over his clammy nakedness and turning away from her. "It's just work—"

Linda reached out and put her cool, smooth hand on his shoulder. He cleared his throat. The box fan whirred and clattered in the bedroom window. Pipes clanked in the walls. The streetlight outside their third-floor apartment, its globe swarmed by an undulating cloud of insects, cast greenish illumination through the darkened room. It had been over 90 degrees for a week. The syrupy reek of garbage baking in dumpsters wafted up from the alley below. Droplets of sweat covered him like thousands of pinpricks.

"Do they have you working in the children's ward again?" Her hand came to rest on the pillow behind him.

"No," he said, and coughed out a laugh. The children's ward of the burn unit would have been a relief after what he'd been seeing every shift. "Just one patient. 23-B. A special case."

"One? Why don't they rotate you like normal?"

"They've only got a couple of technicians qualified to deal with her."

It was the same line they'd given him when he stormed up to the nurses' station, enraged his transfer had been denied. What made him a qualified technician was that he could get within three feet of 23-B without splattering everything in his stomach out across the tiles. His time in Iraq had given him this 'qualification,' along with many others: the ability to follow his training in any situation, to endure endless hours of boredom broken up by blasts of shrieking trauma, and to only think of the dead in dreams.

"What happened to her? Is she bad?"

Another qualification: do not talk about it. How could he explain? If Linda burned a 250-pound meatloaf and then propped it up on a pool chair, she'd start to get a sight of what faced him every day. Except the meatloaf had legs—fat and the color of marbled rye. And it was alive, in pain every second, heaving and lurching, trying to do something it would never accomplish. It was trying to scream.

"Yeah." The bedsprings creaked as he rolled to face her, sheets clinging to his sticky body. "She's pretty bad."

It's all like hamburger, he nearly said. That's what she looked like from the waist up. Ears, nose, eyelids, fingers, tits—all burned away. Nothing but charred meat.

Backlit by the window, Linda still had a teenager's face, the tiny crow's feet around her eyes and thin rivulets of wrinkles on her neck lost in the gloom. She looked the same as when she'd been his senior prom date, though her hair was shorter now and she'd given up the nose ring. Her blue eyes sparkled in the shadows. Her body—firm, small, each perfect breast able to fill a wineglass—was something he could not bring himself to touch.

"You could start looking for another job," she said.

He noticed she didn't say "quit." Not with her only working part-time, not when they were saving for a house, not with a baby planned for next year after being postponed for the past three.

"I don't have time for that, really."

He looked over to the clock. Almost ten. He stood up, walked to the bathroom, and turned on the shower. A baby's wails came like an alarm siren through the vent from the downstairs apartment. In an hour, he'd be back under the harsh cycling light of a white windowless room, watching 23-B try to scream.

***

Ritchie was a skinny guy with a face like a mud-puddle and a queasy smile. He spoke with a drawl and gave everyone in the burn ward the creeping willies. Everyone except Brian. A connoisseur of the fucked up, there was no gruesome medical tale Ritchie couldn't match. He and Brian traded their careers' inexhaustible horrors like baseball cards.

Brian's first call, back when he'd been an ambulance driver, had been to pick up a teenage boy who tried to kill himself by drinking industrial drain cleaner. The chemical was too strong, and rather than finding its way into the kid's stomach simply poured right through his tongue, lower jaw, and throat. It all dissolved away like a clog in a drainage pipe. He hadn't passed out, but was in shock, sitting on the garage floor with a gaping wet hole from his chin to his chest, every breath sending foamy blood spattering out like bacon grease.

Ritchie's first call was a methed-out metal shop worker who committed suicide by cutting himself in half at the waist with an electric table saw. Bottom half on the shop floor, torso on the platform, his guts hanging down "like Chef Boyardee spaghetti." The shop steward explained the guy had still been in one piece when he called the ambulance, that the bottom half fell off after, that he wouldn't have called an ambulance for a guy in two pieces. The shop steward was traumatized. He asked Ritchie if there was anything he could do to help. Ritchie told the guy he'd probably have to buy a new mop and bucket. Brian and Ritchie were the two staff members qualified to care for 23-B.

Brian came into the ward to find Ritchie leaning with his elbow propped on the nurses' station counter, sipping water from a Dixie cup and staring up at the ceiling-mounted television. The happy-faced nurses behind the desk prattled to one another about a mutual friend, or roommate, or someone else who just didn't know how to be considerate to people and seemed thrilled to agree with each other. Under the fluorescent lights they looked like androids, orange-skinned, pink-lipped.

Richie looked away from the muted entertainment news and gave Brian a sickly grin. "Got good news for you, boss."

Oh, thank God, Brian thought. She finally died.

"Naw-uh, she's still alive," Richie said, reading Brian's face. He sipped his water. "But you got a replacement. Gonna have to find a new girlfriend."

"Right. He'll be the same as all the rest."

"Not this one. He's got some iron to him. A soldier. Like you, buddy."

"I was a contractor."

"Well, you both seen some shit. I do believe things are going to change for you."

"What about you?"

"Me?" Ritchie crumpled his Dixie cup. "One crispy is the same as another, far as I'm concerned. Long as I'm getting paid. Speaking of payday, you wanna grab a beer Friday night?"

Brian thought about Linda, back home—the clattering pipes, the greenish light, his limp dick. "Maybe," he said.

"New guy is already in room 23-B. You just need to walk him through the steps, then come on back to find out where you're gonna be tonight, maybe introduce him around."

Brian put up his surgical mask before entering her room. Even with his own mask up, the new kid looked more like a Boy Scout than a vet. Neat little haircut. Spotless sea green scrubs, glaring white orthopedic shoes. Only his army-issue glasses and tattoo of a black cat, hackles raised, on his forearm suggested anything other than a history of family fishing trips and student-council membership. He sat in a molded plastic chair, holding a copy of Black Belt magazine, steadily tapping one toe on the blazing white linoleum.

Patient 23-B sat propped up on her burn bed across the room. The mattress's interlinked inflatable air chambers looked like upside-down Styrofoam egg cartons, meant to evenly distribute her weight and lessen the pain of contact. Fat chance. She twitched, gagged, shuddered—a melted wax person trying and failing to die, or maybe to live. Her body couldn't maintain a proper temperature without most of its skin. That's why the room was heated to over 90 degrees, and it smelled like dirty socks, lye, and beef stew. The first trickles of sweat ran down Brian's back. He squared his shoulders, walked over to the new guy, and introduced himself.

The new guy stood. They shook hands. His name was Will, and he was glad to be able to help out, especially on a case like this, and so on. 23-B sputtered. Will looked over. Her head was a lump of brisket being jerked around on a string. Brian began the rundown of the case, knowing no doctor had bothered to take the time to do it yet, and Ritchie probably just goofed around with him.

She'd gotten stuck trying to climb out a burning house's window, bottom half outside, top half in. Seventy percent total surface area burns, along with inhalation. Large amounts of gray sputum were suctioned from the airway. Debrided. Weaned off the ventilator a week ago. Skin grafting still in process. Escharotomy on all her fingers. Some incidents of sepsis and bedsores, topical treatments still being used. Tracheotomy performed last week. Intravenous hydration and feeding tubes. Loss of all sensory faculties assumed. The pain management interfered with the antibiotic regimen, so it was suspended.

It was all a very clinical way of saying she was deaf, blind, and mute, with tubes pumping her full of water and food to maintain a ceaseless constant state of terror and agony. But she's breathing through the hole in her throat all by herself. Lucky her.

Will kept looking over at her and looking away. He set his karate magazine on the chair. The looks would get longer and longer, Brian knew, until he wouldn't be able to look away. Not until his stomach gave out. God, he hoped the kid could make it.

"Well," Brian said, clapping his hands. "Let's get to it." The walk over to her was like crossing a field of fire every time. Brian explained what to do, Will looking on through his army-issue Birth Control Glasses, keeping his eyes on Brian's hands: Lift her leg to change the IV, sometimes she'll thrash it around, but she's too weak to make it much of a problem. Swap out the bags and tubes. Check for new sores and note them. Get out the "mayo" for the hamburger: a mix of steroids, antibiotics, and Medihoney. Open it up and keep it on the tray. Scrub and glove again. Now comes the tough part.

"You have to apply this stuff all over her," Brian said, holding out a glob of pearly goo on his latex-wrapped finger for Will to examine, "especially where the grafts are still taking. Some of the relocated skin is hers, some from pigs."

"Pigs?" Will asked.

"Genetically altered pigs. Now, this is the part you're gonna have to do yourself. Leaning forward probably hurts her more than anything, but if you put your fingertips on either of her shoulders, she'll do it. The mayo cools the skin and has a topical anesthetic, so she wants it. The hard part is—"

"You have to watch what you're doing closely."

Brian nodded. Watch and feel her, he wanted to tell him. You have to feel all that woman's body, slippery under your rubber hands, the contours all wrong, here like pressing fried chicken, there like hot tofu, the stitches like fly hairs, the sores weeping, her not-a-face just meat and bone with a fist-sized hole full of teeth, and her trying to groan through her trachea-ring, and you giving it your full attention, and then later, after you strip off the gloves and scrub, they're still your hands, the same goddamn hands, and you have to use them to eat a taco, or take a piss, and your wife will suck on those fingers when you're inside of her and you'll think about where they've been and wonder why all the other victims never got to you like this one, and then you remember all the others as a cut up black-brown-red collage and know 23-B is the worst of them because before with the others when you had to debride and cut and scrub away the blistered flesh, even when they screamed and wept and begged you to stop, you felt the life in them, you were pulling all the blackened death from their bodies so they could shine again, so sure of that, but 23-B is like a dark magnet or a black hole pulling the life from you and you can feel it draining out from your fingertips when you touch her and her ceaseless unsleeping pain like radiation poisons you to wonder if this is how it's always been for all of them, even the ones restored, a pointless struggle against unavoidable suffering which will only end when death comes, and it will never come soon enough, and never mercifully.

"That's right," Brian said. "You have to watch it. You do this part, and I'll keep an eye out to make sure you're doing it right. Be careful."

Will did it all, front and back, his steady hands leaving her wetly glistening like a fresh-born baby. By the time he'd finished, his hands shook a little, and his eyes had dilated into black buttons under his glasses' thick lenses. But he was on his feet. He managed to keep his stomach down. He finished the job. Brian wanted to hug him. He wanted to throw his arms around the guy and hug him. "Good work," Brian said. "After that, all you gotta do is sit with her. Let's head on down to the nurse's station. I'll introduce you around, and we'll work out the schedule."

Will swallowed and nodded. Brian wished he could tell him it got easier.

They walked together, the calls for doctors echoing through the corridors, gurneys squeaking by, the room's sickly smell still clinging to them both. Will looked greenish, moving with loose and rubbery steps. They pushed through the ward's swinging double doors and stood before the nurses' station.

Brian smelled the food before he saw it. One of the women sitting behind the counter lifted a heaping spoonful from a bowl of chili-mac, dripping brown with hanging strands of orange cheese, up to her moist, pink-lipped mouth, chewed, and swallowed.

Will's knees thumped against the floor, the slap of his palms followed, and his body convulsed like a slow-motion whip from ass to head. His vomit gushed and splattered everywhere.

"Don't ever eat at the fucking desk!" Brian screamed at her. Everyone froze to stare, holding manila folders and clipboards, hands on gurneys and med trays. The nurse lowered her eyes and put the spoon in the bowl. Will spat as Brian put his hand on his shoulder.

"They're not supposed to eat at the desk. It won't happen again, I promise," Brian said. It sounded like a plea. "Come on, Will, get up."

Will wiped his mouth on the back of his hand and looked up at Brian like a shamed dog, his face white and wet.

"I can't do this," he said.

***

"Hi, baby," Linda called from the kitchen when the front door slammed behind him. "How was work?"

"Same as always." Brian dropped his keys onto the table beside the door. The apartment stifled and suffocated, even hotter than the streets.

It smelled of meat.

"Sit down and take it easy."

The oven screeched open.

Dinner? Linda usually let him cook his own food—she was a vegetarian and he was not. Rather than let every meal become two, they just let one another handle their own feeding. Plus, it was nine in the morning. She only worked part-time, but, if they were going to do a morning together after his shift, they usually planned it together.

It got hotter as he moved inside; the hall was a long throat swallowing him. She'd set the table in the dinette, white plates on a sea-green tablecloth, forks and knives glinting in candlelight. The chair groaned when he sat. He stared into the blue core of a candle flame. Pans clanged in the kitchen. The smell of grease and hot blood swelled as her footsteps grew near.

Rounding the corner, she said, "Voila! I wasn't always a vegetarian, remember. I sneaked a little bite—you'll be pretty pleased, if I do say so myself."

A roast, brown-black in a pool of red juice, steamed on the platter in her hands. Brian jolted to his feet when she held it out to him.

"I have to go," he said.

Her smile melted away, her eyes moistened and blinked, and he turned away before he could see more, grabbing his keys as he ran out the door.

He drove his car through the long-shadowed morning, aimlessly circling this block and that until he parked at a Save-A-Lot and stared at the traffic whooshing by, the news radio gibbering, birds singing their idiot songs until the sun broiled high overhead.

He began to feel sleepy and drove home. He looked at his cell phone. It had been four hours. She had not called.

The roast was in the garbage when he got home, along with the tablecloth. Linda was gone.

***

Brian sat in a booth across from Ritchie in the Pink Cowgirl Lounge's darkest corner. A pot-bellied girl with pancake tits and arms covered in tattoos laid on her back across the main stage, legs in the air opening and closing like scissors. Her skin glowed purple in the floor lights. Radio-metal pounded through the sound system. Brian downed the last of his whiskey and stared into the empty glass.

"Look, I heard this thing on the radio about this guy who was a 'Nam vet'," Richie said. "And he came back all wrecked. Just out of his goddamn mind. Couldn't hold a job, drunk all the time, you know what I'm saying. So, he applied for psychological disability. Wrote out why on the back of the form." Richie craned his head to look at the stage when a new song started, then grimaced. "Ugh. Same girl. Anyway, he was behind enemy lines with his unit, and they were all out of rations. Hadn't eaten for days. And this one day they're going through a village that got hit by a napalm strike or something. So, he smells all this burned meat, and his mouth starts watering, his stomach is growling, but the whole time he knows it's all the people and kids that got lit up in the air strike. But it makes him want to eat."

Brian rubbed his face. "Why, exactly, are you telling me this?"

"Total disability, *compadre*. I mean, total. Never had to work again. You saw shit worse than that over there, right? Maybe you could do the same thing."

Brian looked around. "Where's that waitress?"

"Just an idea. Say, want me to get you a lap dance?"

"No. Waitress!" Brian waved at the server, who gave him an icy glare. "Double jack, please, and one for him, too."

"You ever had to work a crispy with fake tits?" Ritchie asked. "The things melt inside of them."

"Great. Listen, back to the real issue here. Linda's been gone for two days."

"You tried callin' her?"

"I wouldn't know what to say." Brian smiled at the waitress when she clunked two drinks on the table and strode off.

"You two still, you know, screwing?" Ritchie asked.

Not for eight weeks at least, he thought. "I just haven't been able to with her."

"Nothing goin' on down there?"

Brian shook his head.

"Well, Bri, you have been married for a while."

"It's not just her. It's anyone." He swilled the whiskey, and it sent a hot tremor through him. "I can't look at these naked girls without imagining electrodes stuck all over them. Always thinking about having to scrub away their burned-up skin."

"Hell. Why don't you quit?"

"I don't know."

"Ain't that the best answer for everything?" Ritchie lifted up his whiskey in a toast. “Here’s to losing it, I guess. Down the hatch.” Late that night, Brian sprawled naked on the sweat-damp bed as the walls made slow revolutions around him. The clattering fan blew across his face, the mattress a raft drifting in the fetid breeze. His guts churned. A fly buzzed like an electrical short, trapped between the window screen and glass. The streetlight painted its monstrous insect-shadow crawling across the sheets.

The front door creaked open and clicked shut. Brian tried to call out, but his tongue was swollen and his throat raw. He could not move. The floorboards creaked as someone approached. His head lolled to the side, and he saw her shape in the doorway. His own scream sounded distant and thin.

23-B, naked and ruined, crossed the threshold. One swollen foot dragged and thumped. Then, the other. She wheezed through the metal ring in her throat. Her mouth hole opened and closed, gums blackened, the teeth clanking together like a joke-shop novelty in her obliterated face. The fan’s metallic grinding melded with the fly’s buzzing wings into a roaring drone. Her arms lifted as she staggered closer, hands spreading skinless fingers, and Brian lay paralyzed. The acrid stink of burned hair and skin, of boiling blood, flooded the room. The words came shrieking out from him.

“Get away from me, get away! Oh, Jesus, for the love of God, just leave me alone!”

And then he saw her. Linda. His wife. Standing there, hands clasped over her mouth, eyes wide, trembling. Not you, he wanted to say, I couldn’t see you, not in the dark, not now, not with my mind like this. His jaw slackened to let out a long shuddering breath. He closed his eyes. When he opened them, she had vanished.

***

The room’s whiteness exploded like incandescent phosphorous around the two of them. Brian’s hands, dripping with white goo, hovered over 23-B. Hangover ache thrummed behind his eyes. Her head bounced against the burn mattress. Pleasure, anguish, terror, insanity? He could not know. She shimmered, slick with ointment. He reached out and rested his fingertips on her shoulders. His arms locked at the elbow, stiff and shaking, as he stared into her eyeless face. He’d have to grab and stabilize one shoulder and use his other hand to yank her head around, back and away, to snap her neck in a single jerk. She gurgled and leaned forward, offering her bare patchwork back.

A single wet sob barked through his mask.

He was hard. Solid as an iron bar inside his scrub pants, bulging and scraping against the cloth. The rest of him, hollow. He remembered Ritchie's lazy drawl: *You got a replacement. Gonna have to find a new girlfriend.* Brian looked over his shoulder to the door, closed as always—nobody would ever look inside a room like this, or breathe this air, or touch that body, or do something like this unless he had no other choice.

The Language of Bones

Jenna M. Pitman

Inspired by The Killers' *Bones*

"Where are we?" Cadence asked, as she slipped through the passenger door onto the cool white sand of the beach. She didn't sound pleased.

Elwood cringed at the sound of her voice as he too stepped out of the car, absently scratching at his arms. That she still mistrusted him because of the words he'd said last night and in spite of the assurances he's made this afternoon was apparent. He needed her, and he especially needed her tonight, because he couldn't do this alone. He was going to have to try to win her back.

She hadn't made eye contact since they'd started driving. He recognized it as some sort of vindictive attempt at punishment, but it only served to tickle his temper. He struggled to keep his anger in check. He understood that she saw herself as the victim here and felt totally justified in making him the source of her unpleasantness. It irked him, but yelling and telling her off would do him no good and would only further widen the rift between them. He had to stay collected and rely on the connection and the memories they had built together over the last year to bring her around.

Cadence was staring down at the beach, at the waves that lapped noisily at the ocean's shore, inky black against the pale sand. He thought she was beautiful. Out of all of the people in the world, she was the only one he thought he could connect to and bond with; the only one he could see a reflection of himself inside. She was what he needed in his future.

Tonight, her clothes hung off her body, all baggy. She knew he hated it when she dressed like that, like she was apologizing to the world. Like she was telling it sorry that she had been born so beautiful. At that moment, it did not seem apologetic as much as punitive in the way it hid all the curves and crevices he loved so much. It was just another way in which she could express her displeasure in how he'd handled their last encounter. She could be infuriating when she wanted to be.

"I told you," was all he said. "This is where I come to think. Look at the stars, swim...I come here to get back to my nature."

"No," she snapped, a little too quickly for his taste. "I meant *where* are we? Location wise. I didn't recognize the roads; I'm all turned around."

And I don't like that.

The words never touched the air, she never gave them voice, but she didn't need to. He knew how uncomfortable she was when she wasn't totally in control of the situation. There was nothing to be done about that; he couldn't reassure her with solid footing this time. Though even if he could have, it benefited him more if she was off kilter, just a little.

Hoping that he could draw out a spark of her radiance, the luminescence with which she had originally dazzled him, he flashed a smile in her direction. Instead, the glance she afforded him held no hint of the love that they shared. It was as though she had cut off all emotion.

"I'm sorry." He'd said it a thousand times already. And while it wasn't entirely true, he *was* sorry that the truth had hurt her.

She ignored the comment and started down the sandbar, toward the water.

He knew she would like it here in spite of herself. She couldn't help it. Cadence was drawn to nature in a way few humans were—that's what made her an ideal choice. It settled her soul, and he never sensed her worrying about how she could crack and rearrange it to fit her needs. At least not in the way so many others did. He hoped that he could teach her to expand her thoughts on that topic as time drew on. Eventually, she would have to learn to use nature to get what she wanted. But she wouldn't have to destroy in order to do so. And that would be the key.

Slipping out of his shoes, he followed her lead, padding almost noiselessly in her footsteps. The cool grains felt soft and soothing against his aching feet. His bones were itching under his skin, straining toward change. He needed a little more time.

At the water's edge she paused, just out of reach of the waves that rode onto the sand. She was rocking on the balls of her feet, clutching her arms around herself, and staring into the endless horizon of water. There was a dreamy look on her face, one he associated with the good times they had floated through together.

A surge of affection swept over him, and he quickened his pace. This was the woman that was meant for him. The knowledge came from deep inside, from his yearning bones. He needed her.

"Cadence," he murmured when he got closer.

She tilted her head back a little, only her eyes meeting his over her shoulder. "Mmm?"

"The view has never been as beautiful as it is now." He sidled up behind her, their bodies hovering mere centimeters apart but not touching. He swallowed and plunged ahead, the white lie hardly even sticking in his throat. After all, some of it was actually the truth. "You are perfect, my sun and my stars. I wouldn't change you, my love. Not for the world. You're everything I'll ever need."

A half-laugh, half-sob escaped her throat, but he felt her relax and the tension that vibrated between them fade. She loved him, and love caused people to do silly things.

Leaning into him, just barely, she arched her back against his chest. He scooped her to him, holding her softly, resting his face against her cheek, reveling in the smell of her as it mingled with the salty scents of the ocean. "I'm sorry," he said again, so softly the slight breeze that swept in off the water nearly erased the sound.

Cadence sighed and shook her head. "I don't understand why you would say those things to me! Why you would think it was ok? Who tells their partner that they're 'not beautiful yet?' That they 'aren't perfect' or 'too feeble-minded' to get it? Why? What were you thinking?" It was similar to what she had shrieked at him the night before. Then, it had been indignant and full of vehemence, but now she spoke in wounded confusion, looking to him for solace. He liked it that way.

"Shhhh." He nuzzled her ear before gently taking it between his lips and sucking lightly. She stiffened once again but this time it wasn't with hostility; it was undercut with the electric tingle of sex. "That's over now. I spoke out of turn, I shouldn't have said anything. You know I don't mean any of it."

Twelve hours ago, that hadn't been enough but now, out here, away from civilization, standing together on an ancient shore under the stars and the spaces in between, it was exactly what she needed to hear. Cadence melted into him, turning and lifting her head, finding his lips with her own and offering a tentative kiss of forgiveness and reconciliation.

Carefully, he spun her around, without breaking contact with her lips. They pressed their bodies together, her soft curves fitting against his hard planes like puzzle pieces that were never meant to be broken apart.

His restless bones forgotten, Elwood began to shed his clothing, his mouth still covering Cadence with kisses. He moved from her lips across her cheek, down along her neck and back up again. He heard her give a soft moan, delicate and feminine and awakening the human instincts in him that were already starting to tarnish and unravel. They came rushing back without hesitation, and no longer was the alertness of his body nothing more than show; he was as ready now as she. Except that there was no time.

Without rushing, he began to unbutton the baggy shirt she'd buried herself in. Impatiently, she pulled away and whipped it off, tossing it somewhere into the sand behind him. A smile split his face, and he moved to her trousers, the sexless retro tubes she found so comfortable in their fit and he found so irritating in their asexuality. She stepped out of them without hesitation, letting them fall forgotten into the foaming waves that were pooling at their feet. He almost lost control when he realized that she hadn't even bothered with any underwear. Except he didn't have time to lose control.

He reached around for her bra with exaggerated care, tracing feather light circles along her spine and sides with his free hand as he artfully unhinged the clasp. She shrugged out of the straps, completely naked and completely willing to transform her emotional cacophony into physical action. He allowed himself only the briefest of moments to caress her breasts, flicking his thumbs over the stiff pink nipples and momentarily lowering his head to roll each lightly between his teeth. It would never be like this again, he knew. While what awaited them was better, his bones knew that what came next for them was far more enthralling than what they could experience now, his human body ached for just one more chance to touch the rose-petal smoothness of her skin, to feel it shudder as he brushed against it in the right places, to feel her grow warm and moist and hear her breath come faster and louder...

When it grew to be too much, he drew back, allowing a wicked little grin to mask the desire he felt, the craving to lose himself inside of her. She protested with a desperate, yet elegant gasp, and opened her eyes in bemusement.

"Come with me," he whispered breathlessly. There was no acting here. He wanted her with him, more than anything. So, he began backing into the sea.

Her mouth opened in amazement; she too was breathless. He could see that she was full of love, high on endorphins and gliding on affection. This was exactly where he needed her to be. The water crept up his legs, and he just kept moving. It circled his waist and he beckoned her. When it was clasping his chest, she plunged ahead. When he was treading water, she reached him.

It was obvious that she wanted to pick up where they had left off, tangling herself around him, wrapping her long legs around his waist, feeling his stiffness against and inside of her, but he didn't let it get that far. Instead, he took her by the hand and began to lead her further into the ocean.

They swam like seals, rising above and then plummeting back under the glimmering surface. It was pulling at him, embracing him, and urging him to let go, to come back and live beneath.

He couldn't do that. Not yet.

His bones began to itch again, with more intensity this time. The passion of his human nature had blotted out the changes for a short while, but the evidence came back with a jolt. His muscles were rippling, their texture and density becoming something different. Inside, his lungs and heart changed shapes, intent on preparing for their new, older, more natural roles.

Now.

When he drew her to him this time, she was ready, but she didn't understand. She was expecting their tryst to continue, but that part of their lives was over; they would never be going back there. She would understand tomorrow. What he was about to share with her could only be duplicated once a millennium.

It was her hand he wanted once more, and he snatched it up with a swelling sense of euphoria. She didn't have time to react. Where their palms met, her hand sunk into his, siding beneath the surface as neatly as if his flesh were simply a well-fitting glove.

Cadence gasped, and the first threads of doubt began to decorate her gaze. It was too late for that; there would be no turning back. Her own skin dissolved inside of him, until their bones crashed together in a comforting "thump." A dark, wet stain began to twist itself up her arm, sucking from her the blood and color of human life. In its stead remained cold, silver putty.

"What is this?" she demanded, her voice taking on a panicked tone. "Elwood, please! What is this?"

Once again, he smiled and told her, "Shhhh!"

He took her shoulder in his other hand, and another part of her slipped through the seal of his skin, her body melting away until their bones clicked. The cold brush of silver spun away from this contact, down her arm, up toward her throat.

"Elwood," she whispered his name, but the message was just as clear as her scream had been. She was losing control in her last few minutes, panic overriding her senses, her every thought. It thudded through the physical link they were sharing, pounding futilely at his own mind. For a brief instant, he was distracted, but the moment was over almost before it began.

He was still smiling, but now it was frightening, lips pulled back tautly, exposing teeth far too serrated to look comfortable in a human face. He felt love and duty and pride in his work, but his face could no longer convey such emotion. "You'll be fine tomorrow. Tomorrow, you will be perfect."

With that, he took a breath and dragged her under. She tried to resist him, for all the good it did. In the water, her strength was useless. His arms came around her, and the process played out again, the slick silver overtaking her, unmaking her, building her back as a vessel of perfection. After all, no God could survive in anything less.

Thunder concussed overhead, a primal boom in the sky. In mere seconds, it was filled with angry clouds that burst and popped with flashes of light despite the pure clarity the evening had promised. The sea itself grew agitated, and he knew that above them the wind had picked up. The elements sensed what was coming and they were as eager as he to welcome their new queen mother. Like him, they understood what was coming in a way no living being ever could. They rejoiced in what was to be.

Her epidermis was sticky and malleable where it seeped into him, dead and grey and chillingly cold. Ice crystals clung to her where she spilled out of him, adorning her in a glistening robe fit for a starlet.

Their bones were chattering to each other in the queer language known only to bones. Clicking and clattering and whispering to each other the secrets nothing else would ever understand. Humming and thrumming in their communion, reverberating up and down the desensitized neurons of their human forms. It was not an unpleasant feeling for him, but he vaguely remembered when he had been changed and the unbearable pain and horror that had accompanied this new development. He could feel no pity for her, however, not when he knew how it would end. Even as her lungs fought to hold on to the life she knew, and her eyes grew wild with terror, he gripped her tightly, slowly bringing more of her into his grasp, letting his body meld with hers, letting their bones jabber away.

"Elwood?" she tried to ask. Even underwater, he could hear it as though she were laying near him in the peace of a Sunday morning, though now her voice was waterlogged and helpless. It was the first time he had ever viewed her as helpless, and he knew that it would be the last.

When she was remade, she would look back on this and all she would be able to summon would be cool detachment. Maybe a hint of excitement.

But not now. Now was distress so thick, she would feel she was drowning in it. He assumed there was no avoiding that.

There was no comfort he could give her, so instead he pushed her down, letting their bodies slowly drift to the downy ocean floor. He pinned her there, his body swallowing and crushing hers. She was sobbing, her still-mammalian lungs taking in water as they were not designed to. Her tears were lost in the depths, merging with the salt water that encompassed them, then forgotten forever. But it was the bones that were causing her the most torture. They grated against each other now, scraping together as though they were broken and despite the loss of physical nerves the pain felt as though he were flaying her to the core. This was the most important part of it all, the process of the bones, the confidences they shared. Without it, they could never be complete.

The light inside of her began to dim as the silver putty of her skin crawled up her cheeks, slithering around her ears and up her nose.

It was her eyes that went last, those uncomprehending and terrified eyes. They held his gaze for as long as they were capable, and then the humanity that had lived inside of Cadence vanished. Her mortal life winked out in a psychedelic flash of colors and shapes, the shock wave rocking him enough to shake him free from the glimmering, clay-like corpse.

His bones snapped back into their proper places, their messages bestowed and riddles imparted. Inside of that sticky, grey cocoon, she would incubate for a night. Tomorrow she would arise anew, reborn to the planet as its queen and its mother. The humans would call her a God and fear her, but she would feel nothing for them.

"Wait 'til tomorrow," he said with affection. "You'll be fine." And so would he, just as soon as his own transformation was complete. He had been alone too long; it would feel good to have a mate once again.

Saving Grace

Quentin Pittman

Inspired by Screamin' Jay Hawkins' *I Put a Spell on You*

When had she gotten so old? Grace Sherwood stared at the mirror. Thirty seemed like only yesterday. Jimmy had thrown that huge party. Everyone had come. She and Jimmy had flown to the Bahamas for a vacation. It was the best week of her life. Then it was over. Grace was forty, with the laugh lines and crow's feet to prove it. Thank God no one could see the stretch marks on her thighs. Only her boobs were still perfect. That was because they were silicone. Disgusted, Grace opened her purse. Maybe if she used a little more mascara. A little more foundation and lipstick couldn't hurt, either. No wonder her husband had run away with his receptionist. The only wrinkle Grace ever saw on Jimmy's latest twenty-something was the thong riding up the crack of her ass whenever she bent over. No doubt Jimmy had seen that wrinkle too. Seen it more times than she cared to imagine. Grace moved the mascara brush up to her lashes. Would kids have made a difference? She would have liked to have had children. Jimmy was always dead set against them. He said there were too many people on the planet. Like everything he said, it sounded good but was false bravado. Kids demanded time. They needed attention. It was hard to have either when you were busy screwing half your office staff.

It was pointless to be bitter, but she couldn't help it. If Jimmy had left her ten years earlier, five at the most, Grace would have had more confidence. After all, she had been a looker. But at forty, which was not the new thirty, despite what everyone said, she was old. The mirror didn't lie. Pickings were slim when you got old. They were slimmer still if you didn't go to bars or troll the internet. Grace did neither.

A few guys had asked her out, but she had turned them down. They weren't really the problem. She was. Despite everything, Grace still loved her husband. She had spent the last two years hoping Jimmy would change. He hadn't. People never did. There was a knock at the bathroom door.

"Hey pretty lady. You okay?" a voice said.

"Give me a moment, Zachary," Grace said, hoping she sounded natural. She felt anything but. "I'll be in the living room," he said.

"I'll be right there," Grace said. She might still be in love with Jimmy, but February was only four months away. Grace could get through Christmas, but there was no way she was spending another Valentine's Day drinking alone and sobbing to some movie on the Lifetime channel. When Zachary asked her out, she accepted. It wasn't easy, but it was time to get on with her life. She figured a police officer—a really good-looking police officer—was a safe way to start. Who cared if he was fifteen years younger and had a raging Oedipus complex? It made for a nice change.

They had met at the Shelley Point Health Club. Casual banter had led to a few lunches and finally dinner. Now that dinner was over, they were at her place drinking coffee. Grace had excused herself to freshen up. It wasn't working. She felt lightheaded and nervous. After all, the only men she had kissed during the past two decades were Jimmy and her father. Both of those relationships had ended in disaster.

Grace put the mascara back in her purse. Okay, she decided. It was now or never. She gave the mirror a final look and opened the door. Her nostrils flared. Zachary's cologne filled the hallway. It was strong. It was also arousing. Grace couldn't remember the last time she had been aroused by anything that didn't use batteries. Blushing, she took a deep breath, realized she was still holding her purse, and tossed it next to the sink.

She walked into the kitchen, hoping the war paint hid her nerves. She was relieved to find the lights were off. That helped. Zachary had also lit a fire. Grace could feel its heat from across the room. Zachary was on the couch. His large frame covered most of the leather. At his feet, the roses he had brought were in a vase on the coffee table. Two steaming mugs flanked the flowers. Almost everything was perfect. She said, "Did you have to put this music on?"

"You don't like Frank?"

"I grabbed the CD by mistake when I was moving out."

"How can you not like the 'Chairman of the Board'?"

"My husband loves Frank Sinatra. I hate my husband. It's easy."

"That's like saying you don't like McDonald's just because he did."

"Well, now that you mention it," she said.

"If you want me to turn it off, I will."

"No, that's all right."

"Are you sure?"

"I'm sure."

"Come sit down," he said. Even in the fire's unsteady, orange and red glow, Zachary's eyes were still a brilliant blue. They were the first thing she had noticed about him. Well, the first thing she had noticed after she noticed his muscles. "What do you think happened to your husband?"

"I thought you weren't going to be a cop tonight?" she said, sitting next him.

"We're just talking," Zachary said, handing her a mug. "One cream and two sugars, right?"

"That's right. I really shouldn't drink any more coffee. I'll be up all night," Grace said.

"If it's terrible, don't drink it. I'm trying to wean myself from Starbucks, but my coffee is still a work in progress."

"It's perfect," she said, taking a sip. It wasn't. It was worse than the first two cups, but Grace wasn't about to say so. She'd trade bitter coffee for a good date any day.

"So, what do you think happened to him?"

"I think Jimmy and his new girlfriend are in the Caribbean having the time of their lives. Remember, she disappeared too."

"I remember. I also remember he's never touched his bank account. He's never used his credit cards. How do you have the time of your life without any money?"

"The government said Jimmy was sticking cash in offshore accounts for years. God knows how much he has."

"That was never proven," Zachary replied.

"Now you definitely sound like a cop," she said, taking another drink.

"Sorry. Like I said at dinner, I just don't understand how this guy left you for another woman."

"Have you seen the woman he left me for?" Grace asked.

"I've seen her picture. Fake tan, fake blonde and fake smile?

I bet her IQ was as small as her waist and nowhere near as big as her tits."

"I didn't know you knew her."

"I know the type."

"That was Jimmy's type."

"How did you end up with him?"

"We met in college. We fell in love. He went to med school. I worked and paid the bills. Once he graduated, I became less and less important. Don't get me wrong. I liked being a doctor's wife.

I'm not a victim. I was a willing participant until he left for good."

"He'd left before?"

"He'd left years ago. He was just finally moved out."

"What would you do if he came back?"

"I'd divorce him," Grace said. The words came out so quickly that she almost believed them.

"Why not divorce him now?"

"If I divorce him now, I only get half his money. If he doesn't show up in seven years, I can have him declared dead. Then I get all of it. Trust me, I've earned every penny."

"Do you still love him?" Zachary asked.

"I'll always love him. I just don't like him anymore. Does that make any sense?"

"Of course, it does. I'm divorced."

"That fire is really hot," Grace said, fanning her face.

"You want me to put it out?"

"No, don't do that. I like it."

"I like you," he said, leaning his head towards her mouth. Grace flinched and immediately regretted it. She put her cup on the table and took his hand. She said, "I'm sorry. I'm out of practice. I am attracted to you."

"I'm attracted to you," Zachary said. He kissed Grace, sliding his tongue into her mouth. After a moment, she pushed against his chest until he released her.

"I'm sorry. I don't...I don't feel well," she said.

"Was that too forward?"

"No, it's not you. It's me. I feel weird."

"You want me to call a doctor?"

"No, don't do that. I just have this awful headache."

"It's my fault for talking about Jimmy. I'll stop. Turn around. I'll give you a massage. If that doesn't help, I'll tuck you in and leave. Sound okay?"

Okay," Grace said. She turned around. Sweat was running down her face, but she felt cold. She was dizzy. Frank Sinatra's voice filled her ears. God, she hated Sinatra. That was all the band at her wedding had played. Frank Sinatra, over and over. It should have been clue number one that the marriage was doomed. That or when Jimmy got drunk and stuck his hand up the maid of honor's dress.

"Do you think Jimmy has talked to any of his family since he ran off?"

"Can we talk about something else?" Grace said. She felt her forehead. It was damp, she didn't have a fever.

"What do you want to talk about?" he said, squeezing her shoulders.

She rolled her head back and said, "Tell me about this guy you're after."

"What guy? You mean the Angel of Mercy? Now *I'm* going to get a headache."

"Are you close to catching him?"

"They say we are, but I don't see how. I mean the victims were burned after death, so there's no forensic evidence. There's zilch. We've got no witnesses."

"I thought the paper said some lady saw the guy?"

"Some old lady says she saw a guy. We put her with a sketch artist."

"Did you get a picture?"

"Yeah, she described me. It's a perfect portrait. That's what I get for babysitting the old hag all day." Zachary chuckled.

"That's all you've got?"

"That's it. This guy is Jimmy."

"What do you mean?"

"He just disappears."

"If the victims were burned, how do you know he did all that stuff?"

"You mean like tying them up and torturing them?"

"The papers said he used handcuffs."

"The forensic guys can figure all that out. They've even figured out he uses a Taser. They're smart little bastards."

"I thought he strangled them?"

"That's how he kills them, but he does all this other stuff first. It's pretty horrific," he said, pulling her backwards. He kissed Grace's neck, letting his lips linger on her skin before returning his hands to her shoulders. This time, he caressed her, slowly kneading the muscles until Grace lowered her head. "Feel any better?"

"I can't stay awake," she said, batting her eyes. Pain shot through her right breast. Grace looked down and saw Zachary's hand squeezing the front of her dress. She tried to push his arm away but couldn't. He pinched her breast harder. She shuddered and said, "You're hurting me."

"That's the idea."

"Maybe we should call it a night," Grace said, the words catching in her throat.

"It's a shame to end things this way."

"I know, but I can't—"

"I'm not talking about us," he said.

"Oh," Grace said. She felt the slap but never saw it. Zachary's open palm struck her jaw, knocking her to the floor. When she tried to get up, she realized why her arms weren't working. They were handcuffed. She managed to roll onto her back. Pain shot up her shoulder. Tears ran down her face. It was like looking at the world through plate glass. In that reality of soft, muted edges, Grace suddenly saw why she had been attracted to Zachary. It wasn't the muscles or the blue eyes. It was his face. Standing above her, bathed in firelight, Zachary was a young James Sherwood's spitting image. Without looking down, he said, "Do you know why we call him the Angel of Mercy? It's not because he strangled those women before he cut them up. That's just what we told the press so people wouldn't panic. We call him the Angel of Mercy because he fucked those lonely, old bitches before he killed them. Charlie Best came up with that one. Can you believe it? That's the Sheriff talking, Grace. You should hear what he says about you. The Angel gives the grannies one last thrill on the way out. One last thrill for old bitches like you, Grace. And I'll tell you something else. Something no one knows, not Sheriff Best or the forensic boys. The Angel drugs them first. He puts it in their coffee."

"My," she said, fighting to keep her eyes open. She dug her thumbnails into her palms, hoping the pain would help. It did, but not as much as Sinatra's voice. That warbling baritone gave her something to focus on.

"What's wrong? Is it the music? No sweat. I'll turn it off. You want it off? No problem."

"Leave," she said, trying to kick. Her feet were bound. When had that happened?

"Leave Frank on? Okay. You're the boss. I'm a Hank Williams man, myself. I bet Jimmy was too, until you put him beneath a tomb of stone."

"My, uh, my, uh," Grace said. The words clawed up her swollen throat. Knowing she was about to pass out, Grace tried to sit up. He was on her then, his knees digging into her stomach. She saw the knife. The firelight reflected off its blade. The blade was moving up and down. Oh God, it was going up and down. She looked at her chest, relieved to see he was just popping the buttons off her blouse. One after another, like logs on the fire. *Pop, pop, pop.*

Zachary leaned down. He licked her cheek and said, "They're going to find your body in the basement boiler. When they do, they'll say the Angel got you. That will get the forensic boys here in a flash. You bet. That's why I brought a roll of plastic. We've got to be careful what we leave for the forensic fucks. You know what they'll find? They'll find evidence that James Sherwood is alive and well."

"Huh?" she said, head oscillating.

He slapped her and said, "Don't nod off on me yet. This is the best part, Grace. James Sherwood is alive because he is the Angel of Mercy. Sounds crazy, right? Well, I brought some goodies from the evidence locker. When those forensic fucks find it, they'll be convinced. They'll convince everyone else. The evidence never lies. Everyone will be looking for your husband. But they'll never find him, will they? They won't find him because you killed him." Grace didn't speak. She was concentrating on the baritone voice. She was saving what little energy she still had for one final act.

"Here's the best part. You gave me the idea. Always going on and on about Jimmy. I could be his twin. No shit. Even Sheriff Best said so. Blaming Jimmy fixes everything. It explains the old lady's description. It gets everyone off my back. I can stop. I can end it. I can go somewhere else in a year or two and start all over. But that's big picture stuff, right? Before we get to the big picture, you and I have small details to work out. I've been saving you for last, Grace. You're my sweet, saving Grace."

Grace willed her lips to part. The flowers on the mantle behind Zachary's head wilted as she stammered, "K-I-S-S-M-E." Knife in hand, Zachary pressed his lips against her mouth.

Grace's world went black.

***

When Grace opened her eyes, Sinatra was still singing.

I'm dead and this is Hell, she thought. Why else would Ol' Blue Eyes still be singing—how many hours later was it? The clock on the mantle said: 19:38. No help there. She tried to look at her watch and remembered the handcuffs. That's when she saw the toad. He was positioned between her perfect breasts. His skin was a beautiful dark green. It was almost black, which accentuated his bright, blue eyes. The round, cobalt orbs were the color of morning sky after a violent, evening storm. They were also human in their size and intensity.

Grace rolled onto her side. The toad croaked and jumped. It took almost ten minutes of rolling and fidgeting before she finally got the keys out of Zachary's pants. That was the easy part. Finding the right key and getting it into the handcuffs' lock took the better part of an hour. The entire time she did this, Sinatra sang and the toad watched. Finally, the lock opened and Grace sat up. She dug her nails into the duct tape around her ankles and tore her feet free. She stood. Her legs were wobbly. Her head still hurt, but she was determined. Her ears needed relief. She got to the stereo and took the Sinatra CD out. It was hot and broke nicely into tiny pieces. She tossed the Chairman into the trash. Zachary's clothes went on top. She tied the bag and set it on the counter beside the sink. She would make a trip to the basement and the boiler after feeding Jimmy.

Now, where was Zachary? She found him at the front door. He was jumping, trying desperately to reach the knob. Like that would have mattered. Grace snatched him mid-leap. He croaked and peed. Startled, she dropped him. He fled, leaving a trail of urine behind him. His escape was short lived. Paper towel in tow, Grace found him flailing against the patio door. This time, she grabbed and held on. Zachary's eyes bulged as she walked across the living room and into the bedroom.

Jimmy was in the cage beside the dresser. His head turned when he saw her walk into the room. She held up the toad. Jimmy's tongue flicked back and forth wildly. His skin rippled with anticipation. What a difference two years made. Jimmy had refused his first meal. Finally, after five days, he had eaten the small, blonde hamster.

Since then, Jimmy devoured everything. Even as a snake, he was still every bit the man she had married. That was the problem. You could change a person's appearance, but you couldn't change who they were. Their essence always came out. Oh, well, a girl could still dream, even if she was a witch. Grace dropped the toad into the cage and left the room.

Special

Joleen Kuyper

Inspired by Radiohead's *Creep*

He sat in her bedroom, staring at the wall.

"I shouldn't be here," he muttered.

She didn't answer. She couldn't. He had sworn that she wouldn't run away from him again, and he made good on the promise. All she could move were her eyes.

"I'm such a freak, such a complete fucking freak," he said.

She wasn't sure if he was actually talking to her or to himself, or just at the wall he was staring at.

"I don't want it to be like this." He turned to her. "I never meant for this to happen. I love you."

Her eyes drifted up toward her wrists, tightly bound to the headboard.

"Soon, soon," he told her. "I promise. I won't keep you like this forever. I won't hurt you. You know that, don't you?" he asked. Her eyes gazed helplessly back at him.

"You don't yet, but you will," he said. "I'm so sorry it has to be like this. I wish I didn't have to do this to get you to pay attention to me. You're special, but I'm special, too. A different kind of special, though."

She listened. There wasn't much she could do except listen and watch. The sunset bathed him in an orange glow that seemed almost nuclear. It didn't do anything for his features. He wasn't ugly, in her opinion. He just wasn't particularly attractive. She hadn't really paid him much attention before. Now, he commanded it. "I knew you were special the first time I saw you," he continued. "You...there's just something about you. You inspired me. But you wouldn't talk to me, wouldn't get to know me, or even give me a chance to get to know you better than I could from watching you every day."

He sighed. "You called me a freak, and you were right. I am a freak. But we all have our flaws. Maybe that's mine. Maybe yours is that you wouldn't even give a guy like me a chance," he said. "That's a flaw, too.

You're special, and you know it. The way you walk around," he shook his head. "You know you're special, but you think that means you're better than me. Well, you aren't. I guess you know that now. I wish it hadn't taken this, but that's life." He turned back to the wall, then looked out the window as if she wasn't even there.

The sun slipped down over the horizon; he watched it in silence while she watched him. When the sun disappeared, he turned back to her. "Dusk is my favorite time of day," he said, tracing the outline of her cheekbone with his index finger. "See? That's something you didn't know about me. Something that you never gave me a chance to tell you until now." He gently rubbed the smudged mascara away from her eyes and kissed her softly on her left cheek, then her right one.

She inhaled sharply. Something about the way he kissed her showed her how turned on he was. Her eyes darted around, strained to see the window.

"I love you," he said, then kissed her cheeks again. His lips moved to her neck while his hands started to slide down her sides. Her breath quickened as fear started to rise up in her. He was breathing faster too, as his arousal built. She figured he probably thought she was as turned on as he was.

From the corner of her eye, she spotted the moon beginning to rise. Her breathing slowed.

"I love you," he murmured again, as he continued kissing her cheeks and neck. He avoided her lips, probably because they were still bloody from where he had punched her earlier to knock her out when she found him in her bedroom. She was glad he avoided her lips, their shape beginning to transform.

He was so totally absorbed in her—calling her special again and rubbing and kissing harder—that he failed to notice the change taking place until it was too late.

She broke free from the bounds he had placed her in. "I am special," she snarled through razor sharp teeth. "You have no idea just how special!"

She seized his hand, still frozen in place against her chest. He didn't speak this time. He knew the positions had switched. She had the power now. It was easy to tear at his torso with her claws and shred his arm with her teeth.

"Special," she growled as he lay on her bedroom floor, bleeding to death. She threw back her head and howled at the moon before she started lapping up the fresh blood.

Beth Short and the Carnivals of the Damned

Monique Bos

Inspired by Wumpscut's *Angel*

Elizabeth Short was a ghost even before she died.

The people who knew her said no one really knew her. She'd leave them mysteriously and hint at destinations she was too coy to reveal. Perhaps she, ephemeral as a butterfly, didn't know herself, when she left one spot, where she would next alight. Her pale eyes seemed always to be fixed somewhere else, on a dream, another horizon, some other life. She embodied longings waiting to be fulfilled. She was deliriously and desperately eager for love, inventing for herself dramatic roles: fiancée of a fighter pilot, bereaved war widow. She craved a husband, a baby, a house; yearned with desire so deep it sabotaged its own possibilities. She entranced and frightened men. She teased them and obsessed them and became obsessed in turn.

Death opened her up and laid her out, naked and raw. Death granted her immortality and notoriety, sealed her secrets forever between the two halves of her body, abandoned on a vacant lot in L.A. In death she found her new identity, cribbed together from the color of her clothing and the flower she usually wore tucked behind an ear:

The Black Dahlia.

***

The drab man named Oliver had come to Savannah for two reasons. The St. Patrick's Day celebration on River Street—and the girls carried on its tide of cavorting and camaraderie—was the first. Bonaventure Cemetery was the second: the sprawling, picturesque graveyard on the edge of the marsh, with its mildew-streaked marble tombs and lavish memorials, its Spanish moss and azaleas, made famous by *Midnight in the Garden of Good and Evil*. Oliver had not read the book or seen the movie. He did not care who was buried among the camellias and meandering pathways. He simply liked graveyards.

He had rented a canoe, and he approached Bonaventure from the marsh under a florid moon. He would have liked to use the main driveway, flanked by statues of mourning female angels. Oliver found the sorrow of women compelling. But the gates were locked at 5 p.m., and he did not want to draw attention by parking near the entrance after hours. He came instead by water, gliding like an alligator beneath low-hanging branches, slipping onto the muddy bank as fiddler crabs scurried to their holes.

The girl was conscious when he lifted her out of the canoe. Her eyes were darker than Elizabeth Short's appeared in the black-and-white photos he'd seen, and huge, the pupils so dilated that the iris ringing them was a threadlike sliver of blue. She shook her head at him and tried so hard to scream that she gagged against the duct tape over her mouth.

"It's okay," he told her as gently as he could. "I'll try not to let it hurt."

He carried her uphill into the graveyard, past myriad angels: small, gnome-like Cupids peeping around the edges of dogwood bushes; dignified guardians with bowed heads; massive seraphim with wings spread in benediction, as if to comfort the lost and redeem the damned.

Not that the damned wanted redemption, Oliver thought wryly, settling the girl on a flat marble tomb he had chosen the previous day. Even now, the merry and careless hordes would be ending their debauches and drifting into uneasy sleep. River Street would be littered with broken plastic cups, strings of beads with four-leaf clover pendants, feathers fallen off boas, sticky puddles of beer. Well-off visitors—guests, the image-conscious Savannahians called them— would tangle amid strangers' bodies in air-conditioned hotel rooms with views of the river or the spires of downtown or the bridge. The Savannah River would flow by, murky and sluggish, too polluted to reflect pure green.

No sybarite himself, Oliver had spent several miserable hours on River Street before he'd found her. He sported a tacky and colorful Hawaiian shirt; the design splashed liberally with green to ward off unwelcome pinches from strangers. He had fought elbows and arms, feet that stomped on his and beery faces that leered too close. He had endured spilled liquor on his clothes, saliva in his feather boa (so careless, these anonymous souls, with their DNA: so regrettable, for them, that they sloshed their green drinks from the corners of their mouths onto his leprechaun hat or spat onto his beads with their whiskey-slowed tongues). Came away bruised, oddly exhilarated. I have walked among the damned, he thought, paddling his lonely canoe beneath moss-weighted oak branches and crepe myrtles. Drab Oliver—scrawny-necked, scraggly-haired, saggy-gutted—reflected: I have felt their breath on my skin, and still, I am pure.

On River Street he had silently seethed. He hated the revelers with their merry and carefree hedonism, their festive brilliance that so easily degenerated into grotesquerie. Look at yourselves, he wanted to say, to exhort. He wanted to stand on the ancient stone steps, his feet higher than the head of the tallest man in the crowd and cry out: Look at how you degrade yourselves, your beauty, your youth. Tomorrow you'll awaken late and do it all again, and even after you've recovered from this weekend you'll go on; there will be other weekends like it, other carnivals of the damned, other places where you and your fellow lost souls frolic until someday you are dead and your bones disconnect, drift apart in the grave, and then will you matter? Will anyone even remember how you drank and danced, laughed and fucked? No, because a new generation will have passed, and another after that, and numberless pairs of feet will have waltzed on these cobblestones, myriad stomachs emptied themselves of a night's excess in these alleys, infinite anonymous couples mated in the darkness. You don't matter, any of you; you are not making an imprint on this space through which you pass.

Except those, he added in his mind, whom he saved, whom he singled out from the mad masses, whom he etched into time and cast in immortality with his love.

So, no one on the crowded street paid attention to the man who negotiated the spaces between drunken knots of celebrants with careful control. Nothing about him drew notice. He seemed, if anyone had noticed, to watch for someone, to scan faces with a sober alertness, an edge of expectation resisting disappointment. Other eyes skipped over him. Girls looking for a good time barely registered him; he had fifteen years on most of them, his hairline pulling back from a forehead that wore its age in lines and wrinkles.

People poured in and out of the open-fronted bars facing the river. Bedraggled travelers with bandanna-clad dogs begged for change or played hacky sack in the open spaces between the street and the water. Bright white steamships with green bunting rested against docks. Even in darkness, the river beyond wore a sickly shade, the grease-slicked brown of mud and pollution and corruption.

***

Oliver had debuted his signature style in Los Angeles, as was fitting, on a New Year's Eve. No one drew connections to the Black Dahlia murder more than a half century earlier. He left her in a vacant lot, yes, but placed far from the sidewalk and arranged with care. He tucked a brilliant crimson dahlia behind her ear and sprinkled confetti over her white breasts and belly and thighs. He draped a pink feather boa around her neck and coyly arranged it over her nipples and crotch, concealing her most private parts. He placed a party hat on her head and a noisemaker in one hand, an empty plastic champagne flute in the other.

She was not exposed, like Beth Short had been, not defiled. She had not been tortured or raped, and the coroner determined that she died quickly.

That hadn't been his inaugural killing, but he considered it his first mature piece, the debut of an artist operating at the full extent of his powers. He followed it with Mardi Gras in New Orleans, St. Patrick's Day in Boston, the Fourth of July in Philadelphia, Halloween in Salem. After that first scene, he began leaving them in graveyards, nude except for the feather boas preserving their modesty, holiday kitsch in their hands. They shared some of the Black Dahlia's mutilations, but always postmortem: This killer, admitted the stymied forensic psychologists, didn't seem to enjoy his victims' suffering.

Their perfect, beautiful deaths were a gift, his gift to them and to his muse. Oliver saw Beth Short, dead for six decades, denied love and robbed of grace, looking out with the countenance of every silent stone angel who watched, stern and benevolent, over the bodies of the girls he sacrificed to her.

***

"Hush," said Oliver to the girl. She lay on her back, stretched full-length on a concrete slab beneath a cross carved with roses. Her hands, bound together, were tied above her head. Her back arched and her nipples, erect with the chill in the air and her own fright, showed through her bra and thin shirt. He barely glanced at them. A pungent odor drew his attention to the puddle growing beneath her. "Sweetheart," he said, "you should have told me if you needed to go. You don't have to be afraid."

They're always afraid, he thought; they always wet themselves. He wished he could reassure them or perhaps render them unconscious so they wouldn't have enough awareness to register fear. But then he'd miss that final exquisite, terrible knowledge in their eyes.

He reached to the waistband of her jeans. When his fingers brushed the skin of her belly, she flinched away. Her navel ring caught moonlight.

"You're so beautiful," he said.

She fought. He unfastened the buttons and the zipper, slid her pants and thong down her slender legs and over her feet, bare because he already had taken off the pumps she wore. She whimpered, struggled.

"I just want to get you out of these wet pants," he told her.

"I'm not going to rape you."

Tears slickened her cheeks, slid toward her ears.

He stroked her calf, smooth except for a small stubbly patch she must have missed when she was shaving.

"He hurt you," he told her, and, even in her panic, she blinked in confusion. "I'm not going to hurt you."

Around them, stone angels watched with blind eyes or bowed their heads in sorrow.

She started to fight again, kicked at his hands, thrashed, flailed. Urgent noises came from her throat.

He stabbed her quickly in the chest and stomach. Drove the knife in hard, so he wouldn't need to do it over and over again. He wanted her not to have to suffer. He sat and stroked her hair and murmured while she bled.

"They're waiting for you, the angels," he said. "They're holding their hands out to receive your soul, Beth. Don't you see? They'll explain and then you'll understand and you won't be upset anymore. You'll know what I saved you from."

After she stopped breathing, he ripped the tape away from her hands and mouth. He cut off her shirt and bra with the knife. She was beautiful, like Snow White, pale ethereal skin with tangled black hair and crimson blood dripping from between her breasts.

He put her things in a plastic garbage bag, along with the tape. He kissed the air just above her cooling lips.

"I love you, Beth," he said.

Then he took the knife to her again and replicated Elizabeth Short's gruesome smile, edge of the mouth to lobe of the ear. But hers had been made while she was still alive, had been one of the causes of her death, according to the autopsy.

He didn't want her to experience any more pain in this new dying.

He added his own touches at the end: a green feather boa arranged artfully over her body, covering her genitals and one nipple. An open fan covering the other breast. A plastic green derby hat on her head, strings of green beads spilling from her fingers.

He stepped back and looked at her. His eyes blurred. She was exquisitely lovely, and she was his in an intimacy no one else could possibly share.

He touched his fingers to his lips, blew the kiss out into the swamp-tainted air of the graveyard. "I've saved you," he said. "This time I've saved you," and he backed away slowly.

***

Growing up in Massachusetts, she was Betty, a girl next door with dark curls and bad teeth and fantasies. She babysat and worked at a café. Her daddy had left a decade earlier, departed on a train for the West Coast.

Oliver had read all the books about her, the famous Black Dahlia. He grew dahlias—only the dark colors, deep red and purple and various hybrids he produced trying to achieve black—in his garden, in homage to her. He photocopied and enlarged photographs from books about the murder, and her face, framed, immortalized, looked at him from every angle in his small bungalow in a Denver neighborhood as nondescript as its owner.

She was his inspiration, his guardian angel, his fantasy and the source of the only ecstasy he experienced.

In her travels around Southern California, she searched endlessly for love, for identity. She was desperately seeking him, Oliver thought, it was just that she had been born fifty years too soon. He reached back through time and tried to touch her.

Someone burned her with cigarettes, slashed her, beat her head and her face, forced her to eat shit. Someone sliced three-inch gashes from the edges of her lips to her earlobes, leaving her rotten, decaying teeth—teeth that in life she tried to whiten with wax from candles—ghoulishly grinning. Someone sawed her in half and left her naked body sprawled (warning, message, sacrifice, defiance) inches away from a sidewalk in a vacant lot.

She was maddening, paradoxical, impossible, impenetrable. She deserved worship and reverence, not the ignominy of the way she was killed and her corpse flaunted. Not the rumors that lingered decades after her death, that she was a prostitute, that she had infantile genitalia, that she was a consort of mobsters and a calculating would-be extortionist or an abusive babysitter.

She should not have been known for reasons that would have shamed her. She deserved dignity, a quiet death, respect. She deserved angels and solemn ghosts.

Oliver did his best to give them to her as often as he could.

***

In Bonaventure Cemetery, he bowed his head over the girl he'd just killed.

"Beth, my love," he whispered, "I've redeemed another one for you, another damned girl destined to become a tabloid darling dancing through the cruel carnival. I've saved her, saved her for you."

He closed his eyes briefly. Mosquitoes droned in his ears, settled on his neck and arms and face, pierced his skin. He reached a hand to hammer one and then remembered blood: The accoutrements of his latest victim held a feast of DNA he'd absorbed from the rowdy crowd; it was essential not to contaminate the scene with his own.

"How many?" he whispered. The exhilaration ebbed. "How many, Beth, until you forgive me on behalf of all men and come for me?"

He began at last to trudge back toward the canoe. He walked with less purpose but still with deliberation, scuffling the gravel to hide his footprints.

He did not see the stone angel unfold her wings and step down from the memorial into his path. He only knew that when he looked up from the ground where his steps landed, she stood in his path: Beth Short, robed, winged, glorified, beautiful and terrible.

He reached a hand toward her.

Her pale eyes looked at him, at him directly and not at some hazy horizon or distant dream. Even in his exhaustion, he understood the significance. Her mouth, the size and contours a mouth should be, no longer a visceral gash dissecting her face, curved gently.

"What?" he said.

She gestured beyond him, back toward the rose-twined cross and the marble slab where he had left the girl from River Street. "She was for you," he said. "All of them, everything, all of it. For you."

She shook her head. Folded her arms over her breasts.

"What more do you want? What else could I give?"

She looked past him then. He turned too and saw, rising from the slab, the girl, her naked body pale as marble. As she stood, she unfurled magnificent pale wings behind her, and then she walked toward Beth, toward the outstretched hand, without acknowledging Oliver's presence.

Elizabeth Short, whole, graceful, maternal, enfolded the girl in her arms.

"No more," she said to Oliver, "I can't let you take any more; I can't," and he didn't see her stone fist rising above his head, didn't feel it displacing air as it rushed down toward him. He knew only a final anguish and ecstasy as he looked into the face of his love and saw that she did not understand his gifts, did not want them, did not cherish all that he had done for her, all that he'd lived to give her. She left him crumpled there on the gravel path in the moonlight: skull broken, brain slipping out, crushed dahlias around him where her feet had trod.

Beth Short bowed her head in sorrow for a brief moment, and then she followed the girl out of the graveyard. They glided away into a dawn that broke vibrant and trembling over the marsh, silent as angels, merciful as the grave.

Just Another Town

Ben A. Bell

Inspired by The Grateful Dead's *Friend of the Devil*

A big rig swung off the highway onto a rural road, crunching cracked pavement under its tires. A sign, which read: Harmony Bend – population 2317, vibrated in the wind of its passage.

Fields of wheat spread toward the horizon, almost ready for harvest. Along the road's edges, golden stalks shied away from the truck's massive wake. It threw dust in the air and shook the bridge at the town's border. Entering the small community, it rumbled past dirt driveways and farmhouses, nestled like colorful Easter eggs on their lawns.

Clouds slunk across the sky, snuffing out the sun like a gutted flame, and bringing on a premature twilight. The wind howled in mourning at the loss of light. A storm was on its way.

The growling behemoth turned onto Main Street, devoid of traffic on a Saturday, and rolled past a tranquil, tree-lined park. Inside, a child tossed a ball up into the air and usually, but not always, caught it as it tumbled back to earth.

This ain't so hard, Jimmy thought to himself as a breeze ruffled his bangs. Alerted by the snarling engine, his eyes widened at the sight of the approaching truck. The momentary distraction caused him to miss the ball. It struck his sneakered foot and bounced through a flowerbed on its way to the street. He leapt after it, but it was too late. The ball rolled into the path of the oncoming truck and disappeared beneath its heavy wheels.

The tiny shriek that came from the boy couldn't have been any more miserable if the ball had been a favorite pet. The radar ears of his mother, set to receive all incoming childlike squeals as she skimmed a romance novel, glanced over. *Jimmy's fine.* Relief turned to curiosity when she noticed the big rig. Air brakes screeched as it braked at Main Street's single stop light.

From its cab to its taillights, the truck glistened midnight black.

"Mommy," Jimmy complained, scampering up to her. "The truck ran over my ball. He smooshed it!"

"Really, Jimmy?" she asked sympathetically, as she ruffled his brown locks. "I'm sorry." She shot a glance back over to the truck. Brilliant red letters along the sides read: 'Allah Saves. Free books from The Holy Muslim Alliance.' She shivered as a cold wind worked its way in the openings of her damp clothes. Through the driver's window, she saw a dark-skinned man look her way. He pursed his lips and blew her a kiss before baring yellow, misshapen teeth under eyes so dark, they looked like empty holes. A gasp escaped her lips.

His grotesque grin stretched wider as he laughed. The light changed. Still, he sat, watching her. He hawked and spat a wad of phlegm into the street.

Stuffing her book in her handbag, she stood up and grabbed Jimmy's arm.

"What about my ball?" Jimmy hung back.

"We'll tell Daddy tonight, and maybe he'll get you a new one." Child in tow, she hurried away. "And that's not all we'll tell him."

The semi accelerated, trailing dark exhaust fumes, which spread out finger-like across the town's center. At the end of Main Street, it pulled into the Harmony Motel parking lot, dwarfing the small manager's office.

The manager hid her Celebrity Tales magazine under the counter and smoothed her hair when the swarthy trucker walked in. As he approached the desk, one sleeve of his long, dress-like *djellabah* caught a flowerpot on a side-table, knocking it to the ground. His apology, if that's what it was, hid behind a thick accent she couldn't place.

"Don't think twice, it's all right." She smiled at him. Business was slow; she needed paying customers.

He signed the register and handed her grubby, crumpled bills.

"Been truckin' long?" Her friendly attempt at small talk fell flat. He took the key and left, stepping on the bedraggled blooms without a word. She grumbled to herself, eyeing the mess. Walking outside to take down his plate numbers for her records, she noticed a peculiar odor. The truck smelled of oil and something else, something foul. She held her hand over the lower half of her face, trying not to breathe as she walked around the side. She saw the crimson letters, and a quick inhale of surprise sent fumes up her nose. Eyes watering, she trotted to the gas station next door, where her husband worked. When she gave him an earful, his face compressed into sharp lines.

At Jimmy's house, his dad ignored his request for a new ball. He appeared more interested in the trucker and frowned at his wife's description. Jimmy saw his older brother, recently fired from his job delivering hay bales, get a funny angry look in his eyes when she repeated the words on the truck. His father left for his night job at the bar, and his brother went to a rehearsal with his band. Jimmy sat alone in his room, listening to his mother rant on the phone to the other wives, and learned some new curse words to describe the stranger. He slouched in his bed, took a comic book from the nightstand, and wished bad things on the ball-murdering trucker. *Superman would know how to handle him.*

The brewing storm's humidity exacerbated the stench from the truck. It seeped into the night, permeating everything in the town with the taint of wrongness.

From the town bar to the barn where the band practiced country ballads, to the ladies' quilting circle, an ugly tide transformed the town. Peering out from behind lace curtains at the big black blemish in the motel parking lot, eyes smoldered with resentment.

A tangible scent of evil snuck into every nook and cranny.

Stray cats arched their backs and yowled; dogs snarled and snapped at their owners. Rats abandoned their cramped holes, disregarded overturned trashcans, and scurried out of town.

Husbands fought with wives, children whined, and friends hurled insults. An old jukebox in the corner of the bar shuddered to life. Its rusty workings played "Strangers in the Night" at half speed, making Ol' Blue Eyes sound like a ghoul from a nightmare.

"It ain't right," one neighbor griped to another. A few beers later, remarks escalated to "Something's gotta be done" and "We don't have to take this." The phrases echoed around the darkened bar, gaining in rhythm and volume. Clenched jaws became clenched fists. General grievances became irrational accusations. The bartender yanked the jukebox's cord out of the wall, but the hideous music continued to play.

The first roll of thunder rattled windows and loosened a bottleneck of rage. Angry residents charged to their cars, picking up bats and tire irons.

As one, they marched toward the Harmony Motel.

The few who were still coherent hung back. After all, they thought, the trucker would leave in the morning, no harm done. They snuck back to their houses to wait out the storm.

Jimmy's father clutched a bat. He had owned a farm until the bank stole it away. He couldn't give the officials what they deserved, but the stranger at the motel would do.

A wave of anger surged through the town, picked up those who had hard hearts and narrow minds, and carried them toward the motel. Lightning flashed, and a boom of thunder hid the hollow clump of work boots as the pack streamed across the motel parking lot.

After a word from the manager, the men swarmed around the motel door like wasps. They burst into the room, jostling into one another in the darkness and swinging at the form on the bed. Sheets twisted and pillow feathers flew, as bats and tire irons tore into the sleeping shape. Grunts of effort echoed out the open door as neighbors, who couldn't recognize each other through masks of rage, shouldered in to get a good strike.

The bass rumble of the big rig's engine cut across the panting of the attackers. Startled, Jimmy's father turned and pointed. The mob tumbled out the doorway to see the ebony truck roar out of the parking lot. It swerved and clipped a pillar supporting the lighted roof over the gas station's pumps.

The roof spat sparks of electricity as it collapsed, smashing the pumps into the ground. Severed pipes disgorged rivers of gas from underground tanks.

As the truck's straining engines powered it out of the town, a huge fireball lit up the night sky.

In the truck's cab, the swarthy man wasn't shaking in fear at his narrow escape or at the destruction left in his wake. In fact, he had a smile on his face.

The semi rolled down the highway, undergoing a transformation. The writing on the truck's sides morphed and spidered into new ruby-red letters that spelled 'The Book Net. Free Children's Books from Lester, the Happy Clown.' In the cab, Lester shifted in his seat as a cheerful clown costume sprang up and wrapped itself around him in place of the *djellabah*. His face became pale-skinned and jolly. Behind him, small pictures of laughing, playing children appeared along the back wall of the sleeping compartment. Some of the pictures, which were visible from outside the cab, showed children in bathing suits and in unusual poses.

He knew of another little town where the townsfolk would gladly take the bait and resort to violence if they thought there was a child molester in their midst. He grinned in the glow of the dashboard lights, knowing that wherever he went, hell was sure to follow.

Snatch

Bryan Oftedahl

Inspired by Against Me's *How Low*

"Hit me." The words came out sounding like a thumbs up or an 'Okay to go.'

Every muscle tensed. Scott's eyes clenched shut, a full load of oxygen held in his chest. The seconds ticked by, anticipation searing his nerves, his pulse throbbing in his temples, and still nothing happened. His lungs began to burn as the oxygen was harvested, so he released it in one long exhalation through flapping lips. One eye peeled open, followed by the other.

Nothing happened. The hit never came.

Jacob kneeled in front of him with brown eyes pleading. Scott looked down at the needle resting in his vein, a splash of his own red swirling in the chamber, getting high without him while Jacob's thumb hovered over the plunger.

"Hit me!" Scott's shouting, now pathetic and desperate, echoed through the old dining hall of the condemned hotel, frightening the pigeons above into flight out and away from the possibility of danger.

"I already told you," Jacob growled. "I'm not feeling comfortable with this, man."

"It's just a hit, that's all." Scott wanted to shiver from the cold eating at his exposed arm but knew it would dislodge the needle. "I've been good. I've made it like a week now."

"Actually, it's been a day and a half," Stan corrected. "You promised Suzie you would quit yesterday afternoon."

At the mention of her name, the boys glanced toward the corner where Suzie sat on a pile of blankets. She glared through a tattered curtain of badly dyed black bangs with brunette roots. Her eyes, painted with a crusty ring of mascara, stood out against her pale face as she watched them with hate. Her right hand rubbed her swollen belly. All three quickly looked away, feeling her eyes burning into their backs.

"Whatever, Rome wasn't built in a day and a half." Scott let his eyes fall to the dilapidated flooring. "You don't just go clean all of a sudden. Please, hit me."

Heaving a sigh, Jacob pressed his thumb down, forcing the plunger home and the needle's contents into his friend's median cubital, where it was carried along to his heart and lungs. Like a nervous bang of euphoria, the toxin seeped into Scott's muscles and brain. He tumbled backward off his heels and onto the floorboards where he unfurled like a blooming rose. His lungs took in short breaths, while his eyes rolled around in their sockets.

"Oh God, yes...oh, fuck yeah..." A sickening feeling of compression in his upper torso chased the euphoria away. Darkness began creeping around the edges of his sight, slowly blacking everything out. Scott felt as if he were melting into the floor like the candles around him, dribbling out of his body and through the floor. Stan and Jacob stood over him as he started shuddering then convulsing.

Stan whispered, "Is he..."

Jacob stepped back a few paces. "I knew it. I knew this would happen, damn it!"

From her corner, Suzie continued rubbing her belly, perhaps a little rougher. She could only shake her head at the situation as the future appeared so much bleaker.

***

"Death is for the living. It always has been."

Toward the west, what little of the horizon that could be seen through the cityscape was dressed in a thin layer of fiery orange, and, though the east end was quickly falling into darkness, the city glow prevented any stars from showing. A silent ambulance cruised up streets and down avenues, wandering aimlessly through the city, waiting for an opportunity to present itself. James lay on the gurney in the back cabin piloting the airways with a radio against his ear. Debbie, curled in the passenger seat, cradled her Americano and concentrated on ignoring Charlie's driver-side rant.

Aware the others were ignoring him, Charlie felt inclined to take a corner sharper than needed, bouncing off the curb and jolting his co-workers in unison. James was nearly tossed from the gurney, while Debbie screeched as she suddenly became aware of the temperature of her coffee, which splashed out of the cup and onto her hand.

James called from the back, "What the hell was that about?"

"I'm trying to make a very important point and you two are paying no attention, Charlie replied." Debbie expressed her irritation by pummeling his right shoulder. Shoving her away, Charlie wagged a finger,

"Never hit the driver. You want us to get in a wreck?"

"Pull something like that again and 'wreck' will be an understatement when and if they find your remains." Transferring the coffee to her other hand, she slid the burnt and throbbing hand into the sleeve of her coveralls before curling up again.

"Okay, where was I?"

"It was something about death, right?" James continued patrolling the airwaves between police and emergency, though he decided to sit up from then on.

"Right, yeah." Clearing his throat, "Now, it doesn't matter whether you believe in heaven and hell, reincarnation or that death is truly the end of it all. If you're up in God's palace or being reincarnated as a squid, will you really give a damn what happens to your body or earthly possessions?"

After a few minutes with nobody answering, he clutched the wheel as he neared another corner. Without turning to him Debbie mumbled, "Do it and die, my darling."

"Can I get a little cooperation here, then?"

"I guess not," James shrugged. "I mean if I were a squid as you say, then I'd only be interested in fish, right?"

"No," Debbie added. "I wouldn't give a damn."

"Then why do we put so much effort into burial ceremonies or the drawing out of a last will and testament? Is it really for the person who died?"

After being nudged by Charlie's elbow, Debbie finally called out, "I don't know, Chuck!"

"No, that's the answer. The answer is no. We carry out burials or cremations, memorials and all that crap so the living can close off the part of their life that person occupied. The will isn't read so much for the person who died, but so that those still living can divvy up his money and possessions."

"Actually," James cut in, "It could just be out of respect for the dead."

Adjusting the rearview mirror to see the rear of the cabin, Charlie called back, "Respect for somebody who probably doesn't even give a damn about you now that he's occupied with adapting to whatever comes in the sweet hereafter?"

Looking up from the radio, James chuckled. "It was just an idea is all."

Waving James aside, Charlie continued on, "I thank you for the effort. Anyway, the point is—"

"You don't have a point," Debbie interrupted. "You never have a point. The fact is that you're ranting on without a point, as usual."

Half a moment of silence ensued, but Charlie was incapable of letting the matter go. "Okay, I'll jump to it, the *point* is that it's all a waste. I mean the ceremonies and disposal of the body; it's a huge waste of time, money and a very valuable product. Think of what all good that body could be used for, from teaching young surgeons to tissue transplants. That one possession we are born with and eventually die leaving behind could help extend the lives of others, but oh, no, we put on some worthless show, then throw it away in a hole marked by some fancy marble slab."

"Fine, your point is made, could we continue the evening in silence now?" Downing the rest of her coffee, she added it to the stack in the cup holder before finishing. "Please?"

"You're just closed minded."

"Okay, I'm closed minded," she shrugged. "Now shut the hell up."

Before Charlie could pick another topic to ignite, James leapt to his feet, as best he could in the cramped conditions of the rear cabin and gave a whooping holler similar to Slim Pickens' victory call from *Dr. Strangelove.*

"I got one!" He pressed the radio against his ear, nodding to it. "Chuck, go to the corner of Roosevelt and 6th."

"Aye, aye captain," Charlie dropped his foot onto the gas and headed northward, drumming the wheel excitedly.

Debbie remained stagnant. Turning back to James. "What're the stats?"

"Relax, it's that old hotel. The call came through as a blue and holding."

"Another one?"

"Oh, come on," Charlie groaned. "All nearby units are attending that pile-up over on the freeway. We're just a few minutes away."

Debbie threw her hands up in submission, "I'm just sick of these ODs is all. Can't anyone in this town die like a normal human being?"

***

The building, once praised for its Gothic architecture, had been the scene of several high-scale parties, attracting the attention of the prosperous and well-heeled from nearby states, but that was nearly a century ago. As the age of industry expanded, a modern city center of glass towers was established elsewhere, and the building was left to rot with the rest of the surrounding neighborhood. Though neglected, it was not forgotten by all. Despite the occasional team of officers sent in to clear it of addicts and street-kind, it rarely remained empty for long.

Charlie eased the ambulance up to the curb where two kids, not one older than twenty, stood shivering despite the layers of clothing hanging from their frames. Debbie latched onto Charlie's arm before he could open the door, then turned and hissed at James. Her eyes moved from one to the other, burning.

"I'm not in the mood for any shenanigans tonight, you hear me? In and out, that's all."

"Sure." Charlie nodded. "Like a rapist, in and out."

"I mean it Chuck!" She tightened her grip, nails digging through the coveralls and into his forearm.

"Okay." He yanked his arm free, "Time's a wasting."

Debbie stepped in front of the kids before they could crowd in on the others pulling the gurney from the back. Waving her hands at their glazed eyes, she pulled in their attention.

"What took you so long?" The tallest of the duo stepped forward and stated his complaint. Apparently, he was the only one capable of speech as the other one nervously twitched and shivered in the cold.

"We get hundreds of calls every night," she explained. "We take them as they come. So, what's the situation here, boys?" That ignited something, they each broke into a frenzy of excuses and hysterical pleas. "Slow down! We don't want an explanation; we just need you to lead us to the problem, okay?"

Around the corner, a piece of plywood stapled with a 'No Trespassing' sign and strips of police tape was moved aside to reveal an arched stone doorway leading into a long and narrow hallway. The gurney barely made it down the hall as half of the available space was occupied by a train of shopping carts that would probably never see their home parking lots again; the floor was scattered with broken glass and crumpled cans. The hall opened into what had likely been the hotel lobby, and from there, the group hiked an expansive staircase to the floor above.

The kids were familiar enough with the space to continue without light, but Debbie and James both pulled mag-lights from their pockets, pointing them downward to prevent tripping on the stairs.

On the landing above, they cut left and stepped through what had once been a double doorway but, somewhere in time, one of the massive wooden doors had gone missing. The space beyond was enormous and dark; flickering candles melted into the cracked hardwood flooring and failed miserably in their endeavor at chasing the thick darkness away. The kids stopped a few steps outside a semicircle of candles, pointing inward.

Charlie and James rolled the gurney toward the body while Debbie turned to distract the two boys. “Anyone mind telling me what happened tonight?”

They each looked away, then down at their feet, refusing to make eye contact. “Slim-Jim,” she pointed at the tall, gaunt one that had spoken before.

“Jacob,” he mumbled.

“Jacob, what happened here tonight?”

“I don’t know. He just started gagging and grabbing his chest, then fell down and then didn’t do nothing.” Shrugging, “I think it was a heart attack.”

Debbie glanced back at the body. The subject was a wiry teen with graying lips, matted hair. A heart attack was highly unlikely.

She nodded, “Any idea why he may have been gagging and holding his chest?”

Jacob looked down at his feet, shaking his head.

The other boy repeated, “A heart attack?”

“Look, if it was a heart attack, we’ll treat him for a heart attack, but if this was an overdose, then we have to treat him for an overdose. So, which was it?”

Charlie first felt the body’s wrist, then the jugular before resting one ear on the still chest. James peeled open one of the eyes, passing his flashlight back and forth across it.

“Clear!” Charlie’s voice echoed into the dark as he threw his fist down on the subject’s chest with a sickening thud. James played the light over the opened eye again, shaking his head.

The kids jumped at Charlie’s shout, and the smaller one broke into tears. Debbie made a mental note to kick Charlie once they were in the clear, but, for the time, she had to keep the witnesses occupied. Flashing her light into Jacob’s face, “If you don’t tell us what happened, then we can’t treat your friend, do you understand?” He nodded but remained quiet.

“Was he doing drugs?” She pressed.

They each nodded.

“Was he smoking or snorting or shooting or what?”

This time she jumped along with the boys as Charlie again slugged the dead ribcage. "Clear!"

"He was riding the horse, okay." Jacob's voice began to waver.

"Heroin?"

"You gotta bring him back," the other boy spoke up, apparently the youngest of the duo, candlelight reflecting off the tears streaking his cheeks and snot slicking his upper lip. He pointed at a candle flame furthest off to the side.

Debbie's heart skipped, her hands clenching into fists as the outline of a young woman rose in the dark and stepped forward. A ragged blanket hung from the girl's shoulders; her belly was swollen and her waxen face hung almost as slack as that of their departed companion. Debbie relaxed her hands and tightened her throat, cutting off the instinctual curse.

This was not a good situation.

Seeing things worsening, James stood and bowed his head. "I'm afraid there's nothing we can do here." He nudged Charlie and nodded toward the gurney.

Quick as flies, the two lifted the body onto the gurney. Once strapped into place, they began rolling toward the doorway. Debbie did her best to keep the kids out of the way, trying to sooth their rising hysterics.

"No, this can't be happening." The smaller of the two boys clamped his head and began shaking it as if attempting to knock something clear from within. "You have to bring him back, like with those electric paddle things."

"Defibrillators don't jump start dead meat, kid." She started walking backwards, following the gurney outside. "I'm sorry."

"What about one of those *Pulp Fiction* heart needles?" Jacob swung his arm through the air in a motion more Norman Bates than Vincent Vega. "What about those?"

"Sorry, guys," Charlie called from the other side of the corpse. "In reality, dead is dead."

With the whole lot distracted, the girl was able to slink out from the darkness and right up to the gurney with nobody being the wiser. She snorted then spat on the slack and graying face of the departed. Leaping forward, she lifted her fists up in the air, each one slamming onto the body. James wrapped his arms around her as gently as he could, holding back the flurry of fists and cussing back into the dark, leaving Charlie, who was obviously choking back the urge to chuckle, in charge of pulling the gurney out of the room.

Somewhere overhead came the startled flapping of wings as the girl screamed. "You promised you were done with it. You promised!" James had to latch harder just to keep her from wriggling free. “Now what am I going to do? I got nothing! Nothing!”

***

Back on the street, the body was loaded into the cabin, James pulling from inside and Charlie shoving from behind before swinging the doors closed. Debbie stepped in front of one of the two kids who had followed them out. “I’m sorry but we’re all full.”

“But one of us has to go,” Jacob protested. “Where is he headed?”

“If you want to see him again, then head over to the Charles D. Ward Memorial Hospital along the Boulevard.” That said, she jumped into the passenger side just as Charlie pulled away from the curb.

Once away, Debbie turned to Charlie, “Would you mind telling me what the hell that was?”

Charlie looked as innocent and naïve as possible. “What?”

“What?” She mimicked back. “You’re beating up the corpse and screaming ‘clear’ at the top of your lungs. You probably busted his sternum.”

“We pulled it off, didn’t we?”

She could only sit there and glare. “I really hate you.”

“You know, if you just learned to have more fun with things, the world would seem a lot happier.” Charlie flashed a grin that could have sent a shiver up the spine of Lucifer himself. “You do realize that, right?”

Realizing nothing good would come from continuing the argument, Debbie switched modes and looked back at James. “So, what do you think?”

“I highly doubt there’s much tissue or organs of any value. I say toss him at a university as a cadaver or find some medical equipment company introducing a new line of products.”

Charlie glanced through the rearview mirror, “How much, though?”

“If we dice him for parts, I’d say four grand, as a cadaver maybe two.” Finishing his inspection, James picked up his radio again. “Let’s see what else we can find tonight.”

For a moment they were silent, something Charlie could never stand for very long. “You know who the biggest psycho killer is?”

Debbie threw her hands in the air, “Can’t you ever keep that trap shut?”

“God, that’s who, I mean there’s the big flood then Sodom and Gomorrah...”

***

Stan looked up to Jacob as the ambulance disappeared around the corner. "I didn't know there was a hospital on the Boulevard."

"There's not, it's just marketplaces and—"

Their attention was suddenly drawn down the street where an ambulance with flashing lights and wailing siren rushed toward them. The gleaming white and red vehicle skidded to a stop as two burley men leapt out.

"Okay boys, what's the situation here?"

They both stared at the men, then up to the corner where the other ambulance had disappeared from view. Behind them, from somewhere in the depths of the old hotel, Suzie's screams turned from anger to sudden horror.

One of the paramedics stepped forward, "Did you guys make the call? What's going on here?"

"I don't know," Jacob shook his head. "We called and an ambulance already came and—"

"Wait, somebody already came? Did they take anybody?" The other paramedic pulled a radio from his belt and started yelling into it. "Nancy, call the cops down here. It happened again.

Another one got snatched."

Suzie waddled out of the hotel, her inner thighs soaked. "For God's sake, my water just broke. Help me!"

For a second, the world was silent and still.

The paramedics rushed toward Suzie, leaving the boys alone. Finally, Stan looked up to Jacob. "What the hell just happened, Jake? I mean, if it's what I think it is, that kind of thing doesn't happen."

Synthetic Messiah

Marc Sorondo

Inspired by Depeche Mode's *Personal Jesus*

It was hot beneath the huge, billowing tent that served as the nomadic home of the Lord's Fire revival as it worked its way slowly across the south in a serpentine path as crooked as its leader, Reverend William Flemming.

Carson James stood amongst the faithful—the gullible—assembled that morning and took note of the beads of sweat as they moved from his hairline to his eyebrows. The sheep wore lighter cloths than he, breathable fabrics that allowed the humidity within the temporary sanctuary to mix with that of their own sweaty bodies. Carson did not. He wore a black suit, a blue shirt with black pinstripes, and a blue tie. His clothes were like a bio-dome, keeping him separate. His moisture was his own, as was his truth.

He, like those who surrounded him, had always been one of the faithful, the credulous, the susceptible. His mother had raised him to believe, to trust that the flock was watched over, even after her husband had abandoned her to care for their newborn child alone, even as the cancer painfully devoured her, turning her bones to splinters and her own blood to poison.

Thinking of his mother always brought tears to his eyes, tears that in these settings were doubtless misconstrued as ones of joy, as a mark that he'd been touched and that Jesus' invisible print had been etched onto his soul.

The Reverend William Flemming quoted from the book of Revelations from his place at the pulpit—his exalted place on high—on the stage at the center of the tent like the ringmaster of a circus with only a single act, surrounded by his legion of freaks who would swallow almost anything.

Carson was the sole spectator. He alone would not swallow. He'd seen the act before, he'd stood amongst the fooled, listened to the words of liars and false prophets, of synthetic messiahs who created their own air of divinity in the minds and eyes of their followers.

Their name, too, was Legion, for there was no shortage of them all over the world, spreading their message of self-glorification.

But they were good, Carson had to give them that. Even now, after all he knew, he could see why people were so easily fooled. Good people who just wanted to believe, asses who chased the carrot dangled in front of them, held always just out of reach.

Carson looked around at faces that smiled and faces that wept, at hands held up, grasping for holiness that was as out of reach as that carrot: just barely.

The reverend bellowed into the microphone, "The time draws very near. The Lord's hour is almost come, and it is time to come clean, to make ourselves right with our savior. We cannot be lukewarm, for he will turn us away. We must be more vigilant than ever before, in our prayers, our lives, and our resistance to the sin that runs rampant in this day and age. We must be faithful and steadfast. We must be witnesses of the truth, devoted to Him above all else. We must be generous to aid his works on Earth, the preparations for his return..."

Ah-ha, a slight revelation of truth amidst the propaganda: a call for generosity. Carson was well aware that for all of their talent, regardless of how good their façade could be, the truth always slipped out, it broke free. Veritas, it could not be contained, it is irrepressible.

One such bit of truth had opened his eyes, revealed whole truths to him just by the slip of a minor one. It had been years ago, after they'd diagnosed the cancer that decimated his mother's body. Back then, he still saw the world through the veil that his mother had tied over his eyes when he was a baby, the same veil that she wore herself, the veil that obscured her vision until the moment of her death.

The truth that tore the first rip in Carson's veil had been revealed, quite by accident of course, underneath a similar tent in sweltering heat. Jonas Martin, not a reverend, was well known for the gifts that he'd been given, which he claimed included the ability to spread the Lord's healing fire, to burn away both sickness and sin through a laying on of hands, a few words of prayer, and just a bit of help from the man upstairs.

Carson and his mother had gone to see Martin while he was stopped just outside of Atlanta, driving from their home in West Virginia even though Mrs. James' brittle bones ached after sitting up for too long.

On the drive down, his mother had assured him that the Lord would care for them, that Jonas Martin wielded enough of the Almighty's grace to cast out the demons that ate away at her.

And Carson had believed.

Martin had called up those who were in need of the healing flames, and Mrs. James was among them. The choir sang on as Martin preached and prayed into a microphone stuck to his too vibrantly colored suit jacket.

One by one he prayed over the infirmed, laying his hands on them gently at first, but shaking them as his words built in intensity, finishing with a short but forceful push that sent them to fall backwards into the waiting arms of Martin's healthier followers.

Carson's mother went up, she was prayed over, and she smiled as she slowly fell into the arms of other believers.

On the drive back to West Virginia, his mother still looked uncomfortable. She grimaced when she moved, and she took long, deep breaths now and then, with closed eyes, when the ache would briefly spike into severe pain.

"Don't you feel any better?" he'd asked.

"You can't rush God, Carson. He does things at the pace that's best. You know that," she'd said.

"I know. I just thought you'd feel better right away." She was dead less than two months later.

But before she died, once it was clear that the evil within her had not been purged by preachers or by doctors, she and Carson had gone to see Jonas Martin again.

They drove into the heart of South Carolina, where Martin's tent and ministry had since moved, and waited until the afternoon meeting had ended, and the others dispersed before approaching the healer.

They asked him what had gone wrong, why she was still dying, if he would ask the Lord again to heal her.

Martin's answer was but a sentence long, after which he simply turned and left, leaving Carson and Mrs. James to stare at his back, silent, as he walked away.

"You must not be right with the Lord, sister, if he chose not to heal you," Martin had said. His eyes were lit up from deep within, a blazing fury of religious zeal. That was the real fire wielded by Jonas Martin, and it burnt away lots of things, but sickness was not one of them.

Days later, Mrs. James had died, in terrible pain both physical and spiritual. Her belief that she was somehow out of God's favor, that she'd offended the Almighty in some way, made her spiritual anguish even more excruciating than her physical suffering.

Carson James had seen a glimpse of truth unobstructed. He decided that he would do the Lord's real work.

But that was years ago, and Carson had become a regular on the revival circuit, as a Dr. James Cannon at the River of Life revival in Mississippi, as Connor Jager esquire at the Way of the Light revival in Arkansas, and as numerous other names at revivals that have since ended abruptly.

He traveled wherever necessary. It wasn't a problem, as he had few possessions to bring with him nowadays. He had sold it all off to follow Jesus after his mother died, to be a disciple and spread the word.

Carson's eyes squinted a bit, and he stopped thinking about the past when he noticed a gradual shift of tone and semantic patterns in Reverend Flemming's speech. He was beginning to wrap things up. He'd only heard Flemming preach once before, but they all sounded vaguely similar, and, after the years spent amongst the wolves, he could almost instinctively tell when the sermon was winding down.

He was to meet with Flemming right after the service.

Carson walked out of the tent and into the cooler, dryer air outside. He made his way around the tent and towards the small, dingy trailer that Flemming used as a mobile office.

Not long after, herds of people began to leave the tent. The service was over. Carson figured he had at least twenty minutes before the reverend would be able to get out of the tent.

Flemming was no different from the others. Carson arranged the meeting yesterday and knew that Flemming was supposed to be the next, knew that Jesus had led Carson here to do His work. Carson knew it from the way the reverend's eyes glazed over the minute he mentioned that he wanted to discuss a large donation to the cause—a very large donation. With his fairly new ability to see the truth, greed was easy for Carson to spot.

Carson leaned against the off-white trailer. He cleared his throat and said, "Wonderful sermon, reverend." Very good. Only someone with a well-trained ear would make out any hint of his southern twang. Now he sounded like a northerner, New York maybe, or at least New Jersey. Practice makes perfect. Praise the Lord. Carson waited patiently for what turned out to be twenty-five minutes before he saw the reverend come around the tent and towards the trailer, towards Carson.

"Good evening, Mr. Carlstadt," Flemming said with a wave as he got closer.

"Wonderful sermon, reverend," Carson said.

The slight breeze toyed with the reverend's white hair, which was already a mess from the fervor and enthusiasm of his preaching. The reverend pushed open the door to the trailer and said, “Come on in. Make yourself comfortable.” The door hadn’t been locked, and Flemming did not bother to do so after Carson stepped inside.

“So, what did you think?” Reverend Flemming asked with a smile.

“I wouldn’t have thought it possible, but I think tonight’s meeting may actually have been more moving than yesterday’s. You could really feel the Lord’s presence among his people tonight.” Carson smiled and made unnecessary adjustments to his tie.

“Ha-ha! I thought so too,” Flemming said, lightly smacking his hands together for emphasis. “I could really feel the fire tonight. I could almost see it burning through the congregation, purifying flames...” Flemming trailed off and his eyes seemed to go with his words, off into some memory.

“I don’t mean to rush, reverend, but about my donation...” Carson said, pulling Flemming back in.

“Oh, yes. I’m sorry. Very generous of a young man like yourself. So often it’s the older folks who hear the Lord’s call to generosity. Especially with you being from the Big Apple and all. Unusual, but that is often the way He works,” Flemming said, pointing to the roof of the trailer.

“Well, I only work in the city. I live in the suburbs, if that makes any difference.”

The reverend chuckled and said, “It may. I wouldn’t really know.”

Carson reached into his pants pocket and pulled out a silver pen and a small pad of paper.

“I would like...” Carson said as he scribbled on the paper, “...to offer something in the region of this amount. I believe you’re doing good work and want to see it continue. It’s the least I can do.” He tore off the sheet and handed it to Flemming.

The reverend took it, and his eyes widened at the sight of the figure. Along with his tousled white hair and grin, Flemming’s wide eyes made him look like a maniac for a second.

“Mr. Carlstadt—”

“Please, call me Jackson. Jack if you’d like,” Carson interrupted.

“What exactly do you do that you can offer this kind of money?” Flemming sat down, still holding the paper up in front of his face.

“I head a private equity firm. Why? Is that too much? Because if you couldn’t use it all, I could always donate less.” Bait.

“No, no, I’m sure we can make good use of it. There’s just no end to the work there is to be done. I’m just taken aback by your generosity.”

Carson started to pace a bit, and said, “You see, reverend, I like to think that I also have a purpose, a duty that has been assigned to me by God Himself." Carson's smile slipped away, his eyes took on a wolf-like reflectivity which gleamed in the evening light.

"I agree," the reverend said amiably.

"As you said, there's no end to the Lord's work. Can I ask you something, reverend?"

"Of course, Mr. Carlstadt."

"Jackson, please. The healings that occur in revivals of this kind..." Carson began to cover a greater distance now in his pacing, and he undid one of the buttons on his suit jacket, leaving it held closed by a single one. "How do you do it?"

"I don't. I'm no more able to heal a man than you. The Lord chooses to heal his faithful, and he just so happens to choose sometimes to do so at these meetings."

"So, it is a matter of faith? Of being...right with the Lord?" Carson moved completely behind the old preacher now. Flemming did not follow him with his gaze but rather looked forward with the same nostalgia as earlier. "I believe that Jesus can and does heal people wherever he sees fit; could be in a ditch on the side of the road or in an airplane at thirty thousand feet..."

Carson, still standing behind the reverend, had heard enough. He reached into his jacket, taking care not to unbutton the last fastener holding the jacket closed.

"...However, when a congregation gets together for prayer and worship, when the flock is joined together and calls out the Master's praises and asks for His grace and mercy..."

It was a huge knife. It had taken Carson a while to get used to the feel of it pressed against his abdomen, concealed in the jacket of his suit. It was actually fairly small for a Bowie knife, but any collector of the type will tell you that small for a Bowie knife isn't very small.

The handle was ivory, carved from the tusk of some long dead elephant, and the blade seemed to glisten in the light of the trailer. It was the only thing Carson's father had left behind. Sometimes Carson thought that had been part of God's plan.

"...It just seems to me that the Lord wouldn't ignore the prayers and praises of His people, especially all together like that. That's why I think healings take place so often at the meetings, because..."

Carson ran the blade across the soft skin of the Reverend William Flemming's throat, careful not to let much of the blood get on the sleeve of his suit.

The reverend gurgled, but only for the briefest of moments, and then his head fell forward.

Carson closed his eyes and lifted his face towards Heaven.

He took a deep breath and held it. He could feel it, the mark of the Lord, pressing Jesus' invisible print deeper into his soul. His body quivered in a nearly sexual ecstasy in his communion with the divine. His act had been a prayer, an offering, a sacrament.

When Carson finally opened his eyes, there were tears in them.

He felt around on Flemming's chest for a moment, the still warm blood coating the tips of his fingers before he found what he was looking for.

He lifted a small gold cross, now slicked with a scarlet sheen, from the thatch of grey chest hair.

Carson pressed the blade of his knife against the delicate gold chain, and with minimal pressure, a few links popped open and he held only the cross.

Carson found the sink and rinsed the piece of jewelry, his hands, and his knife. He slid the knife back into the sheath that he'd sewn into the lining of his jacket. From the inside pocket of the jacket he pulled a small velvet pouch, black with a pearly white cross stitched onto it. He opened the top, and crosses of gold, platinum, and silver, some jeweled and others plain, reflected the yellow light of the trailer back at him in slivers of gold and silver hues that slashed across his face.

He dropped Flemming's cross in with the others and returned the pouch to his pocket. He quickly checked his hands to make sure they were thoroughly clean. He turned out the lights in the trailer, locked the door, and listened to the latch click into place as he pulled the door shut.

Osaka's Fallen Son

Natalie L. Sin

Inspired by Queen's *Bohemian Rhapsody*

Dear Mother,

Today I killed a man. I hope you will forgive me. The money is not for myself, and I was promised that he was not a good person.

Your son,

Zenshiro

When he was done writing, Zenshiro carefully folded the letter and put it into an envelope. He always wrote to his mother, after doing something bad. There was no way to deliver them; she had died during his birth, so Zenshiro would tuck the letters into a tin box that once held packets of dried noodles. After that, he didn't feel guilty anymore.

His mother, he was sure, understood that he didn't enjoy killing people. She knew what his father was like. He always favored Zenshiro's brothers and made it clear that Zenshiro had never been anything but an inconvenience. For years, Zenshiro thought it was because his life ended his mother's. As he got older, and wiser, he came to understand that his father wasn't romantic enough for such sentiments.

At twelve years old, Zenshiro's father informed him that it was time he started to pay back the family. He had three older brothers, after all, all of whom showed 'great promise' and were bound for higher education. Good schools cost money, and why should they have to neglect their studies to acquire it? Every spare penny was necessary, his father explained, so it would be best if Zenshiro left immediately to begin acquiring funds.

Job opportunities did not abound for those who hadn't even gone through puberty. Zenshiro was homeless for five years, during which time he made money as a pick-pocket and overall thief. Luckily, he was broad for his age and, though on the short side, looked older than he really was. He lived in Kamagasaki, where the day laborers would sometimes take pity on him and share their lunches. Zenshiro was always immensely grateful, as it meant he could send a little more money to his father.

By seventeen, he was recruited by a man called Hosei, a braggart, who liked to act as if he was a Yakuza boss, instead of a low man on the totem pole. Hosei wanted Zenshiro to help with what Hosei called his 'side business.' Hosei explained that he was often approached to aid in matters that were, quite frankly, beneath the Yakuza's concern. It was a shame, he felt, to let so much easy money go to waste. The solution was to become an agent and scout talented young men to do the work for him.

To keep his employee close at hand, Hosei put Zenshiro up in an apartment, the rent for which was deducted from Zenshiro's share of the money they made. Given how much people were willing to pay to see someone else die, Zenshiro still made more than he had as a thief. He told himself that, if the victims were doomed to perish, it was better that the money not go towards selfish ends.

Zenshiro's only rules were that he would not kill women, children, or animals. His most recent assignment had been to kill a man who ran out on his pregnant wife. The wife needed her husband dead, so she could collect the insurance money and use it to raise her unborn child. At least that was what she told Hosei. When Zenshiro asked him how far along she was, Hosei laughed.

"Why the fuck do you care?" He asked. "She had money, that's what counts. The kid is going to grow up without a father either way."

It would have been nice, Zenshiro thought, to hear that she had definitely been pregnant. He wondered why she bothered to tell Hosei anything. It wasn't as if Hosei had moral qualms about murder, or much of anything for that matter.

Whatever the real story, the woman's husband was dead, shot twice in the head, and once in the chest. Zenshiro spared his mother the details, as only the confession was important. Soon, he would need a bigger tin to store them all. Along with four years' worth of letters, it also held two pictures: one of Zenshiro's mother and one of himself.

The picture of Zenshiro was taken shortly after he started to work for Hosei. He bought it from a homeless man, who had somehow acquired an old Polaroid camera, which he used to take snapshots of people on the street. Most kept walking when he tried to sell the polaroids, but Zenshiro felt bad and bought one. Sometimes he took both his picture and his mother's out of the tin box and held them up side by side.

A few days after the pregnant woman's husband died, Hosei brought Zenshiro a new assignment.

"I almost didn't bother taking it," Hosei said. "The guy was weird, all twitchy and nervous. Like he thought I was going to kiss him or something."

"What does he want me to do?"

"Same fucking thing as always: kill someone he doesn't like. You're going to have to take the subway to Umeda."

"When?" Zenshiro asked.

"Tonight. The client said it absolutely had to be while it was raining."

Both men looked out the window. It was the rainy season, and it had been pouring for hours. The next day was supposed to be humid and hot, then rain again.

"I told him it would rain tomorrow night, but he started arguing with me." Hosei sat down on one of Zenshiro's chairs and lit up a cigarette. "Can you believe that bastard?"

"Why does it have to rain?"

"How do I know? He wouldn't tell me!" Hosei waved his cigarette around like a conductor's baton. "He kept saying that it has to rain, it has to rain! He can go to Hell. If he ever asks me for help again, I'll kick him out."

Hosei threw an envelope at Zenshiro, who caught it before it fell off his lap. There was money inside, along with a piece of notebook paper, and a picture of a man in a tie.

"That's for you. He paid pretty well, for a weirdo. You can take yourself out to a nice dinner, when you're done. Or spend it on a girl."

"I don't have a girlfriend," Zenshiro said absentmindedly. He was already planning out the trip in his head, which station he would leave from, and what time he would be likely to arrive in Umeda.

"I didn't mean a girlfriend, I meant go pay for a girl!" Hosei shook his head. "Do you even remember where to find your dick?"

"I remember," Zenshiro said, as he scanned the paper a second time. "Why are there two addresses?"

"The guy you're looking for has an erratic schedule. You have to wait outside his office, to make sure he leaves at all. Sometimes he sleeps at work. I told the client if that happens, he's shit out of luck. Office buildings have security cameras."

Zenshiro looked at the picture and tried to memorize the man's features. He was middle-aged, with a benign expression and large, black framed glasses. Zenshiro was reminded of a math teacher he had in primary school.

"I meant what I said about paying for a girl," Hosei said. "You're no good to me if you're all tense. You need to release your energy!"

Hosei thrust his fist upward and slapped the muscles on his left arm. Zenshiro's chest ached. The last time a woman had touched him, he was still living on the streets.

"Look at me, Zenshiro-chan, I'm a beautiful male specimen! You find a woman to take care of you, and someday you can be, too."

"You make me sound like a little kid. I've been with women before."

"Not enough." Hosei got up and readied himself to leave. "Go do our job and then find a girl to do a job on you. It's good advice!"

Zenshiro said he would think about it. He wanted to be agreeable. Whether it was his father, Hosei, or a beggar with a camera, Zenshiro was happiest when he gave people no reason to complain about him. Hosei joked that Zenshiro was like bamboo, he bent whichever way the wind wanted to blow him. Zenshiro appreciated the comparison. Bamboo bent, but it also survived while other things snapped.

After Hosei left, Zenshiro went over the details the client gave them. Hosei was strict about keeping clues around. He said a smart hitman burned the facts into his brain and destroyed the evidence before he left to do the job.

Zenshiro didn't like to think of himself as a professional killer. He was more like the day laborers; a man for hire, whatever the job might be. It wouldn't be forever, only until his brothers were done with school and any debts they incurred were paid off. After that, Zenshiro would be free.

***

From Kamagasaki, Zenshiro walked to Namba station and took the Midosuji line to Kita. The station wasn't far from the office building where his target worked, but Zenshiro took a taxi anyway. He worried that if he didn't, he might get the address confused and wait outside the wrong one. Numbers were never his strong point. Any stress, or surprises, and they flew from his head like frightened moths.

The plan was to wait in the lobby of the building, until the man left. Zenshiro would wait fifteen minutes, to give him a head start. In his experience, some people were very sensitive to being followed. Once the man was inside, and his guard was down, Zenshiro would strike. The client said that the target lived alone: no wife, lover, or roommates, so for Zenshiro it would be a straightforward affair.

Since he would be among office workers, Zenshiro dressed for the occasion. Despite being in his closet for years, the clothes were clean and almost new looking. Even so, he couldn't help but feel self-conscious. His haircut was wrong, and he didn't wear a fancy watch like so many men in the building did. Anyone who paid close attention would know he didn't fit. Zenshiro was greatly relieved when the person he was waiting for appeared across the lobby. The man looked tired and eager to get home, as he exited the elevator.

Fifteen minutes later, Zenshiro collected his umbrella and left the building. Despite the bad weather, he didn't mind the walk. It was still light out, and he liked the way the rain made the air smell. He circled the block once, for prudence as well as pleasure, before entering the target's apartment building. The man had clearly chosen it for proximity, as opposed to luxury. Eight stories tall, it had no doorman, nor did the building require a key or access code to enter. Zenshiro kept his eye out for security cameras but saw none. He got out of the elevator on the top floor and casually strolled down the hallway.

At the target's door, Zenshiro picked the lock and slipped noiselessly into the small apartment. From that vantage point, Zenshiro could tell the living room and kitchen were empty. There weren't any sounds of water running or urination, so he approached the bedroom, to which the door was partially open. He stopped when he saw the man's silhouette against one of the bedroom walls. It looked like he was changing into his house clothes. Zenshiro waited, gun ready, as the man sat down and pulled his shirt over his head. A second later the man's body fell back onto the mattress, yet the shadow of his head remained fixed in place.

Zenshiro closed his eyes, then looked again. The shadow continued to hover, well above the bed and the body laid across it. Zenshiro clutched the gun to his chest in the hope that the feel of something solid and familiar would calm his thinking. He wanted to believe that the shadow was from a lamp or some other benign household fixture. Anything but what it really was.

The shadow moved. It fled across the wall and disappeared as its source flew out the bedroom door. The head stopped short when it saw the unexpected guest in its apartment. Zenshiro's body went cold, as if his spine had become encased in ice.

"Strange," the head said. "I never thought I could order in." To hear it talk was too much, yet instead of becoming overwhelmed, Zenshiro went numb. His hand left his chest, and the gun fired. The first bullet went through the head's open mouth and tore out the back of its skull. The second sliced into its temple, as the head spun wildly from one wall to the other. Brains burst out and onto the floor, and the emptied skull landed on top of them with a splat. The head continued to gape and silently gibber for a few seconds, then went still. Zenshiro walked around it and went into the bedroom, where he shot the man's decapitated body once in the chest. The silencer muted it all. Zenshiro left the apartment unobserved and returned to Kamagasaki the way he came.

He told himself to forget what happened. He didn't doubt it was real; however, he valued his sanity too much to indulge the notion. It was easier after he wrote to his mother. For the first time, he told her everything. Having someone else know, and believe him, allowed the night's events to sink into the mire of his subconscious. The effect wasn't complete, but it was enough for Zenshiro to fall asleep. He even forgot his dreams, and the shrieking that stalked them, by the time Hosei came knocking on his door.

Zenshiro's employer was smirking, the way he always did when he had something funny or clever to say.

"Guess what?" He asked. "I don't have to worry about that weird guy bothering me again."

"That's good," Zenshiro told him.

"Don't you want to know why?"

"All right."

Zenshiro scratched his stomach and went to find a clean shirt in the pile of laundry by his bed. His body ached, along with his head. He wondered how much aspirin cost, and if it was selfish to spend money on a bottle.

"The bastard died!" Hosei announced. "It was on the news. He jumped off a building late last night."

Zenshiro paused, to filter the information.

"Maybe he felt too much remorse," he said.

Hosei scoffed. "Sure, whatever. Anyway, it must have been after the fucking rain finally stopped. The reporter said the guy's clothes were dry when they found him."

Hosei snickered and offered Zenshiro a cigarette. The client's death had him in an especially good mood. Hosei rarely shared anything other than his opinion. Zenshiro accepted the gesture and thanked his boss.

"No problem. So did you have sex last night?"

Zenshiro shook his head, and Hosei groaned.

"You know what you need? A big brother, to teach you how to be a man. Did you grow up with all girls, or something?"

Zenshiro knew that Hosei wasn't really looking for an answer. He liked to theorize aloud and liked it even better when he was right.

"I'm the youngest," Zenshiro told him. "The only boy."

"I knew it," Hosei whooped. "Someday, I'm going to take you out for drinks, and we'll go get massages. Your treat." Zenshiro flinched inwardly at the thought. Hosei had appetites Zenshiro couldn't afford, even if he wasn't supporting his three brothers. With any luck, Hosei would forget the idea. It wasn't as if he needed another companion. Hosei had his Yakuza brothers, and a collection of women he called his girlfriends.

"Are you in a hurry?" Hosei asked. "You look like you're waiting for me to leave."

"I have to go get medicine," Zenshiro told him. "For my head."

Hosei grinned. "So, you did have a good time last night. Too drunk to pick up a girl!"

Zenshiro laughed along with Hosei and went to find the rest of his clothes. As Zenshiro got dressed, Hosei took out his cell phone and began to scroll through the numbers.

"I've got to go," he said. "People to call. Everyone wants a piece of my time; it's a great inconvenience. These are for you." Hosei tossed a plastic bag onto the table. It was filled with bootleg CDs, of popular Japanese and American artists. "Sell those while you're out today. I'll come back and collect the money tonight."

It was another one of the "little chores" Hosei liked to give him. The problem with selling bootlegs was that Zenshiro wasn't any good at it. There were forty CDs in the bag: At best, he expected to move ten. Since Hosei had little patience for failure, Zenshiro would have to throw out the CDs and steal the rest of the money. Though he would always fail at salesmanship, he excelled in sleight of hand.

Of course, he would still try to do what Hosei wanted. It didn't help that Zenshiro had to avoid anyone who worked for Hosei's bosses, which meant forgoing the best locations. By dinner time, Zenshiro was tired, hungry, and dehydrated. He had only sold eight CDs. He decided to risk going back to the apartment long enough to eat something and renew his strength, then go back out and hit the nighttime crowds. If he saw Hosei, he would explain that he was only on a break and beg forgiveness.

Zenshiro was about two blocks away from home, when he noticed the people. There wasn't anything peculiar about any of them, rather that there were so many. Zenshiro was used to the faces around his corner of Kamagasaki. It made him uncomfortable to see dozens he didn't recognize, all going in the same direction as him. No one acknowledged Zenshiro, or each other, in any way. They simply formed a languid crowd that slowly grew as Zenshiro got closer to his apartment. If anyone else in the neighborhood noticed, they minded their own business, even when the two parts of the crowd accelerated and split off to flank Zenshiro on each side.

He wanted to run. It seemed like the sensible choice, except that it was unlikely he could stay ahead of the entire mob. Being in public was no guarantee of anything, other than having witnesses to whatever the crowd did to him. Zenshiro waited another block, until he was close enough to see his front door, before he bolted. He glanced back, once, as his hand wrapped around the doorknob. The crowd had gone completely motionless. Their faces were impassive as they stared forward, through Zenshiro, instead of at him.

Zenshiro dug out his key, only to find the door unlocked. His first thought was that Hosei had come early, to collect his money. Zenshiro entered the apartment backwards, in case anyone in the crowd made a surprise move and engaged the door's cheap chain lock. He turned to see Hosei sitting on the futon that doubled as Zenshiro's bed. Hosei's throat had been cut from ear to ear, and his body was held up by two men dressed in suits and ties. A third man sat at the table, his legs crossed and his hands folded neatly in front of him. Unlike his friends, he had no tie on, and the top two buttons of his dress shirt were unfastened.

"I must ask you a question," he told Zenshiro. "Why, when you destroyed Sato-san's head, did you also shoot his body?"

"I don't know that name," Zenshiro said, his voice barely above a whisper.

"Have you shot so many men, that you get them confused?"

"Yes," Zenshiro said. "Only my mother knows how many."

"I see," the man said. "And how many could detach from their bodies and fly about the room?"

Every buried memory rushed back to him. Zenshiro's throat went dry, and numbness spread through his fingertips. This time there was no gun to save him. The man at the table looked up and sighed. Red symbols circled his neck. Zenshiro was sure the other men had the same marks, as did everyone in the crowd that had stalked him.

"We could have used Sato-san's body," the man at the table said. "Losing it was a terrible waste."

"I only did what I was told," Zenshiro said.

"I believe you." The man got up from the table. "You do not look like someone who understands what he has done."

The men on the futon rose to join their friend. Hosei slumped to the side and rolled forward. Zenshiro's eyes teared up when his body hit the floor. Meanwhile, one of the men handed the man from the table a small black case. There was a needle inside, filled with green fluid. Zenshiro didn't fight back or try to get away. He wasn't ready to die, but it didn't matter. Death had come for him. The man from the table stuck the needle into Zenshiro's neck. Whatever the liquid inside was, it worked fast. The last thing he recalled was being caught in arms of strangers and carried away.

***

"Is it over?" A strange voice asked, out of the darkness. "Are you letting me go?"

Zenshiro opened his eyes, unsure why he was still alive, much less where he was. The details got clearer along with his vision. It was the biggest cave he had ever seen. Stone walls ascended upward, for what seemed like miles. The cavern itself was the size of a soccer field. The voice came from an elderly man. He was dressed in rags and was talking to the man from Zenshiro's table. The old man held a large wooden bowl in his arms, and one of his ankles was tethered to a chain, the end of which was sunk into the stone floor. "Your service with us is no longer required," the man with the red markings said. "We are going to release you to your ancestors."

The old man's face fell, along with the bowl he had been carrying. It rolled to the side, and a thick red substance spilled out. It smelled like copper and something else that Zenshiro found sweet, yet unwholesome.

"Please," the old man said. "Can't you let me go? What harm could there be?"

"It would be very confusing," the other man said. "Your wife has remarried, and your children are all grown with families of their own. Why would you wish to disrupt them?"

There was a hissing sound as five ovoid shapes descended from above. When they were low enough, Zenshiro saw that they were heads. Unlike the one he shot, these seemed sickly. Their cheeks were sunken, and their skin was waxy, as if they were half dead. They began to butt and bite at the old man. He cowered, his rail-thin arms a pathetic shield against the head's aggression. The old man's body was already covered in scars, imprints of teeth layered across each other.

"You see?" The man from the table said. "They're hungry, and you dropped their food all over the floor. If they are to stay alive, they need a more vigorous caretaker!"

He pointed at Zenshiro, who rose clumsily to his feet.

"Let the old man go," Zenshiro said. "He should see his family again, before he dies."

The man from the table chuckled. "You are a hard person to stay angry at."

He took a key out of his pocket and used it to unshackle the cave's elderly prisoner.

He approached Zenshiro next and knelt to the ground.

"Good," he said, as the shackle closed around Zenshiro's ankle. "I worried it wouldn't fit."

The old man wept openly. The heads gave up nibbling on him and turned their attention to Zenshiro.

"I'll show you how it's done," the man from the table told him gently. "Watch carefully. Without bodies, they can't get proper nutrition, and their minds have become unbalanced. They get angry if you take too long or make mistakes."

He picked up the old man, who could only wail as he was taken across the room to a hulking metal monstrosity. Zenshiro couldn't make any sense of it. It looked like two deep, rectangular bins connected by a closed off section of machinery. The old man was dumped into the bin on the right side and the machine rumbled to life. There was a sucking sound, along with the groaning of gears. The old man screamed like an animal about to be slaughtered. It took Zenshiro a moment to realize that he was.

A loud crunch cut off the screaming. The suction increased, along with the whine of gears, and culminated in a wet whoosh at the other end. A chute over the bin on the left oozed the same red sludge Zenshiro had seen in the old man's bowl. The man from the table took Zenshiro by the arm and pulled him to the side of the bin. "You dip the bowl in there," he instructed. "They can only take a few spoonfuls at a time, so they are always hungry."

Zenshiro watched what was left of the old man splash and mingle with the atrocious brew already inside the bin. Behind him, the heads resumed their hissing. The man from the table turned him around, to face his new responsibility. The heads bopped up and down. Occasionally one would look towards the bin and snap at the air.

"You should get the bowl," the man said. "They want to eat."

End of the Road

Neil Willis

Inspired by Jonathan Richman and the Modern Lovers' *Roadrunner*

One came out of nowhere, two showed the way. Three lifted; four and five, grounded. Six...

Route 128 ran through Richard Mann like a vein. Memories from childhood always featured the Yankee Division Highway, daytrips to the coast, Boston Harbor, or deep into the heart of Massachusetts. Often his family would cruise the highway just for the love of it, his father at the wheel and his mother in sunglasses and headscarf, trying for all the world to look like Audrey Hepburn. His most vivid memory, the worst and the most persistent, always pushed to the front of his mind.

When his parents asked where he wanted to go for a tenth birthday treat, Richard didn't hesitate in his answer: dinner at Howard Johnson's. All he loved about the modern world was symbolized in those bright orange roofs and 28 flavors of ice cream—as the slogan said: A Landmark for Hungry Americans. He and his parents took a booth near the jukebox and ate clams and grilled franks, followed by a sundae with three scoops: strawberry, peach and peanut brittle ice cream, cherry syrup and candies the color of anti-freeze.

You only live once, his father said.

Within the hour, Richard was upside down, wedged and suspended between torn vinyl and twisted metal. From this perverse vantage, he watched a lifeless abstraction of his parents fade to black. The Chevy, which had drifted drunkenly across the median, looked for a moment like it might miss the Mann's car and send some other random victims spinning into the path of an oncoming Mack. But Fate picked them.

Years slipped by. Richard never celebrated another birthday. His grief became eternal, caught in a moment of things that could have been: if only they had taken another route, or stayed for another soda. What if he had not had that sundae?

***

Snow fell in fat, lazy lumps. Richard watched the flakes float to the ground and vanish without a trace, swallowed greedily by the wet tarmac. A pip of a car horn snapped him from his reverie. The lights had changed to green, and a line of traffic was forming behind his car. Had he been an ordinary motorist, the slightest delay would have been met with angry blasts and abusive language, but he was no ordinary motorist, and at times this lonely distinction was more than he could bear. He adjusted the rear-view mirror and pulled out into the flow of traffic. The steely determination of the rush hour had melted into early evening. Remaining cars on the northbound passed in erratic batches, whispering of secret destinations as they flashed beneath the neon lights of a Quick Stop. The lot was empty except for a few cars huddled by the sliding doors: faithful hounds eagerly awaiting their owners.

Richard parked and went in for donuts. Shoppers' footsteps squeaked on the linoleum in adjacent aisles, but he managed to avoid seeing anyone face to face, or they managed to avoid him. The checkout girl served him with cold indifference. She wore a gold chain around her fat neck, so taut it looked as if it might slice her head clean off. The pendant against her pallid skin bore the image of St. Christopher, patron saint of travelers. Richard doubted she had ever been outside Massachusetts and then remembered that neither had he.

"Doesn't that music drive you mad?" He offered, nodding at the portable AM radio beside the cash register. He felt bad about judging her and hoped small talk would assuage him.

"It keeps me company, I suppose," she replied flatly, already busy with the next customer.

Richard's headlights probed the dark corners of the parking lot, as he weaved between discarded shopping carts towards the exit. A ragged bum, rooting around the dumpsters, ducked into the shadows at the sight of his car. Richard wondered what crimes the bum had to hide. Or had word of Richard spread among Boston's underclasses? A network of tin cans and string, humming with fear: there's a killer on the loose.

***

Richard hadn't set out to kill. The first came out of nowhere—panhandling, slurring and stinking of booze. The dark fantasy appeared in Richard's mind, usually a fleeting thought, soon discarded by the roadside. On that night, as Richard headed to his car after a long shift, a wrong turn led him into a dead-end alley with the drunken vagrant between him and the open road. The old man's lank hair was greasy in Richard's grip, and the blood, so much blood, tacky beneath his feet. Months passed, and no one seemed to notice or care about a battered down-and-out left to die among the rubbish. Guilt ate away at Richard's soul, but the deed was done; there was no turning back. Slitting the throat of a violent crack dealer filled the guilty void with something like purpose and meaning.

By chance, or fate, Richard found the third slumped at the wheel of a Buick beside the deserted turnpike. It was so simple to bundle his semi-conscious prize into the back of his car, drive the short distance to Cambridge Reservoir and roll the weighted body beneath the dark mirrored surface.

Then and there, Richard found the peace he had searched so long for. He drove the highways with the radio on, waiting for the missing person reports to come crackling over the airwaves. It pleased and amused him to picture himself as the tragic hero: The Roadrunner, driving the highways, avenging the memory of his parents, and protecting others from suffering his same lonely fate. Revenge, thought Richard, smelled like heaven.

His kills became clean and efficient. Richard had no appetite for blood. He dispatched the fourth and fifth in quick succession, suffocating them with a plastic bag, gasping in their own alcoholic breath. He buried his guilt along with the bodies, leaving no trace other than their abandoned cars. Then, for months, Richard patrolled without incident. Thanksgiving would surely bring the inebriated out onto the streets once more; all he had to do was wait and drive.

***

Richard reached the suburbs of Quincy around midnight. The sky had cleared to a scattering of tatty clouds, oily smudges against the moonlight. He had a mind to stay a while and watch the lights across the bay, but the road called him on. He made a U-turn and headed back towards the 128, back past the factories and the power lines, past the modern suburban houses and the families and the lovers. The streetlights petered out. Up ahead, a Chevrolet grabbed his attention as it joined the main highway. After fifteen years in the job, he had learned to read the subtle signs of a possible DUI in the body language of an automobile. He followed at a distance. A service road branched off the highway and Richard made his move. Accelerating, he caught the car before the junction and flashed his lights. The Chevy pulled over with weary resignation. Still, Richard rode close to its tail, pushing further up the single lane track to the base of a radio tower, obscured from the highway by bushes. For a moment, both drivers sat patiently waiting. Richard ran actions and words over in his mind like an actor on first night. He knew he was duty bound to open the performance. The red lights of the radio tower winked at him knowingly as he approached the Chevy. If this wasn't justice, then there was no justice. To serve and protect; wasn't that what the public expected from him? They feared him, ducked into the shadows and avoided him, but it was him they turned to for justice. They saw the car and the uniform—never the man inside.

"Step out of the vehicle!" he called, silhouetted in the headlights of his cruiser.

A stocky male stepped from the car, clearly agitated but with no outward signs of intoxication. He lay face down on the asphalt as directed, craning his neck to plead with Richard.

"Please, officer, what do you want from me?"

What did he want? Richard's mind raced a thousand miles an hour. A rock 'n' roll tune drifted from the Chevy's open door. Richard thought of the highway, the suburban houses and the power. You only live once, his father had said. He dropped hard with his knee into the small of the man's back, wrapped a cord around his neck and pulled. He thought of cherry syrup, his broken parents, the checkout girl with the St. Christopher and how she didn't want to talk. He pulled harder. The thrashing subsided. His sixth lay limp in his hands and the scent of pine trees hung in the cold night air.

***

State Trooper Richard Mann sped along Route 128 to a place he could hide another body. His hands ached from the cord, and his eyes stung with torn, twisted memories. Already his sixth had joined the others in his mind: a grotesque gargoyle set like stone. He tried to recall his father's laugh, his mother's eyes; he saw silent screams and dark, shattered lenses.

Richard turned the radio on.

"—blue Chevrolet. Child is a Caucasian male, five years old. Missing person is Caucasian male, mid-thirties, stocky build, dark hair. Request backup."

End of the Road

The faintest suggestion of a new dawn, pink like strawberry ice cream, crept above the lights of Boston. Richard pulled to the side of route 128. He had reached the end of the road.

Don't Tell Mama

Belen Lopez

Inspired by Radiohead's *I Am a Wicked Child*

The first time Mayra saw him was at the park. She stumbled across him on a cool, almost icy fall night as she cut across the park on her way home from work.

Mayra stayed on the path; made sure she passed straight under the yellow light of the lamps. The thick heel of her shoe on the gravel made quick, violent snaps as she hurried. She kept her face directed forward but glanced at her sides and listened for the sounds of anyone following. No one had ever followed her before, but she remembered her Mama's words.

"Bad idea," her Mama told her each time she got home. "It's a bad idea for a girl like you to be walking out there at night."

No one, in particular Mama, listened when she explained about the evening joggers, the officer named Ben who patrolled the park once every hour, or the fact that there were lamps every thirty feet on the path and most of the trees were still babies, not yet tall enough to tower or obscure at five feet.

"Don't matter," Mama said, "trouble can find you in the brightest places. What makes you think it won't find you in the dark?"

Mayra never answered this question, always letting her mother have the last word. Better that way, Mayra thought; Mama will only get angry if I talk back.

Mayra didn't see him till she was in front of him. She almost tripped when she spotted him on one of the few iron benches that had been set up in the bends of the path. He made for an odd figure, leaned against the bench's back, his right arm on the too small curve of the arm rest, his legs splayed. His eyes were closed, pointed up to the sky, his shoulder length brown hair was loose and swung down over the bench's back, and his mouth was tight, puckered.

Mayra continued forward, unwilling to let her steps falter from the path. Asleep, Mayra thought; it's better to let him be.

Mayra didn't see anyone else by the time she made it out on the park's other side and soon enough, as she neared her front door, she forgot about the man altogether. She didn't hear or see the man on the bench click his boot heels together, pull at his dark jeans, and smooth his threadbare gray t-shirt as he got up and followed behind her until the last lamp at the park's edge. Mayra walked the rest of the way home distracted.

Good girls don't walk out at night, Mayra imagined her Mama saying. Sometimes, Mayra thought as she tried to come up with a good answer, sometimes they have to.

***

She was on her way to work when she saw him again.

Each morning, Mayra made her way through the park to the third floor of the corner building in the center of town where she filed away reports she wasn't allowed to read for the officers. She took each file—some thin with only one sheet stapled inside, others thick with twenty pages and pictures—and gave it a number, entered it into the computer, and then placed it in a drawer by crime, last name and date. Sometimes when she was alone, and if it was a slow day, she would glance at the ones at the top of the pile. Most were innocent. A local kid had been caught with marijuana last week, not even enough to really charge him with anything. Others were worth not opening at all for what it told her of her neighbors. For two weeks now, she'd been unable to look George Miller in the eye because of what she'd read in his file.

Mayra tried to push George Miller's face out of her head. She looked up and saw the man again. He sat under a tree, the thin limbs barely casting a shade over him, and watched the people that walked by. No one seemed to notice him, except Mayra.

He was wearing a gray T-shirt smeared with a line of mud across the chest, his brown hair threaded with grass. His mouth was pulled into a rectangular smile; the teeth that showed were white and poking at his lower lip.

Mayra was not startled by any of this—instead, it was his eyes that made her want to run in the other direction. Sharp shards of blue glass encased the circles of his iris, too bright and round to be natural. She glanced at him sideways as she got closer. He looked familiar, but she couldn't place him, as if she'd dreamt of him long ago.

Mayra saw the smile grow wider.

All he said was, "My, my, my."

***

Mayra had one friend at the station, Ben, the officer who patrolled the park at night, and, as soon as she walked through the door, she went to find him. He had just poured himself a fresh cup of coffee, wrapped an apple into a paper towel and stuffed it into his coat pocket, when she came up behind him. Ben jumped. Coffee sloshed over the side of the cup and burned his hand, but he only hissed and wiped it away.

"Sorry," Mayra said.

Ben nodded. He tried to hide the smile that formed on his lips each time he saw Mayra.

"No problem," he said. He stood straighter, something about Mayra's small frame and wide brown eyes made him want to be better, even if only for the moment he was in front of her. "What's going on?"

Mayra told him about the man she'd seen in the park. Ben shook his head. He rubbed the back of his neck. None of it really made sense. If others had seen him, they would have gotten reports already. With the history the park had, no one took a stranger in the park as normal. They'd been called out just last month over a backpacker passing through town who had crashed in the park to sleep, unable to afford a room in the motel. Ben thought this over but didn't mention it to Mayra.

"I haven't seen him," he said. "And I don't have park duty till after six, but I'll tell Mark. He's got park duty in the morning."

Mayra nodded. "Thanks."

Ben smiled. He tried to ease away the frown that had formed. "Don't you worry," he said. "It's a small town. I'm sure it'll turn out to be someone we know just playing a prank."

Mayra smiled, the muscles in her cheeks felt tight and strained. She watched Ben go through the double doors. His stride was smooth, long, unmarred by the momentary worry she had seen in his face.

"I don't think so," she said.

***

When the town council had voted for the park to be laid out, for grass and trees to be planted, for a man-made pond to be installed, no one had protested. Lobo Creek had few attractions: an ice cream shop that stayed open late even in the cold of winter and a movie theater that was always full. A park twice the size of the high school's football field had been a welcomed break to the boredom that often settled over Lobo Creek in the slow summer months.

Most people believed that Juniper Park, named after the town founder's daughter, would be the best thing to happen in over twenty years.

Lobo Creek's pride in the park, though, didn't last long. Shortly after the swings had been bolted into the ground, and the slide had been polished to a yellow shine, a five-year-old boy named Darryl Martinez disappeared. One minute he was kicking his legs back and forth to gain momentum, the next the swing slowed to a stop, the seat empty.

By the time the police came, Darryl's mother had lost the ability to speak. She stood silently in front of the swing, her arm reaching outward as if to catch an invisible object. When a medic had passed his hand in front of her to rouse her, she had closed her eyes. They'd had to carry her out of the park.

The other mothers and children could not recall anything; it seemed that in the moment that Darryl disappeared, a kind of blindness had settled over anyone who was in the park.

Darryl's disappearance had been the first in nearly eighty years. In answer, the sleepy police force had risen. Patrols went out at all hours, and the park was under constant watch. No one ever found Darryl. In the six years since then, one person went missing each year with the same results.

Darryl's mother was so small now it seemed she had shriveled into herself. She hadn't spoken since. When she opened her mouth, all anyone could hear was a low, screeching hum that seemed to be coming from outside her.

***

That night, before Ben went on his patrol of the park, he made Mayra promise to get a ride from one of the other girls. When she questioned him, Ben just shook his head. He ran a hand over his short brown hair.

"Just do it, will you?"

There was something dark in his eyes, a shadow, crouched low, that passed over them as he watched Mayra. She felt that if she said the wrong thing, he might lash out and strike her.

"Okay," she said.

Ben nodded. He walked away without saying anything else, his focus already directed somewhere else.

Mayra went home with Patricia, a girl with dark red hair, who worked in the evidence department.

Patricia smiled too much; it seemed permanently molded onto her face. Mayra wondered if it hurt to smile so widely. Mayra turned to look out the car window.

"I was surprised when Ben asked me to give you a ride," Patricia told her, "But I figured he's worried. There hasn't been a disappearance yet this year. And you know how superstitious people are. Figure there's one coming soon."

Patricia turned on the heater; the air inside the car had become frigid.

"He said he didn't want you walking around that park at night." Patricia glanced at Mayra from the corner of her eye. She didn't know what Ben saw in Mayra. It wasn't like the girl noticed him unless she needed something.

"Why do you like walking there anyhow? I wouldn't want to. I mean, every person that's disappeared is last seen in that place. Bad idea if you ask me."

Mayra's breath fogged the window. She wiped away a circle so she could see.

"Hey, are you awake?" Patricia said. She shook Mayra's shoulder when she didn't answer.

When Mayra turned to face Patricia, her eyes were open, but empty, their gaze unseeing. "What?" she asked.

Patricia shook her head. "Forget it," she said. She turned on the radio and switched it to a country station. She'd heard somewhere in the office that Mayra didn't like country music. She hoped that rumor was true.

Mayra didn't hear the music. She tried to catch a glimpse of the park as they drove by. If she had been listening, she would have heard a slight, windy voice saying, "My, my, my. Don't tell Mama about what I've done tonight." She would have noticed that Patricia hadn't heard the voice, just the old country song she was singing along to.

***

Mama waited in the living room, all the lights, even the corner lamps that no one used except when reading, were on. The TV was on too, but muted, and Mama's eyes left the set as soon as Mayra clicked the door shut.

"Did you lock it?" Mama called.

Mayra shook her head. Damn it, she thought. She turned mid stride to lock the door.

"Just did," she called.

Mayra hovered in the doorway to the living room. Mama stared at her. She wore the same clothes she always wore: a moth-eaten cardigan that changed color once a week—this week it was gray—, a flowered shirt with buttons the size of quarters, and gray Capri pants. Her feet were in flip flops, her long black hair in a braid. Mayra remembered the one time she had said something about Mama's clothes.

"You're so young Mama, why don't you try a dress or put your hair up different," Mayra had told her. She'd been thirteen at the time and eager to have a mother like that of the other children; a mother that baked cookies on Friday nights and told Mayra what color went best with her skin.

But Mama had only frowned and stood. Mayra had been so focused on that frown that all she'd heard was the flap, flap, flap of Mama's flip flops on the linoleum floor, then the snap of Mama's hand as it hit Mayra's. The blow stunned her; she hadn't even thought to cry.

"Don't ever say anything else like that to me," Mama had said. Her voice had been so quiet, Mayra had been afraid she was missing something important.

"You hear me?" Mama had asked.

Mayra had nodded. "Yes, Mama," she'd said.

Those two words had become part of the limited lines allowed in her part as daughter.

"How was work?" Mama asked. She pushed back a strand of hair that had come loose.

Mayra smiled. "Good, Mama." She pulled at her coat.

"Anything happen?" Mama asked.

Mayra shook her head. "No."

"You didn't walk through the park today, did you?" Mama asked. Her eyes went up and down and scanned Mayra as if the lie she expected would manifest itself physically.

"No, Mama. I got a ride."

Mama stood. Her cardigan slipped off her shoulders.

"Who from?" Mama's voice was so quiet that Mayra had to force herself to suppress the cringe that was beginning to creep up her back.

"A girl named Patricia," Mayra said. "She's nice, Mama."

"I see." Mama continued to watch Mayra. She waited to see if Mayra would change her story.

Mayra stood her ground, she smiled, looked at Mama from under her lashes, until she saw Mama's shoulders relax.

"Well, then, think it's time for bed. Don't you?" Mama said. She walked to the TV and turned it off. Mayra heard her finger crack as she pushed the button down. One by one, Mama shut off the lights.

"C'mon," Mama said.

Mayra followed her up the stairs. Mama's steps were quick, and Mayra had to take the steps two at a time to catch up to her.

"You may read for an hour if you like," Mama said as they reached the top. "No more."

"Yes, Mama," Mayra said. She pushed open her bedroom door and closed it behind her. She could hear Mama go into her own room. Mayra waited until she heard Mama turn on the fan she kept by her bedside to lock the door.

When Mayra finally took off her coat, a single eye-shaped leaf fell down. Mayra picked it up and turned it over in her hand. It was just a leaf, the surface waxy, the underside soft. She stuffed it into her coat pocket, so Mama wouldn't find it and get the wrong idea. Tomorrow, on her way to work, she would toss it in the grass.

***

On the way to work the next day, she heard his voice. She knew it was his. His voice was thick, heavy, the edges of it rough as if someone had forgotten to smooth them down. Someone could cut themselves on that voice, she thought, and they wouldn't know it till it was too late.

"My, my, my," he said from behind her. Mayra sped up, but he was at her side. He was tall and the top of Mayra's head just reached his shoulder.

"Aren't you pretty," he said. There was a question there that lingered, as if he was unsure of what he was saying.

His gray T-shirt had a new stain, this one streaked across the other to form an uneven cross. The grass in his hair was joined by a small branch that hung down near his left ear. Up close, Mayra saw, his eyes really were glass, stained and filled with light, as if there was a flame hidden inside. He smiled the same rectangular smile as the day before.

Mayra swallowed thickly, and his smile stretched as if he could hear exactly what she was thinking.

"Who are you?" she asked.

He raised a hand to push his hair out of his face. The hand was stained brown; mud clung to the nails and stretched to his elbows.

"Don't you recognize me?" he asked her.

Mayra didn't have to think to answer. "No," she said. "I don't know who you are."

"My, my, my," he said. "That's too bad, because I know who you are."

"How?" Mayra asked. She was walking faster with each word that passed between them, but he kept pace with her, one step of his matching three of hers.

He didn't answer her question. Instead, he said, "You have such nice hair. You don't dye it, do you?"

Mayra frowned. She stopped herself from reaching up to touch her hair. It was black, just like her Mama's, but Mayra kept it twisted up in a neat spiral. She shook her head. "I don't like that sort of thing," she said. She wanted to keep him occupied long enough to make it out of the park.

"Yeah, I suppose it's for the best. I've never been a big fan of illusions." His eyes were illuminated, the glass clicked as he blinked.

"Have you talked to your officer friend? If you see him, I bet he'll have some interesting stories to tell."

Mayra stopped; gravel skidded across the path. "What are you talking about?"

He sighed. The smile remained in place. "He saw some things he shouldn't have, but you already know that. Don't you?"

"Ben is fine," she said, but something inside her cracked and pounded. No, no, no, it said. "You're crazy," she said, no longer sure who it was directed at.

She began to walk away. He didn't follow her.

"My, my, my," she heard him say. "Brown-eyed girl, you're gonna be harder than I thought to take back."

***

The previous evening, as Mayra had passed by in the car with Patricia, Ben had taken one step, and the next one never came.

Mayra wandered around the police station all morning and waited for Ben to come in. She paced in the break room, expecting him to come in for coffee or an apple.

All day, from her desk, she glanced at the door. The files piled up. Only Patricia, her figure blocking the doorway, roused Mayra. She blinked.

"Are you ready?" Patricia asked. Her blue eyes were pinched, and her red hair had begun to become undone from the knot at the nape of her neck. She wished she hadn't promised Ben to give Mayra a ride home every day.

Mayra shook her head to wake herself and stood, her hands moved to gather her coat and purse.

"Yeah, sorry," she told Patricia.

Patricia shrugged and led the way to her car. The ride to Mayra's house was passed in silence, not even the sound of the radio was there to buffer the quiet.

As Mayra reached to open the door, Patricia gripped her arm and held her in place.

"Take the day off tomorrow," Patricia said. She tried to make her voice kind, but she knew she was failing. "I'm sure Ben will turn up," she added before Mayra could protest.

Mayra shook her head. "How do you know?"

Patricia smiled; it was easy if she thought of Mayra as a child. "It's Ben, remember. He's probably just sick and didn't bother to tell anyone."

Mayra couldn't believe that, but she forced a smile.

"Sleep or something," she heard Patricia call after her. "You look like you're dying."

***

In the living room, her mother, her long hair braided, her shoulders covered by a brown cardigan, sat in front of the television. Even in the dark living room, illuminated only by the blue light of the television, Mayra could see that, though Mama smiled in sync with the laughter coming from the TV set, her eyes were glazed as if the person behind them turned off all the lights. Next to Mama sat the man from the park. A new stain ran down his torso, his long hair was tangled with clumps of soil, and his hands, folded neatly in his lap, were encased in a layer of mud.

"Mama?" she said.

Mama smiled but didn't turn to see her.

"She's occupied at the moment," the man said. He patted her mama's shoulder, where a stain appeared the moment he lifted his hand. "Aren't you, Mama?"

Mama nodded.

"This is very funny," she said. She opened her mouth as if to laugh, but the sound came from the man.

"What did you do to her?" Mayra asked. She knelt in front of Mama. Mayra waved her hand in front of Mama's eyes, but she didn't even blink.

"My, my, my," the man said, smiling. "I didn't do anything at all."

Mayra shook her head. "Stop saying that," she heard herself say.

She heard the sound of broken glass again. This time it came from inside her. "Who are you?"

The man grinned, his mouth a full square. "You should know," he said.

Mayra shook Mama. "Wake up. C'mon, snap out of it."

Mama closed her eyes and grinned just like the man.

"Why don't you tell her why you go walking out in the park at night, Mayra? Go on, tell her what happened to Ben," the man said. He closed his eyes, leaned his head back.

Mayra turned to face him. The TV clicked off and the room went dark. Mayra shut her eyes while she adjusted to the change.

"I don't know what happened to Ben," she said through gritted teeth.

"No. Course, how can you? I'm the one that does all the dirty work." He opened his eyes and held his hands up, examining them in the light of his eyes. Mama stared at the TV's black screen. "Here I am, all muddy, and you haven't even offered me a chance to wash my hands of all this mud and grass."

Mayra shifted her weight from one knee to the other. All she needed was a little time, just enough to figure out a way to get out of the house or call for help. "If I let you wash yourself, will you wake Mama up?"

He closed his mouth tight but nodded. "Why not?" he sighed, the sound scratched at the air. "It might be nice to have her here."

Mayra led him into the kitchen, pulled out a washcloth from a drawer, and turned the water on for him. She watched him set the plug and fill the sink with water. When his hands slid under the water, he winked at her. Mayra felt her own eye, out of her control, wink back. He smiled as if that was the exact reaction he had been hoping for.

"I'll be in the living room with Mama," she said. Mayra wanted distance between them.

"Up to you," he said. "It's not like she's good company at the moment."

As Mayra walked back to the living room, she saw the footprints, his, on the carpet in the light coming from the kitchen. When Mama does wake up, Mayra thought, she isn't going to be happy about those.

***

Mayra waited in the living room. She sat in a chair that faced the doorway so that she could see him when he came in. As soon as she'd gone into the living room, she had tried to call the police, but when she picked up the phone all she heard was a hum, as if someone were on the other end singing.

She waited now. She guessed that, if he kept his word, around the same time he finished scraping away the last of the mud Mama would wake up, but she didn't. He came into the living room, his pale hands clean, his hair wet but clear of grass, and sat down next to Mama again. If it weren't for those eyes, the fact that his shirt was still dirty, and now that she knew to look for it, the mud clinging to his boots and the ankles of his jeans, he might have passed for handsome.

"You said you'd wake her up," Mayra reminded him. He nodded. The rectangular smile was gone. Mayra wondered if he'd scrubbed away more than just mud.

"I want to remind you of a few things first," he said. He patted Mama on her back, and she fell forward, her head in her lap.

Mayra sprang up, but he stood and stopped her. He didn't say a word, but Mayra felt herself lowered into a chair, her feet firmly planted in the carpet.

"You're awfully good at forgetting," he said. He sat down again, the heels of his boots bumped against each other and the sound was loud, like someone stomping up and down the stairs.

"Lucky for you, I've got a very good memory—the best memory actually." He smoothed down his shirt, flicked away a pebble of soil. Mayra couldn't get her mouth to work long enough to ask him what he was talking about.

"Now," he said. "I've played this little game with you for long enough. I want my payment."

He waited for her to say something. Mayra sat still, her throat caught in a vice she couldn't see. He smiled; his mouth slipped into right angles.

"Right," he said, and Mayra could speak again.

"Payment?" she asked.

"'Don't tell Mama,' you said. And I haven't; I kept my word. Let you carry on without consequence. But I'm tired of hanging round the park, tired of having to get my hands dirty." His smile grew wider. "I have beautiful hands, you see, and I don't like seeing them covered in mud, especially when it's not my work that's getting done."

Even in the dark, Mayra could see he was right. He did have beautiful hands: the wrists slim, the fingers long, the skin so tanned it highlighted each vein and tendon. Stop, Mayra told herself. Don't look at him. She directed her eyes past him to the wall.

"I don't remember making a deal with you," Mayra said after taking a slow, practiced breath. "I've never seen you before a few days ago."

"No, no. This isn't the way it works, Hon. You owe me and there's no way out of it." He shook his head and leaned forward.

"I didn't do anything." Mayra squirmed in her seat, unable to get up.

"Oh, yes you did." He winked at her again and the light in his eyes flickered. "You'll remember soon enough."

The man stood and Mayra stood with him. He raised his arm and Mayra raised hers. Every movement he made, she mirrored.

"I'm gonna have a little chat with Mama here," he said softly. "You go outside and check the park. Go check it out," the words floated from his rectangular smile.

Mayra did as he directed, powerless to stop. She couldn't scream, couldn't even push her muscles to fight the involuntary movement. She felt herself, watched herself, unlock the door, close it behind her, and begin walking.

All she heard in her ears was a hum, so loud it sounded like the buzz of bees ready to sting.

***

Afterwards, Mayra waited for him at the park. She sat on a bench, the same bench she had first seen him on, her hands neatly folded in her lap. Her hair was caked with mud; the strands hung like string and covered her eyes. She didn't see him till he pushed the hair off her face. He sat down next to her and leaned his head back.

"Know who I am now?" he asked. "Remember what we agreed? What I allowed you to do for the past six years?"

Mayra was looking ahead. The lamp here had gone out, and no one had bothered to replace the light bulb.

Mayra nodded. She remembered now. She didn't know how she could have forgotten any of it: the mud that clung to her skin, hard to wash away, the grass and leaves tangled in her hair, stuck to her coat and face.

"Can't say I didn't give you time, you know. I always worry about giving people more time. Most of them squander it. You kinda did."

Mayra nodded.

"At least it's all worked out now," he said.

He took her hand in his. "My, my, mine," he said.

"I'll dirty you," she said, looking at the mud covering her hands.

"Don't worry about that," he chuckled. "I'm used to dirt. Used to all those nasty things most people find untouchable."

He scraped away mud from her fingernails. Mayra's skin prickled at the touch. His hands were so cold. "You found them all?"

"Yes," she said. Her hands itched from having touched the bodies. Someone would see them in the morning, and it would all be over for Mayra.

"Good," he replied. He stood and pulled Mayra with him. "We're gonna go now. Alright?"

Mayra followed him. She felt hot now, her skin sweltering under a fire she could not see, and she knew that only his cold hands would put it out.

"Don't tell Mama," Mayra said. "Please."

He led her down the park path. Mayra didn't want to ask where he was taking her.

"Don't worry," he said. The glass in his eyes clicked as he winked. "Mama won't know a thing."

Messages

David Renfrow

Inspired by Disturbed's *Ten Thousand Fists*

Craig Robertson awoke with a start. The dream was always the same. The machine gun fire, the exploding of the IEDs, and the screams of dying soldiers mixed with the terrified cries of injured civilians. He ran the back of his right hand tiredly across his brow. Sitting up, he looked at his alarm clock and discovered that he had awoken a full hour before he needed to. He tried to lay his head back down, but between the sweat that had soaked his pillow and the fear of having that dream again, he decided that the best thing to do would be to just get up and get ready for the day.

Since coming back from Iraq, Craig had found himself a changed man. He had always been the class clown, the type of guy that could diffuse any situation with merely his presence and a quiet word. Lately, he just wasn't that guy anymore. Instead, he found himself jumpy and liable to overreact to the slightest provocation. What is wrong with me? He thought silently as he stared at his reflection in the mirror. I just want my old life back.

Craig dressed in his military uniform; on days that they had public appearances, that was the way that Craig's boss, the senator from a southern state, liked it. It was important for his political image to be seen out in public with a true war hero, a winner of the Silver Star and all that. Craig hated public appearances the most. His job usually consisted of sitting in the senator's office on Capitol Hill and handling complaints from constituents. That kind of stuff he didn't mind, it was what he had expected to be doing when he had applied for the job after coming home from overseas, but out in public, standing on a stage with all those old guys who had fought in World War II or Vietnam, he always felt like such a fraud.

"Maybe I'll try to talk to the boss again today," Craig said to an empty apartment. "Tell him that I really need to start getting more time in the office." Craig grabbed his drab black briefcase and slipped out his door into a chilly spring morning.

***

Craig arrived at the office well before the senator and the rest of the staff. Craig liked it that way; he could usually get more work done at this time of day than he could when the office was full of people. He poured himself a cup of coffee from the office communal pot and turned on his computer. The picture posted above it drew his attention, as it did every single day. It was a picture of the eight of them together, a picture that had been taken a full day before the event that had changed Craig's life. He knew that if he lived to be a hundred, he would never forget that last mission. The one where he had gotten his seven best friends in the world killed.

The mission had been cancelled and then rescheduled seven times over three days. His squad was up for a recon mission, and the company commander had called Craig into his tent. He had told him that someone at the Pentagon had decided the mission was too risky, but the commander still thought that it would be worth it, if they could get some good intelligence. The commander had left the decision up to Craig as to whether or not the mission would be a go or not.

At first, Craig had considered not going, but he was going to be up for promotion in a few more months and decided that the mission was worth the risk. The squad had been wiped out in a small village just outside the gate by a combination of explosive traps and a small group of well-armed local insurgents. Craig had only survived because the initial explosion had thrown him a short distance away from the kill zone. Somehow, he had survived with just minor injuries and found his way back to the firebase.

***

The shrill ring of his cell phone pulled Craig out of the memory. He fumbled and dropped it on the floor before picking it up and flipping it open.

"Yeah?"

"Craig, it's Mindy. Are you seeing this?" Mindy was the senator's scheduler. Her habit of asking dumb questions had irritated Craig since his first day.

"What are you talking about?" he asked. "Seeing what?"

"Where are you?" Mindy asked.

"I'm at the office. Cut the shit, Mindy. What are you talking about?"

"Just turn on the television. I'm on my way in now. There's some kind of disturbance or demonstration going on at Arlington."

Craig picked up the TV remote as she hung up. He turned the TV on and immediately tuned it to one of the national 24-hour news networks. Jumpy cameras showed a large group of people in and around the cemetery. The talking heads at the anchor desks were attempting to figure out what was going on, but no one was getting close enough to tell. Whatever was going on, the group of people were just standing in the cemetery with their fists raised in the air.

Craig's phone rang a second time.

"Yeah, Mindy, I'm watching."

"Robertson, is that you?" It was a deep male voice.

"Oh, senator, I'm sorry sir. I thought you were Mindy. She called me a few minutes ago to tell me something was going on."

"That's why I'm calling, Robertson. I'm on my way in and Mindy is here with me. I want you to get out there to Arlington as quickly as you can. I will not have today of all days disrupted by some dirty beatnik hippies holding a demonstration at one of the most sacred spots in this country."

Craig interrupted, something that he rarely did when speaking to his boss. "I'm sorry sir, what do you mean today of all days?"

"Jesus H. Christ, son! Don't you know what today is?"

Craig looked at the small calendar hanging just above the squad's picture, and he knew immediately. "It's been ten years," he said softly.

"Yup, ten years ago today, son, we invaded Iraq. What a great day it was too, backing that invasion was one of the first things that I did as a junior senator, and I will not have this day ruined. Weren't you there, Robertson?"

"Umm, no sir. I wasn't there during the initial invasion. I was still in high school. I got there about five years later."

"Alright, alright, son. I didn't ask for your life story. Listen, you just get out there as quickly as you can, and, if you get a chance, you park yourself right in front of those TV people and just keep reminding them how many times I have said in public that I am proud to live in a country where our young people have given so much against seemingly impossible odds. You got that? Really talk us up on this thing, son, and don't let any of those hippies get a word in." Craig tried to respond but found that the senator had already hung up on him. He really hoped that he would not have to get in front of the camera; the senator had other people for that. Making sure that he had his car keys, he raced out of the building to his car.

***

The road out to Arlington was clear this time of morning, with most commuters heading into the district as opposed to leaving. Craig showed his congressional ID to a cop who was directing traffic around the growing crowd at the cemetery. Craig was able to park next to the news vans. He was amazed that so many reporters were standing around, and no one seemed willing to walk into the graveyard. Craig looked closer and instantly understood why. The people standing at the graves weren't protestors, they were soldiers. Not just any soldiers here to mark the day either; they looked like soldiers who were supposed to be resting in their graves. All of them holding their fists in the air just like the news stations had been reporting. The silent show of solidarity made Craig hesitate, but somehow, he knew what he had to do.

Craig slowly entered Arlington. He had attended so many funerals here; friends and comrades killed at such a young age. He also knew that somewhere deeper in this place lay seven graves of the men that his decision had put there. He wondered if they were standing outside of their graves with the rest of the soldiers. Craig turned back at the entrance to watch the TV crews. All of them were pointing their cameras at the lone man entering the cemetery, but no one made any moves to follow him.

As he walked through the graveyard, Craig saw that not every single grave had been disturbed. Instead, judging by their modern dress, Craig realized that the only soldiers who were leaving their graves were those who had died in Iraq. Sometimes, a soldier would try to crawl out of his grave and find himself stuck and unable to move due to a lack of limbs. Craig was amazed to see the other resurrected soldiers reaching down to help their comrades escape the soft fertile earth. None of the soldiers said anything to Craig or even looked at him; they instead just stood stoically with those hands raised.

Craig approached a soldier who wore the silver oak leaf of an Army colonel.

"Excuse me, sir." The colonel looked at Craig. "Can you tell me what's going on?"

Instead of answering, the colonel looked at Craig and then at a massive wound on his right side. The uniform was torn away, and Craig could see into the colonel's chest and abdomen. The colonel looked away from the wound and back at Craig, a lone tear sliding down a pale white cheek. Craig walked away, feeling a strong urge to see if his squad mates were out.

It didn't take long to find them. He had visited this section of the cemetery every chance that he had, at least once a month since they had been buried. They stood in a small cluster off by themselves, not saying a word, just standing there, oddly silent and still. They looked up as Craig walked closer and Craig hesitated for just a moment.

Craig's best friend, Bill Vandiver, opened his mouth. "Craig," the dry throat cracked. "Step closer." Craig did and Bill reached out to touch his shoulder. Whether from fear or guilt, Craig fell at Bill's feet.

"God, Bill, I'm so sorry. Please, I didn't mean to." Craig was momentarily ashamed as he began to cry.

"Craig, we forgive you." Craig looked up and saw that the entire squad was nodding as one. It seemed that Bill was speaking for them all. "We forgave you a long time ago. Yes, you may have made a wrong decision, but war and hate and intolerance, those are the things that killed us. Go on and live your life."

"But why, why is this happening?"

Bill looked around at the thousands of soldiers who were standing as still as statues with fists raised in the air. "We do it to remember those who came before us, and those who will come soon. We're tired, Craig. Tired of welcoming new brothers and sisters who die too young. Die before having families and die before they get to make their impact in the world. That's what you can do for us Craig; we'll only be here today, but we want you to tell the world how tired we are of all of it."

Craig nodded. "I'll do what I can." He looked down at the ground, no longer caring if the tears fell from his face. He wiped his eyes and looked back up at Bill. "I'll tell them."

Bill nodded as he helped Craig off the ground. He looked around at the entire squad before continuing. "I just want you guys to know that you are the best friends that I ever had, and I will carry that day with me forever."

He noticed Bill giving him a slight nod. "You were a good friend, Craig. Don't let your guilt eat you away. Just remember to tell them all that I told you."

Craig's phone rang as he started to walk away. He could see from the screen that it was the senator calling him. His boss, a politician just like the rest, who throughout history had sent young men off to their deaths on foreign shores with no clear objective. Craig knew what he had to do; he had a mission and purpose in life again. He pressed the answer key on the cell.

"Hey senator, I'm glad you called. I just wanted to let you know that

I quit." The senator's agitated voice was so loud that Craig had to move the phone away from his ear. "Well," he said, looking back at his friends, "let's just say that I got a better offer." The senator was still yelling as Craig hung up the phone; he smiled for the first time in a long time as he walked to the waiting cameras.

The Rule Breaker

Chris Samson

Inspired by The Ramones' *The Crusher*

When I was nine years old, my world ended.

I was with my dad in Boston Garden when it happened. Ivan 'The Beast' Molotov had the guile to try and take the championship from my hero, Ricky Blackhawk. He might have been confident as he asked us to show respect for the Soviet national anthem, and he might've hunted Siberian Tigers back in Russia, but Ricky Blackhawk was an American Indian warrior. He fought with honor, played by the rules, and was the best champion I'd ever seen. When he came to the ring, I remember cheering my lungs out as his headdress and gold belt adorned his muscular body.

The bell rang. I sat in my seat, ready to see my hero send Molotov home a loser. It was only a matter of time. Good always triumphed over evil. That was the way it worked.

Twelve minutes and one bear hug later, everything changed. All sixteen thousand of us booed Molotov as he raised the belt in one hand, the Soviet flag in the other. He roared in triumph, in Soviet superiority. I asked my dad if Ricky Blackhawk would win the belt back. Dad looked at me. He could tell how upset I was. "Someone will, son."

That was when I knew I wanted to be a professional wrestler. After twenty years, I was ready to face the man who had inspired me all along, Ivan "The Beast" Molotov. But I never expected it to be like this.

I wanted to fight him for the title. Molotov hadn't held one in years.

I wanted to wrestle in the Boston Garden. It was destroyed before I reached high school.

I wanted to wrestle in front of thousands of fans. We might crack one thousand tonight.

Topping it all off, The Beast was late.

"You got any cigarettes?" Leviathan asked.

I stretched on the dressing room floor. The show had already started, and I was watching the clock. "Cigarettes?"

"I had some in my bag," Leviathan said, looking over at the gym bag on the folding chair. Leviathan was nearly three hundred pounds, had eight tattoos, and wore black face paint to the ring. At the moment he looked like a sixth grader, suspicious someone had stolen his pencil.

"I didn't see anybody."

As he grumbled off, I looked back at the door. I wanted Molotov to show up, but I wasn't sure what we'd have to talk about. It was sad sometimes, seeing these older guys on the smaller venues. Now their bodies couldn't pull off half the moves they used to, and the ones they can are dull. Truthfully, the Beast just wasn't scary anymore. As I waited, I tried to come up with some ideas for the match I'd dreamed of for the past twenty years.

My name's Todd Norenberg. Growing up, I knew I'd need a different name if I wanted to be a champion. Who'd pay to see Ivan "The Beast" Molotov vs. Todd Norenberg? I went through as many imaginary names as I did imaginary matches with The Beast. I was Kid Knockout, Apex, Johnny Smash, and a thousand others. None of them felt right, until one day I realized who the best man to beat The Beast should be. If Ivan Molotov stood for Soviet superiority, I should stand for American values. After years of training, Todd Norenberg became D.C. Washington, a guy who went out there and still stood for all the American values of big muscles, big cars, and stomping out evil. Finally, after twenty years, D.C. Washington was going to face The Beast.

"Washington," a voice said to me. I looked up from my leg stretches. Leviathan was back, standing in the doorway.

"What?"

"He's here."

"Molotov?" I cast a quick glance at the clock.

"Yeah. I was out smokin'. Saw him come in."

I rose to my feet. "How'd he look?"

"Big." Leviathan walked past me, putting his cigarette lighter back into his gym bag. "Didn't know he was still alive." There was a murmur of agreement from the rest of the guys in the room, trading rumors and snippets of information they'd heard over the years.

The footsteps down the hall were distant, but heavy. The rumors quieted down as those footsteps came closer. The first real-life monster, the supervillain so many of us took turns pretending to be in playgrounds or backyards, was finally here. Outside, you could hear the roar of the crowd as Prince Vince and Archie Cruise battled in the ring. The crowd thundered with boos and cheers, flip-flopping like mad during the pace of the match.

That's when The Beast appeared.

That giant shape filled the white doorway. We stopped at once, startled by his appearance. There was a collective tensing, as if we'd all seen a car crash, but we turned, sighing with relief when we realized everyone was still alive. We all exhaled, some lightly chuckling at how Molotov startled us like that.

He looked down at us as he stepped into our dressing room. He was huge, bigger than I remembered or expected. Most wrestlers add a couple inches to their height to seem more impressive, but Ivan Molotov was easily six-eight. He had a shaved head with stubble still dark enough to make it look like an eternal shadow crowning his skull. His Lenin-inspired goatee still framed his face, accentuating his already square jawline. His eyes were steely black; his neck muscles bulged under his leather jacket and turtleneck. He looked us over like a substitute teacher examining a suspicious class. He cut to the left, going through us like a knife through butter. The rest of the guys milled around as The Beast turned his back on us, taking a free space on the wall and placing his massive travel bag down on a chair. Holding my breath, I walked over. His black leather jacket spread over his wide shoulders like a cobra's hood. I slowly stepped into his field of vision, not wanting to sneak up on him.

"Hi," I said. "I'm D.C. Washington. I'm working with you tonight." His black eyes scanned me up and down. Then, ignoring me, he reached down and unzipped his bag. I extended my hand. Maybe I wasn't showing the proper respect. This guy was a legend; if I was going to work with him, put my body in his hands, I was going to have to make it clear I knew he was the boss. "I'm honored to work with you, sir. You're why I got into wrestling."

He pulled out a bottle of vodka and placed it on the chair next to him. The clear liquid sloshed around. He turned and looked me over again, staring down at my hand. "You strong?" he asked, the Russian accent rippling underneath his words.

"Yeah." My hand was still extended.

He gripped my hand, not shaking it, but gripping it like a man in a butcher shop examining a piece of freshly slaughtered beef. Letting go of my hand, he looked back into his bag. "Good." There was something about that bag—the heft he carried it with, the depth of its contents—that made me think of Dracula's coffin, carrying it with him across the ocean.

Taking a pair of boots and some kneepads out, Molotov began setting his equipment next to the black bag. Vodka. Kneepads. Cup. Boots.

Singlet. All ordered and ready to go. An artist with his tools.

"Do you have any ideas about the match?" I asked.

"You lose," he replied.

"Yeah, but, uh, do you have any spots? The bear hug—"

"You not break bear hug," he said, still not looking at me.

"Right, but these people paid—"

"You not break bear hug," he said again. It wasn't even up for debate.

"Look, if I give up, it's like America gives up. I think you should cheat..." I stopped as he reached down with his hands and pulled off his shirt. Ivan Molotov had that old-time physique where you could tell a guy was strong without seeing him flex. He had that frame, those muscles you get from years of hard labor. These were muscles that weren't huge, serrated, defined, or honed with supplements and gym equipment. These were real world muscles. Some of it was gone, taken with time, but some of it you never lose. The Beast still had that, but what stopped me mid-sentence were those scars.

Wrestlers take bumps all the time. Scars come with the territory, but these were different. Four or five parallel scars from his left shoulder down to his navel; the scars' pink flesh stuck out on Molotov's skin like stitches on a rag doll. Everything holding him together seemed to come from those scars. I saw him looking at me as he held his turtleneck in his powerful hands, wringing it like a chicken's neck.

"Those scars—," I asked, looking at him.

"Bear," he said. Nodding his dark head to the side, he indicated our conversation was over. I walked back to my little portion of the dressing room and tried to stretch. After a few minutes, other wrestlers walked up to him, trying to pay their respects, thanking him for coming to our little show. Molotov didn't even respond to them. In between stretches, I looked back at him. He sat on his chair, next to the bottle of vodka, watching me. I can't prove he was drinking, but every now and then I'd look up and see the vodka swaying back and forth in the bottle.

I was starting to worry. Granted, you didn't have to go over the match before you went out there. You could improvise the whole thing, and yeah, the heel or the guy with the most experience usually calls the match in the ring, but no plan for the audience can lead to an awkward match. The idea was that I'd lose, but I'd be so good during the match that the dastardly Russian would have to cheat to win. This way, the old guy—the rule breaker—gets the win, but the young guy looks good too, and America's honor is preserved because I played by the rules.

A kid poked his head in the doorway. "Washington, Molotov, next."

There was something about seeing the way Molotov stood up, so straight, so purposeful, that just didn't seem right. This was a guy who put his body on the line three hundred nights a year for twenty-five years. I've seen guys like him before. They don't walk; they shamble. They don't stand up; they pull themselves up. You hear the cracks in their joints, and you see the lumps in their knees from surgery after surgery. By all rights and measures, a man like Ivan Molotov should be in constant pain.

He moved like a surgeon. Every move was precise and crisp. He made it to the door first. Honestly, something about seeing that mountain of scar tissue and muscle leave the room made me want to get out. Something told me the smartest thing to do would be to get out, go to the car, and just drive away.

I could feel the sweat already coming through my pores. My heart rate tripled and I had trouble swallowing. I cast a glance over at my gym bag. I could grab it and leave. I looked at the zipper on my bag, muscles in my arm twitched.

No.

I turned for the door, swallowing and feeling only a pinch in the back of my dry throat. As soon as I was alone in the hall, I desperately wished I'd listened to myself. The long walk to the curtain was worse by the fact that I didn't see Molotov, and I didn't like being alone. My stomach felt like it was being pulled through a vice. I've never been the biggest star, but I've had my moments, and I've traveled a fair bit. In this business, where egos, testosterone, and muscles are as big a part of the job outside the ring as they are inside the ring, you develop a sixth sense when someone's trying to take advantage of you.

As I walked to the curtain, I felt that warning going off in my mind. There was something here I didn't like, but I had no idea what. When I finally reached the curtain, The Beast was waiting. No flag this time, just those bulging muscles and the scars that seemed to shine in the darkness. He looked back at me as we stood there, freezing me with his eyes. As the Soviet national anthem played over the arena, he threw open the curtains, stepping out into the bright arena. In that second, as The Beast emerged, there seemed to be nothing else but him and the light. The spotlight of the arena blinded me backstage. I couldn't see anything out there. No ring, no fans, no guardrails, nothing. Nothing but that huge shadow of The Beast. When the curtains fell back into place, I was alone in the darkness. Soon they'd play my entrance music. Until then, there was still time. He was out there; I was back here. I could run. I could leave. My already uneasy nerves were now a fever pitch.

My music began. There was a cheer from the audience as the announcer's booming voice filled the arena. I stepped out. Normally, I play it up for the crowd, fist-pumping, posing, all that stuff, but not tonight. Tonight, I simply walked to the ring, staring at The Beast and the ridges of scars across his chest.

The music cut as I passed the ropes. As the referee explained the rules of the match to us, I could just make out the white noise of the crowd telling me to crush this guy. I nodded in agreement. On the outside I was still D.C. Washington, American hero. If I acted unafraid, maybe it would actually sink in.

"Okay, so, how we gonna start?" I asked.

Nothing.

The ref continued talking.

"Ivan, how do we play this?"

The ref turned his back to us to start the match.

"Ivan," I said one more time.

"Go," was his single response.

The bell rang.

Right from the beginning he was stiff. You're supposed to take care of each other out there, but he chopped my chest so hard you could hear it in the balcony. He twisted my joints out of place when he applied a hold and rammed his body into me like I was a tackling dummy.

Usually, if you nail the old-timers once, they back off. Not The Beast. He just kept at it like a freight train. About twelve minutes in, I came off the ropes. Twisting, he grabbed me as I came in, wrapping his arms around me in the tightest bear hug I've ever felt. The crowd rose to their feet, shouting with concern. I tried breathing, but my lungs were pinched together. It felt like I was in a shrinking barrel. I braced my hands against his shoulders, trying to push out.

"Ease up," I said through gritted teeth.

No answer.

"Ivan," I said, opening one eye. I felt deflated, like every inch of air in my body had left me. I was an empty balloon. I tried breathing in and it felt like a marble was stuck in my throat. The blood rushed into my face as I tried pushing out.

"You not break bear hug," he said. His voice was lower now, there was a strength to it that wasn't there before, like he'd suddenly had twenty years of smoker's lung removed. He squeezed tighter. I almost choked. The noise from the crowd got louder in my ears, then grew distant. I was lightheaded; black spots flashed in my eyes. I looked down at Ivan

Molotov one last time as I began passing out. His face was a mask of intensity. "Your strength," he said, "be in me."

I suddenly became tired, like someone pulled a plug inside me. My neck rolled like a grapefruit and my arms went limp. My legs felt like they'd fallen asleep. "Ivan," I said one more time. Through cloudy eyes I looked at The Beast's face. In my hazy vision, all I saw were two ovals of darkness. "Ring it," I said to the referee, with all my remaining strength.

"This isn't the finish," he said.

My arms were tingling now. "Just end it," I whispered. Was it just my vision, or did he really have those black eyes? "End it," I said, pushing again. The bell rang. I didn't hear it so much as feel the vibrations somewhere in the distance. Everything was like I was underwater. "Let me go," I said.

"Your strength be in me," The Beast said.

"The match is over," the referee said. "You won. Break the hold."

"*Noagh...*" he said. I wasn't sure if his voice was garbled or if my hearing was just gone, but the ref started tapping Ivan to get him to ease up on the hold.

No dice.

That was it. I'd had enough. I smacked The Beast in the face as hard as I could. It landed awkwardly, but as soon as I pulled away, his face went back to that grimace. "Let go," I said, with another hard strike. I felt the smack of my fist glide off his sweaty face. Things were flashing now. I hadn't taken a breath in almost a minute. Heart pounding, I reached out with my left hand, gripping his sweaty face, jabbing my thumb into his left eye. With a howl that silenced the crowd, he let go.

I collapsed onto the canvas, gasping. The ref knelt next to me. "Are you okay?"

"Wouldn't break," I said, my skin finally feeling the canvas. "He wanted—"

Something slammed into my still-sore ribs, knocking me on my back. I stared up at the ceiling lights as a chorus of boos arose from the crowd. I turned my head to see the ref step in front of a shadow.

The shadow reached out, swatting the ref aside. The ref landed with a loud thud. The boos escalated. Someone threw a soda into the ring. "Alright," I said, fists clenched. "You wanna..." That's when things started to change.

Those stoic, black steel eyes had morphed. There was a fire behind them, a blaze of uncontrollable fury, like something had been unlocked and exploded into Ivan Molotov's soul. His blazing eyes seemed further back than they were before. His skin looked clammy and malleable. His nose and jaw looked like they were in different places, and muscles began pulsating under his skin. The scars seemed smaller, and he looked like he'd put on a year's worth of muscle mass in two seconds. Blood streamed from his nose where I'd hit him. It dripped to the floor, pooling at his boots. Hair was growing on his chest and arms, wriggling like a thousand little worms. Raising his head to the ceiling, he bellowed into the arena. His cry was like an explosion. The ref rolled out of the ring, and the crowd fell silent. I stepped back as The Beast returned his gaze to me, his misshapen jaw disfiguring his face. I stumbled backwards.

"Your strength," he snarled, reaching out with his hands, blood staining the white canvas as something sharp edged through his skin. I stepped back into the ring post. "Be in me." He lunged, but I rolled out of the ring. The Beast slammed into the turnbuckle; below, I started backing away. The crowd rose to their feet, beginning to share that sense of dread in my body. Staggering on my twisted knees and breathless body, I backed up to the dressing room, catching snippets of conversation from the audience.

"Hurt—"

"—looks real, I don't—"

"—going on?"

"The way it's supposed to—"

"Blood—"

"—happening?"

"—went wrong—"

"—scared, Dad."

I chanced a glance back at the ring as I made it to the curtain. That shadow of The Beast was still there, but it was different now. It moved out of the ring like a cat stepping down from a windowsill. This huge black void, this mass, in the middle of light seemed to stretch its darkness out down the aisle. I thought I felt its breath.

I stumbled through the curtain, the black fabric sticking to my sweat. I made my way down the hallway, trying desperately to get my breath back. I glanced back again; the curtains ripped open as something behind them violently slashed through. My mind struggled to reconcile what I was seeing with what I thought I knew to be true. There were rules in the world. A natural order. Man followed these rules.

But somehow, Ivan Molotov was breaking these rules. As I approached the dressing room, my gasping attracted the attention of Leviathan and Flex Rodriguez. They stepped out.

"What was—"

"Jesus, what—"

"Beast," I gasped, my teeth chattering. My arms felt cold, and the throbbing welts forming on my skin were buzzing and tingling like a swarm of wasps hatching underneath, frantically punching their way to the surface.

Another roar bellowed through the hall, killing the wasps under my skin, stabbing lightning into my heart. I pushed past Flex and stumbled into the dressing room. Flex and Leviathan stared down the hall at whatever was coming through those curtains. Collapsing on the dressing room carpet, I turned to the doorway. A crowd of the wrestlers in the dressing room stood up, unsettled by the inhuman howls from the hall.

"Get in," I gasped, waving to the two in the hall.

Something fell to the ground, shattering on the tiles, rousing Flex and Leviathan from their fixation. They stepped inside as The Beast stomped closer. Flex shut the door, but not quickly enough. There was a crack of wood splintering across the air like a gunshot. We looked at the door crumpling inward, brown splinters bleeding out like torn muscles.

CRACK!

A second shattering. The door split open. I looked at the doorway, the gateway between the world of the show and reality. The Beast stepped through, his haunches shaking, upper body snaking in. He was oversized now, his torso misshapen and stretched, bulging out. Molotov's skin was dark brown, furry, and his entire skull had elongated. His teeth, too large for the still stretching skull, were jutting out of his mouth, cutting into his own face as the bones and cartilage re-shaped in the hideous visage of a bear.

The Beast lunged forward, smacking wrestlers aside. I backed up, stumbling over bags and gear. The bear pivoted to follow me as I backed to my left. Wrestlers panicked and rushed for the door. As The Beast stepped again, more sure-footed this time, my fingertips brushed against something cold and round. Looking back, I saw a folding chair with a black bag on it.

I swiped Leviathan's bag off the seat, scattering a cigarette lighter, gum, and his wallet to the floor. In one swift move I collapsed the folding chair into a flat weapon. I swung just as The Beast lunged in.

SLAM!

It felt like the chair was going to wrench out of my hands. I could see the metal indent with the outline of his misshapen skull. Ignoring the shock wave traveling up my arms, I pulled the chair back again.

SLAM!

The dent expanded; I could feel the screws loosening in their joints. I pulled back one more time, bringing it down on The Beast's head.

The chair buckled; the bear shoved his snarling head through. Whatever human qualities Ivan had were almost gone now. The thrust of The Beast's body tore the chair out of my hands. He stood there with the broken chair around his still-changing neck. The chair framed his face, making him look like an evil painting coming to life, reaching out from the world of oil and pastel to the world of flesh and bone.

In the few seconds the bear struggled with the modified choker now trapped around his still-expanding neck, I looked around the deserted room. Contents of Leviathan's bag were on the ground, but there were no other chairs within reach. The Beast turned back to me. To my right were the overturned contents of Ivan Molotov's belongings. Leather jacket. Turtleneck. Bottle of vodka.

Vodka.

I darted out with my right hand as The Beast came in. My hand reached that bottleneck, fumbling with the cap. Remembering a trick another one of my favorite wrestlers used to do, I took a swig as The Beast swiped out with his arm, knocking me down. I landed on my tailbone, feeling something shatter. My stomach clenched; I desperately fought to keep from swallowing. The Beast reared back, raising its claws. It was a great evil god, a pagan statue from an extinct age brought to life. The remains of my weapon hung around his neck like a war necklace of skulls. He howled in triumph, filling my world with his inhuman wail.

I flicked the lighter once. The flame swayed like a belly dancer as The Beast came down. With all my strength, at my limited angle, I swung the bottle of vodka like a club. I don't know if it shattered on the chair or his skull, but it broke in my hand. As the glass shredded skin and fur, I dropped the bottleneck, blowing the vodka in my mouth into the lighter.

It ignited a fireball blazing into The Beast's looming face. My hand was scorched, but when the fireball hit the vodka soaking into the bear's fur, it exploded. I could feel The Beast's howling breath. I rolled out of the way of the flames as the bear stomped in anger. It tried to reach its face with its paws, but the chair around its neck got in the way. Stumbling to my feet, staggering out of the dressing room, I pulled the fire alarm.

I ran down the hallway as the blare of the fire alarm merged with the moans of evil and pain. In the parking lot, I could still hear the howl in my ears. I watched every figure that stepped outside through those doors, waiting to see that hideous silhouette, but it never came.

That was six months ago.

No one's seen or heard from Ivan Molotov since then.

There are supposed to be rules. Someone dies, there's a body, evidence of a body at least. But once one rule is broken, once a man can become a true beast, why should anything adhere to the rules?

We act like we know what's going to happen, but we don't know. We stand in the light, confident that what has always happened will continue to happen; our rules will hold. That noise in the darkness is just old pipes. It can't be anything else. The world has rules. Everyone, everything, in the world is bound by those rules. Why should a dead man stay dead? Why shouldn't a body disappear?

Why should The Beast, still hungry for me, stop searching? I don't live my life in fear, but I don't take anything for granted anymore. Our world—our lives—are on the edge of a very deep abyss every moment of every day. The natural order—the rules—keep us from falling in. They keep us safe, but we must watch out. We must keep ourselves safe too. We have to be ready for anything.

Because once in a while, the rule breakers will do something terrible.

Sometimes, the rule breakers win.

Under the Watchful Eyes of Los Abuelos

Aaron Polson

Inspired by Bob Dylan's *Shelter from the Storm*

John Hardaway sat in the driver's seat of a stolen car. He weighed a gun in his hands, a pistol, 9 mm, assembled in the United States from parts manufactured around the world. The grip was black, and the barrel cold. Ten cartridges waited in the clip. His eyes shifted to the window, resting on the sign above the small building. The final "a" faded from the painted sign, leaving only the truncated "Cantin." Behind the building, a thunderhead rose into the blue sky like a vengeful ghost.

John swallowed and his fingers tightened around the grip. He had been warned about this town and the old men that watched over the people. Los Abuelos. Stories of the unnatural reach of Los Abuelos chased him to Guanajuato just as he chased his quarry. Two children ran into his field of vision, one pursuing the other with a soccer ball. In front of the cantina, they slowed to a walk—almost on tiptoe until they moved past the door. A few drops of rain pattered against the windshield: a light, easy rain that came down despite the bright, almost cloudless sky.

John opened the glove compartment of the car, an Impala from the late '60s. He never had much skill with makes and models of cars, let alone identifying body style by year, but his grandfather had owned an Impala once. The glove compartment was empty save for a few yellowed papers and a rag stained with grease. He looked at the gun in his left hand and shook his head.

For six years he had waited for this moment, and now hesitation? No. With a quick flick of his wrist, he snapped the box shut. Six years was a long enough time to play hide and seek. It would end this afternoon.

He climbed from the car and straightened a pair of sunglasses over his eyes. The shades were cheap and plastic, purchased that afternoon from an old woman with a booth near the beach. His eyes swept the street on both sides of the cantina. The pistol tucked snugly inside his pants and under his cotton shirt. A tall man, John strode to the door in easy lopes while a war raged in his stomach.

The bar was dark inside—dark enough that he slid the glasses from his face. The air hung in clumps, reeking of old wood, rot, and another odor—a foul, earthy odor. As his eyes adjusted, shapes took form. Three men sat at a single table in the back of the room. All three smiled. Old men with jagged teeth. One hand sat on the edge of the table, gnarled and boney like a raptor's talon. John nodded and stepped to the bar. The eyes of the men followed him, white spheres like clouded marbles.

They reminded John of his mother's lifeless eyes, screwed up toward her scalp as she lay dead on the kitchen floor. The shadows across the old men's broken teeth looked to him like a mouth full of blood. Like his father's mouth full of blood six years ago.

"*Señor?*" The bartender set a glass tumbler before John and raised his eyebrows.

"I'm looking for a man named Alvarez." John's left thumb traced the pistol grip beneath his shirt.

"Ah. Mister Hardaway, *si*? He said you would be coming soon." The bartender smiled, his fat face parting into deep crevasses around stubbled cheeks. "Through to the back." He pointed to a thin curtain hanging across a doorway.

John nodded. His palms began to sweat. So close to the end of his journey, but the old men conquered his thoughts. Those teeth. His neck prickled as he pushed through the canvas into a sort of kitchen, sure that they were watching. Various bottles—dark glass containers with darker fluids inside—sat about on shelves along with a butcher's block of knives. A few wooden crates rested in a corner, covered with a torn bed sheet.

On a steel table against one wall, a body. A figure melted out of the shadows.

"Hardaway?" a voice growled with a heavy accent.

"Yes." John's eyes were fixed on the corpse. "Is this?" He asked, but he didn't need to. John Hardaway recognized the body. The face was a bit bloated, but the nose was crooked and forehead scarred from a motorcycle accident ten years ago.

"*Si*. We do our best, *Señor* Hardaway."

John stepped closer to the body and yanked down a sheet that had covered the bottom half. Three dirty bullet wounds, like swollen cigarette burns, marked the belly. "I expected him alive."

Alvarez shifted his weight from one foot to the other. He crossed his arms, heavily inked with tattoos—the Virgin Mary, dragons, and assorted skulls—the sacred and the profane stitched in blues and reds and greens.

"This man," he nodded once to the body, "we found him like this in the alley, *Señor*."

The gun weighed twice as much as it had in the car when John Hardaway pulled it from his pants. He set it on the metal table with a heavy clunk. His eyes flickered between the bullet wounds and the gun. "Shit," he muttered.

"What was your business with him?"

A moment passed. John chased a fly from his face.

"He was my brother."

John closed his eyes, pinching the bridge of his nose between forefinger and thumb. Memories surfaced like billows of mud in clear water. Six years ago, John Hardaway came home from college to find his parents slain in their home, the house ransacked for cash and easily liquidated valuables, the doors unlocked, and his brother's keychain hanging from the garage lock. His brother, the junkie, the waste. The corpse on a table in front of him in a dirty bar in Guanajuato. Six years he burned with revenge, and now he only thought of burying his brother.

"Ay." Alvarez took a step toward John and held out a hand. "Sorry for the loss, but the fee, *Señor*. In dollars, *por favor*."

"Right." John turned away from Alvarez, pulled the sheet over the dead man's torso, and tucked it around the head and neck.

It was time for Travis Hardaway to go home.

"*Señor*?"

"I can't carry him to my car uncovered."

"No. No, *Señor*. You can't carry him out at all."

"What?" John glanced at Alvarez over his shoulder. The tattooed man's eyes were fixed on the gun as he backed away.

"Los Abuelos, *Señor*. They want the body." Alvarez pointed to the curtain. "The townspeople always bring them here."

John straightened and faced Alvarez. In his mind's eye, he saw the jagged peaks in the mouths of those old men. Their white eyes watched him through the wall.

"I don't think I understand."

"For Los Abuelos. They keep us safe, give us shelter, if we...take care of them. They have certain...appetites." Alvarez's eyes drifted to the filth on the hardwood floor. "Guanajuato is a dark place, *Señor*."

John's hand reached back and touched his brother's leg. A nervous smile shimmered on Alvarez's face. He put his hands up at his sides. "They only eat the dead." Sweat began to gather on his forehead. "I thought you only wanted to see the body..." In a slow, sweeping motion, John's left hand slipped behind him and found the pistol grip. A short while ago, he imagined shooting his brother, exacting vengeance for his parents. Now, the gun pointed at Alvarez's chest.

"Help me get him out of here."

The tattooed man shook his head. His voice cracked. "*Señor*...that will not work on Los Abuelos. They have no fear of guns." The cantina was too quiet. John imagined the sound of clawlike hands scratching through the wall, white eyes burning into the core of his brain, sharpened teeth clicking together.

He pulled the trigger, breaking the silence like a sledgehammer against plate glass. Alvarez crumbled, just a bag of meat. John waited for a moment, listening for the sounds of Los Abuelos—of anyone. Then he stepped over the dead man, heading for the butcher knives on the shelf.

"They will need something else for their bellies then," he said as he pulled a long blade from the wooden block. Rain began tapping a beat against the corrugated metal overhead; John felt the thunder in his chest. "My brother has been away from home for too long."

Him

Mark Taylor

Inspired by Judas Priests' *Night Crawler*

The Midwest town of Callion was shrouded by early evening darkness, as the lines of the rural countryside had started to blur into the deep blue sky. Jacob looked out of the window of his thirteenth century farmhouse. In the distance, clouds, distended and grey with fury, were rolling across the sky at an unnatural rate. In the front yard, trees bent and bushes were nearly uprooted by the increasing winds. It was a storm that this town knew all too well.

"It's a dark one tonight. He'll be coming." Turning, Jacob looked at his father, now in his sixties, and his four-year-old son, both sitting at the kitchen table. "Dad, take Michael downstairs." He looked around at the windows. "I'll put the shutters down up here; be down in a few minutes."

Without speaking, the slightest nod of his head was enough to signify to Jacob that his father understood. He picked the boy up in his arms, swung him around his shoulders and carried him off to the basement, leaving Jacob standing in the kitchen, looking out onto the street. That's when the rain started, lashing against the sides of the old house and creating tiny rivers of mud.

The neighbor's house was a good three hundred feet away and still wearing its lights in its windows, like medals on a hero. "Damn fools." Jacob shook his head and picked up his shotgun from beside the sink. Breathing out a long sigh, he walked from window to window, checking to ensure that they were all closed, with the shutters down—where they still worked—and were locked. Ending up at the front door, he slid across the deadbolt as quietly as he could. Standing there, he could hear the wind rustling around the porch, and the water starting to run out of the gutter into the mud. Blowing out the only candle that lit the kitchen and gathering up a plate of food from the refrigerator, Jacob left the ground floor and locked the door to the basement behind him as he tread quietly down the stairs.

Jacob's father, Daniel, sat in the corner of the dark basement with the single window above their heads shedding what light it could from ground level—the only illumination coming in spurts from the lightning flashing outside. Michael had been put down on the cot in the corner, which had been dressed in clean sheets only this morning, in preparation. He laid there, eyes wide open, afraid to speak or even ask why they were there. He was too young to remember the last time they had hidden.

Jacob rested his gun down by his chair and sat. "The Johns' still got their lights on."

"You've told them. It's their choice."

Jacob looked at his father, watching over his grandson. He was a proud man, and Jacob had hoped that he was still proud of him—even after what had happened with Annie and Mother—not that it was his fault. "I didn't know what else to tell them." He tried to keep the conversation flowing with his father. "It all sounds like crazy talk."

"I said, you did what you could." Daniel shot a glance toward Jacob that could have cut through ice. His father was a religious man, forever quoting the Bible, God's word, as he put it. But Jacob believed that everything had changed last year, on a night just like this, and he wasn't sure now if his father even believed anymore.

Jacob pulled the gun up from beside him and rested it across his lap. "You see anything?"

Daniel got up and peered through the window, shaking his head slowly. "Can't see much through the rain."

"See the Johns? Still got their lights on?" Jacob asked.

Daniel nodded. "Yeah. Gonna get themselves in all sorts of trouble."

Jacob caressed the hilt of the gun gently. "I wish they'd just turn them off."

Daryl Johns was new to the town, moved in seven months ago, and didn't yet know about Him. Last week, when the weather had taken a turn for the worse—as it did once a year, every year in preparation of him—Jacob had tried to explain it to Johns. But who's going to believe it? Looks like a man, sounds like a man, hell, even bleeds like a man. But he's not of woman. Not of this earth— sounds crazy? Sure does—and Daryl had made sure that Jacob knew it, too. He'd had it all thrown back in his face, like a cheap joke.

Daryl didn't understand that Jacob was just trying to save his life... and the lives of his poor family.

Daniel had started to mutter under his breath as he returned to his seat, his soul being beaten into submission by the passive words of the church that had been force fed to him his whole life. As he sat, watched by

Jacob, Daniel stared blankly into an abyss; Jacob wondered briefly if the look of torment on his face was due to something inside him begging for salvation. He shook his head, realizing he didn't really care. Honestly, Jacob just wanted the night to be over, the wind and rain gone, and hopefully, Michael, himself and his father, to be unscathed.

***

And as the rain continued to cascade down, a black '65 Mustang pulled into the town of Callion...

***

Daryl Johns sat at the dining table with his wife Grace, and their two daughters, Elsie and Dena. The crashing thunder that had started up from the skies outside added to the chorus of the rain playing on their roof. Dena, the Johns' youngest, had said a short prayer—as was the tradition—before they had started on the dinner that Grace had lovingly prepared. The four of them fed from the pot in the center of the hard wood table, ignoring the lights around the house flickering occasionally, in time with the lightning strikes.

Daryl's attention was pulled away from his dinner by the lights of a car pulling up outside the house. He looked at Grace. "Stormy night for visitors?"

She nodded an agreement, unnecessarily, as Daryl had already slid his chair away from the table, stood, and was going over to watch from the window. As he looked through the water that had started to deluge from the porch roof, he could just make out the form of the car idling against the equally black night. The lightning flashes illuminating the dark steel before once again bathing it in shadows.

"Is he coming out?" He questioned rhetorically, rubbing his short stubbled chin with a rough hand. As he went to the door of the house and opened it, he was greeted by the chilled wind gusting in and the flowered curtains of the front door dancing. Daryl took a step forward, protected from the elements by the porch overhead, and squinted down at the car; its unseen driver killed the engine. The door of the Mustang swung open, and Daryl could finally see the dark figure behind the wheel, unfurling himself into the storm.

He stood in the rain, a long leather coat and a dark Stetson protecting his body and face from the downpour. He strode towards the entrance to the Johns' house, as Daryl waited patiently on the porch.

"What can I do for you, Mister?" he called out to the stranger, his voice raised above the spattering of the hard rain on the ground. The Stranger didn't respond but instead kept walking towards Daryl. As he reached the steps to the porch, he brought down his heavy boots on the soft wood. Almost in time with the weather, a methodical rhythm rose deeply from his step, until he was brought to eye level with his host.

Daniel watched the scene from the basement window. "Someone's going in."

Jacob crossed the basement to the window, shooting a quick wink to his son, Michael, as he watched anxiously from the cot. "Is it him?"

"Can't see."

Jacob leaned up, pushing his face closer to the window, peering through his own reflection. "I can't see the car clearly from here. I need to warn them." He stepped backwards away from the window.

Daniel grabbed out, taking Jacob's arm, "No." His voice cracked with fear and his scowl showed his anger.

"Dad!" Jacob tried to pull away, but his father's grip held firmly.

"You've already done what you could," he hissed through his gritted teeth.

Jacob knew that fighting against his father's will was unwise, as the consequences of past actions had taught him, but he felt responsible for the welfare of his neighbors—stubborn as Daryl was. What if he'd done a better job of persuading him? What if...? It had become a recurring thought ringing in Jacob's head of late. What if he hadn't let him in? What if he hadn't left him alone with his wife and mother?

Jacob pulled hard against his father's grip and released himself. "Look after Michael." He took a glance at his son, and then back to his father. "I'll be back." He hurried across the room, picking up the shotgun from by the chair on the way. After the first three steps of the stairs, he stopped and turned. "I *will* be back," he reassured.

In the rain-hazed night, Jacob stood, shotgun in hand, looking over to the Johns' porch from his own. He could see the car clearly from here—it was him. His reticence held him back—honestly, he was afraid—but he pushed himself forward, stepping down from the porch, into the heavy downpour. As he walked towards the lights of the Johns' house, he cocked the gun. He wasn't about to let history repeat itself. The closer he got, the tighter his fear gripped him, but Jacob wanted to be brave, wanted to try and stop this monster—once and for all.

As he reached the road line, a hundred feet from the house, the door of the Johns' home burst open, and two small figures dashed out in Jacob's direction – it was Elsie and Dena. They ran towards him as if Death himself was close on their heels, their nightgowns drenching quickly in the torrential rain.

"Girls!" He called out to them. They ran over to him, and he could see the rain merging with their tears. "What happened?"

The two of them halted in front of him. Dena wailed, her face curled up, terrified; Elsie, the elder of the two, looked dispiritedly at Jacob, then turned to look back at their abode and pointed. Jacob knew it had happened again. "Go to my house." He shouted above the rain, "Go down into the basement. Old man Daniel's down there. He'll look after you."

Elsie nodded and grabbed Dena by the arm. She took flight, dragging her sister behind her.

Jacob looked up, back to the house. The front door was now flapping in the wind. *Creak, thud, creak, thud.* He willed himself forward, fighting against the now vicious wind and rain towards the house. As he reached the porch, he paused, took a breath, and climbed up to the front door, ducking under the embrace of the dry porch. He leaned against the wooden frame and braced himself for what he might find inside. Sucking in one final breath, he turned and pushed the door open with the barrel of the gun. Light cascaded out of the house, casting long shadows across the porch.

He peered around the doorframe into the chasm of the house, looking for signs of life. The front door led into the living area and, leaning against the couch, only a few feet from the door, was Daryl, sitting on the floor. From behind, he looked like he might be resting, drunk even, slumped to the floor, unable to stand. Jacob looked around cautiously and then walked up behind the sprawled figure. "Daryl?" He didn't move—not much, at least—but his head lolled slightly. Jacob noticed blood on the floor around him. He sidled around him to take a closer look.

The sight of Daryl horrified Jacob; the skin around his neck was torn, exposing tendons, the blood running from the deep wounds seeped into his clothes. He tried to speak, but all that came out was a gurgle, blood bubbling around his mouth and throat. His eyes pleaded silently with Jacob for help; but Jacob pulled away, sickened, gripping the shotgun even tighter than he already was. "Oh, God..." He looked around the expanse of the ground floor, near naked in its sparse furnishings. He hadn't had a good relationship with his neighbors and was unfamiliar with the building layout, but the kitchen, lounge, and dining area were all open—and empty. He looked back at Daryl, "Where's Gracie?"

Daryl's eyes simply rolled in response, his head battling to stay upright.

Jacob knew it was no good and turned back into the room. His eyes scoured the layout, looking for a sign; something...anything. The scream that echoed from upstairs was almost drowned out by the storm lashing down outside. Instinctively, Jacob looked up at the ceiling. *Where are you, you son-of-a-bitch?* He crossed the room, stepping around the rug that had been disturbed and folded over to the stairwell and looked up the wooden stairs leading towards the bedrooms. "Gracie?" He called out. "It's Jacob." His calls were met with nothing but silence. His shotgun only had two shells loaded into it, and it didn't make him comfortable. It took all of Jacob's courage, but he managed to put one foot in front of the other, climbing the creaking stairs. At the top, he surveyed the surroundings; all the bedroom doors were shut—he couldn't see into a single room.

"Gracie?" He called out again, this time more urgently. "Where are you?" Again he was answered by silence.

Slowly, he crept up on the first door and gently laid his ear to it. The absolute silence was deafening—then, another scream rose from further down the hallway, the far end of the house. Jacob hurried down the corridor.

"Gracie!" he screamed, kicking his foot square into the center of the door.

Jacob stood—the door splintered and hanging from its hinges—in one of the girl's bedrooms. He was affronted by Gracie, cowering, half naked, and painted with her own blood at the feet of The Stranger—him.

He was looking down at her, his Stetson covering his face, his body hidden by the folds of his long coat—just as Jacob remembered. The Stranger looked up, his actions defined—deliberate—in order to show his gaunt features. His hollow eyes, lifeless, cut into Jacob; his thin lips curled up into a smile, revealing rotten teeth. Wind blowing in through the open window parted his hanging trench coat, exposing the body of a long dead corpse.

"Jaaacobb," his voice seemed to play around the room, as if it were the very wind itself. "You caaame for mee."

Fear gripped him like a vice, and Jacob nearly dropped the gun. He was unable to look away from the thing before him but somehow found the strength to raise the gun at The Stranger. "Get away from her." He wasn't proficient with the weapon and didn't want to fire just yet for fear he'd hit Gracie.

He stepped forward—over Gracie—a hand held out, as if greeting an old friend.

Jacob didn't think—couldn't. As soon as The Stranger was clear of Gracie, he just squeezed the trigger without aiming. The shot was deafening, ringing around the room like a carnival ride. It staggered backwards, but the force of the impact wasn't enough to knock it over. After an initial reel, the monster steadied itself and came at Jacob once again.

Paralyzed by fear, Jacob could do nothing as The Stranger reached forward, grasped the gun barrel, and pulled it from his hands. Jacob stumbled to the side, trying to get away from the monstrosity while at the same time not taking his eyes off it; he flailed for footing, struggling to retain his balance.

The Stranger looked at the weapon in his hand, and whilst his face displayed no signs of emotion, he somehow exuded disdain. Tossing the gun through the open door into the hallway, he turned back to Jacob, now sprawled on the floor. "Jaaacobb," his voice rang out again.

"What do you want?" Jacob screamed back. He was helpless on the ground, and glancing over at Gracie, he knew that she wouldn't be of any use either. She was still sprawled on the floor, unmoving, but he was fairly sure that under the blanket of blood she was still alive. He looked back into the eyes of the monster, a tear rising in his own. "Come and get me, you son-of-a-bitch!" The Stranger leaned over, toward Jacob, his rotten face pulling into a ludicrous smile—so ludicrous, that Jacob almost found it funny.

"DIE!" Daniel's voice erupted as he burst through the door into the room, crashing the butt of the gun down as hard as he could on the monster.

Shocked, Jacob spun around to see his father, a look of hatred and disgust on his face, bringing the discarded shotgun down onto the back of the beast.

Losing its balance, the creature fell forward onto Jacob. Jacob fought against it, kicking and clawing, as the thing struggled to regain its footing. Daniel continued to release a year's worth of hatred down onto the beast with the shotgun, causing it to wail out painfully. Jacob managed to raise his feet into the belly of the beast and launched it with all his might backwards—howling—into the air.

"Dad! Shoot it!"

Daniel spun the gun around, training in on the fast-moving prey—he was a much more accomplished hunter than his son—and fired the remaining round; the slug rammed into the head of the beast, and it fell lifeless to the floor between Jacob and Gracie. The blast echoed briefly, then vanished, leaving the room silent.

Jacob looked first at the beast, and then at his father. He didn't know what to say or do. Slowly, he clambered up and edged his way around the room to Gracie. She was still motionless, apart from her shallow breathing. He didn't remove his eyes from her; whilst he listened to his father reload the shotgun.

"Gracie?" Jacob put his hand gently onto her shoulder. She muttered and mumbled, a look of unimaginable fear and torment in her eyes. Jacob looked over to his father, but Daniel was fixated on the monster lying still on the floor. Turning back to Gracie, he uttered some comforting words as best he could. He wished that Annie was here to say them for him; she was always better at it than he was.

Daniel approached the beast cautiously; the shotgun trained on the unmoving figure. He nudged it with the barrel of the gun, keeping as much of a distance as he could, but it still didn't move. He crouched down and rolled the body onto its back. Its eyes were dead. It was gone.

Jacob came over and crouched next to him, "Is it dead?"

Daniel shook his head. "No, son. But it's gone—for now."

Untethered

Morgan Dambergs

Inspired by Cobra Starship's *Good Girls Go Bad*

When Kayla leaned over the counter and ripped out the bartender's throat with her teeth, it became suddenly and abundantly clear that something had gone wrong with the lust spell.

Andrew never found out what triggered the change—if the bartender ignored her too long, or wouldn't accept her ID, or just didn't know how to make the drink she wanted. All he knew was, one moment he had one of the other Ice Queens—besides Kayla, he could never keep their names straight—pressed up against the bar, grinning over at his friend Blake as he slid his hand under her shirt. Then there was a scream, and a jet-spray of what looked like grenadine splashed over them, covering Andrew's face and the back of the girl's blonde hair.

Andrew turned to see what had happened, and there was Kayla a few feet away, face still buried in the bartender's ruptured jugular, arms hooked around his neck like a lover as she dragged his limp body over the top of the bar. Blood ran down her chin and chest, funneling between her cleavage.

The crowd around the bar erupted into panic, but Andrew barely noticed. He watched in mute shock as Kayla turned in his direction and spat out a piece of gristle. It bounced off the toe of his Keds, leaving a dark splotch on the canvas. For a moment, she was staring straight at him, and something in her eyes caused Andrew to stumble backwards, heart rate spiking as his body shifted into flight mode. Andrew's back hit something soft yet solid, and when he glanced over his shoulder to see what was blocking his escape, he found himself staring through clumps of blood-streaked bangs into a pair of green eyes—eyes that were every bit as predatory as Kayla's. The Ice Queen grinned at him, lips parting to reveal perfect white teeth. Andrew's breath caught. She slid her body up against his back, her arms snaking over his shoulders. Her hands moved languidly down his chest, coming to a halt just under his sternum, and, as her carefully manicured nails tore through his shirt and began to dig into his flesh, Andrew's lungs finally hitched in enough air for him to scream...

Someone grabbed his wrist, wrenching him forward. Andrew cried out again as his body fought against the girl's nails. She hissed angrily as her hands finally gave way, and then he was stumbling through the club behind Blake.

The dance floor was in total chaos, people scrambling to escape. Andrew couldn't tell if the DJ had turned the music off or if it was simply drowned out by the screams. And no matter what direction he looked, he saw injuries from the massacre. To the left, a man shrieked at the sight of his own hand, its fingers reduced to tattered ribbons; to the right, a girl tried desperately to replace her lower lip, which hung off her chin in a loose flap. One girl stopped to help her friend, who had slipped in a puddle of blood or booze—only for two slender, bling-laden hands to claw their way over her face and drag her, flailing, back into the mob. Blake pulled Andrew through the carnage so fast, he didn't get to see if her friend managed to stand up before she got trampled.

Through it all, Andrew's mind reeled with the knowledge that the Ice Queens were the force behind this slaughter—the same six pretty little wallflowers who Blake had half-joked were so uptight they'd probably have a natural shield of prissy protecting them from anything as base as a lust spell. All he and Blake had wanted was to screw with them a little bit, or at most, just plain screw them. It seemed impossible that one spell, one—admittedly, not the most innocent—spell, could turn the Ice Queens into monsters.

Though maybe he was being naïve. After all, it was clear from the first time the Ice Queens walked into Club Sur, months ago, that they had the market cornered on repression. The six of them invariably arrived together and left together—a little swarm of couture and interchangeably pretty faces whispering to each other at the back of the club. Five of the girls maintained a constant orbit around Kayla, as they watched the dance floor over drinks that looked more like food coloring than alcohol. Although they were pros at the catty turn-down—as Blake and Andrew discovered the first time they asked a couple of the girls to dance—the right song could get the whole group out on the floor; shaking their tight little asses, in a tight little circle, backs facing out to let everyone know how welcome they were to cut in. One time, they even saw Kayla fulfill the ultimate cliché of throwing her drink in some guy's face when he smacked her ass. That was when Blake made it a personal challenge to get Kayla to blow him instead of just blowing him off again—or at the very least, dance with him willingly.

When Blake suggested the lust spell, Andrew went along with it primarily for shits and giggles. Not that he minded the idea of getting into one, or more, of Kayla's hot friends' pants, but for all Blake's assurances that he'd been collecting 'grimoires,'—as he insisted on calling them—for years, Andrew had never seen him read anything longer than an issue of *Maxim*. He found it hard to believe that Blake could pull a rabbit out of a hat, much less pull off an actual spell.

So, it came as a pleasant shock tonight when they walked in and saw the Ice Queens actually hanging all over a bunch of guys on the dance floor. When Kayla made a beeline for Blake, he grinned so wide Andrew thought his lips might split. In turn, Andrew quickly picked out the blonde Ice Queen, who had been grinding very enthusiastically on her dance partner, in the hopes that he'd have the makings of a threesome by the end of the night. Then Kayla decided an Adam's apple made for a tasty bar snack, and it all went to hell.

Blake yanked Andrew to the left and Andrew almost lost his balance. He saw one of the Ice Queens skip past, covered head-to-toe in gore and slurping up a mouthful of what looked like someone's small intestine. Next thing he knew, Blake shoved them through the door to the men's washroom, paused long enough to throw the deadbolt in place, then stumbled across the room and collapsed against the back wall. Andrew started after him but stopped as his eyes swept across the four windowless concrete walls.

"Blake, what the *fuck*? The main entrance was right over there! Now how are we supposed to get out?"

Blake looked up at him wearily. "Main entrance? Do you remember where we are?"

Andrew grimaced. Blake was right. Club Sur was an entirely illegal operation set up in the basement of an abandoned warehouse. Its shtick of being both literally and figuratively underground was what made it one of the hottest clubs in the city. Even the men's washroom was just a storage room fitted with a couple urinals and a wall-mounted hand sanitizer pump—anyone in need of more complete facilities was quite literally S.O.L. Sur had no official address, no liquor license, no fire exits—hell, most people couldn't even get cell reception. There was only one way in or out, and given the mob scene, there was virtually no chance he and Blake could fight their way up the stairs to street level before they were either eaten alive or crushed underfoot.

"And not even a fucking 'thank you.' I don't know why I bothered saving your sorry ass. You deserve to be out there cleaning up your mess."

Andrew gaped at Blake. "*My* mess?"

Blake pushed himself up and strode over to Andrew, getting right in his face. "You brought the wrong ingredients, didn't you? The spell said, 'blood of a virgin,' Andrew. *Of. A. Virgin.* I knew chicken blood wouldn't cut it, but you convinced me—"

"So, you're saying I caused a bloodbath by refusing to murder a virgin for you? How does that even make sense?"

"Everyone knows that messing with a spell's ingredients can make it unstable—"

"Oh, yeah, Blake, 'cause you know all there is to know about magic." Andrew gave Blake a shove, and he stumbled back a few steps. "Some master fucking warlock you are! If chicken blood was such a problem, why cast the spell at all?" Blake backed further away and Andrew stalked after him. "And what about your stupid incantation? 'O Great Demon Gods, for just one night, please make the Ice Queens go very, very bad.' Maybe you could have made that a little *more* ambiguous."

Andrew shoved Blake again, slamming him against the wall hard enough that the back of his skull cracked sharply against the concrete. Andrew raised his hands for another go, but stopped short when Blake cringed, face crumpling up like he was about to cry. Andrew balled his hands into fists and forced himself to turn away. After taking his rage out on a garbage can, Andrew made his way through the scattered trash to Blake's side of the room and sat down next to him on the floor. His stomach stung a little, still tender where the Ice Queen had clawed at him, but the cuts were already scabbing over. They sat in silence, listening to the screams and shatters of breaking glass that filtered through from out in the club. After a while, Blake spoke.

"The spell should wear off by morning. From the sound of it, we're probably better off in here than trying to escape."

Andrew nodded. "And if we're lucky, there's enough out there to keep the girls occupied that they won't try to break in." He pulled a face. "I can't believe I just said that."

Blake just shrugged. Andrew tipped his head back to rest against the wall, wincing as some poor, doomed soul gave a particularly bloodcurdling shriek right outside the door. Dawn couldn't come soon enough.

***

It was just past five in the morning when they finally ventured out of the bathroom, almost forty-five minutes after they'd last heard any noise from outside. It took a while for Andrew to convince Blake to let him open the door. He might not have been so hot on the idea himself, but he couldn't shake the thought that maybe someone else had survived. Hell, even if it was just the Ice Queens, coming back to themselves as the spell wore off...there might be someone out there they could help.

The smell hit them first, a thick tang of iron cut with shit and sour sweat. Andrew pulled the door wide; his stomach lurched. Blake took one look out and stumbled back to puke on the bathroom floor. The club was a bloodbath, a wall-to-wall sea of bodies, many so mutilated they looked more like slabs of meat than human beings. Andrew had to step over a small pile of severed heads to get out the bathroom door.

It was eerily silent, and absolutely still. No movement, no one crying out for help. No sign of the Ice Queens. Andrew forced himself to start walking towards the club's entrance, stepping gingerly over corpses and body parts, Blake at his back. He locked his eyes on the shadowed arc of the metal staircase and refused the horrible urge to look down at any intact faces. If he recognized anyone, he didn't want to know.

They saw the blonde Ice Queen first, half-decapitated in a pool of what seemed to be her own blood. Andrew shared a wide-eyed glance with Blake, then peered around the rest of the club, aware of just how perverse it was to pray for more dead bodies in the middle of a massacre. But there she was, propped against the left-hand wall: another Ice Queen. Her head lolled like a broken marionette's, the gaping hole in her skull glistening wetly under the club's dim mood lighting.

"Fuck." Blake ran a hand back through his hair. "You think they're all...?"

Andrew swallowed hard, hating Blake for the relief in his voice, hating himself more for understanding it. He nodded at the staircase. "C'mon. Let's go."

It felt somehow poetic when they were stopped short by the sight of Kayla kneeling at the foot of the stairs. Her head was tipped forward, a dark curtain of hair obscuring her face. She didn't seem aware of them. Her left-hand lay palm-up on her bare knees; her other arm hung limp at her side. Hard as he looked, Andrew couldn't tell if she was injured—she was just too soaked in blood.

Blake glanced at him, and Andrew didn't need to ask what he was thinking. Unless Kayla was catatonic, there was no way they could get to the stairs without her noticing. And if she was catatonic, they couldn't leave her behind.

Andrew took a tentative step toward her. "Kayla? Can you hear me?"

She didn't move. Andrew took another step forward. Kayla raised her head, blinking up at him—and he stopped in his tracks as a Cheshire cat grin spread slowly across her face. Her teeth were tinged with red.

"I didn't realize there was anyone else left." She tilted her head to the side in a way that under normal circumstances would have been pretty damn cute. "Where did you come from?"

"We, uh...were hiding out. Are you okay?" Andrew started to reach out to her, then hesitated, not entirely sure why. "I mean, fuck, I'm sorry, of course you aren't. But—"

Kayla gave a high-pitched giggle. "Oh, I'm fine. I'm...mmm..." Her left hand made a rolling motion in the air. "I wanna say fabulous, but that's not quite it. Glorious, maybe?" She laughed again. "I'm glorious!"

"You're..." Andrew shot a look at Blake, who had come up beside him, but Blake's eyes were fixed on Kayla. "Do you remember what happened?"

"How could I forget?" She closed her eyes in an expression Andrew could only describe as rapture. "I've never felt like that before, so...untethered, unleashed, un...something. Un-me." She opened her eyes and smiled at Andrew. "I know you think I'm a fucking prude. Until tonight, I never understood why."

Andrew's mouth went dry. His eyes flicked to the trampled and eviscerated bodies lying all around them, and he shook his head like he could somehow dislodge Kayla's words from his mind. "This is not how you let go! You fucking *ate* people, Kayla!"

"I know, right?" She raised a finger to wipe away the blood caked at the corners of her lips, then stuck the tip in her mouth, sucking it like a lollipop. Andrew heard Blake give a disgusted little groan. "Hopefully the chase burned some of them off already or I swear they'll go straight to my thighs. So not hot."

She rose to her feet; Andrew took a couple steps back. Kayla clasped her hands behind her back and shot him a coquettish little pout, then turned to Blake, who seemed frozen where he stood. Andrew saw the blood drain from Blake's face when Kayla's eyes met his, but still, he didn't move.

"Your friend's acting like I'm already Pudgy McPudgerson. But you still like me, right?" She moved slowly towards Blake, her gore-soaked babydoll dress clinging wetly to her curves. "You've always liked me."

She raised her left hand and ran her index finger down Blake's chin to the hollow of his throat. He swallowed hard. "You still think I'm pretty like a model?"

Blake gave a jerky nod, and Kayla graced him with a glowing smile.

"Good. That makes me glad I didn't eat everyone I killed."

"No?" Blake rasped.

"No. My girls, I just killed like this..."

Before Andrew had even fully registered her words, Kayla's right hand flashed out from behind her back and plunged a paring knife up to the hilt in the side of Blake's neck. Blake cried out, his hands jerking up to grab Kayla's arm. Kayla smiled sweetly, kissed the fingers of her free hand and pressed them to Blake's lips. Then she twisted the blade sideways and sawed halfway across his throat with two jagged pulls.

A gush of blood exploded from Blake's severed carotid artery. Kayla turned her face up to it, mouth open, tongue extended, and as her eyelids fluttered shut in ecstasy, Andrew finally found the presence of mind to run. He sprinted for the staircase, ignoring Kayla's angry shout behind him, the heavy thump that must have been Blake's body hitting the floor, and the slap of her bare feet on wet concrete.

He vaulted over a small pile of trampled corpses, felt his foot hit the first step...and slide right out from under him. Andrew caught a split-second glimpse of a girl's long, dark hair, spread like oil across the bottom step; then he was hurtling backwards, snatching hopelessly for the railing he knew he couldn't reach. A sharp pain shot through his kidneys as he hit the floor and he cried out, rolling away from whatever he'd landed on—the tips of someone's shoes, by the feel of it.

He scrambled to his hands and knees, biting his lip against the throbbing in his abdomen, and then Kayla hit him like a wrecking ball and knocked him on his back. He shrieked as he tried to squirm out from under her, legs kicking, fingers clawing at her arms. Kayla dealt him a surprisingly powerful backhand across the face, and straddled his waist, anchoring him to the floor. She tucked the tip of the paring knife under his jaw; Andrew forced himself to lie very, very still.

Kayla leaned over to kiss the tip of his nose, then sat back and shook her head. A few drops of Blake's blood pattered onto Andrew's face.

"Oh, no, sugar. You're staying right here." She gazed down at him, absently tracing the tip of the knife across his throat. "If you go, I'll have no one left to play with. That's no fun."

Kayla tilted her chin up, indicating the club. "I should've taken my time with my girls. But when we started to come down from—whatever it was—they were being such whiney little bitches! 'Oh, boohoo, blood on our hands, mortal sin.' And I..." Her lips formed a dreamy smile. "I didn't want it to end. So, I got a little, uh, overeager. Doubt it took me twenty minutes to take them all down." She looked back at Andrew. "When you and your friend showed up, I thought I could make it last a while; but his throat was so smooth...I couldn't help myself." She giggled a little. "So, I guess it'll just be you."

Andrew began to shiver uncontrollably. He turned his eyes away from the horrible spark of joy in hers, but it didn't help. Wherever he looked, all he could see was his future amongst the blood and mangled bodies. There was a tension welling in his chest, and he couldn't tell if it was another scream, or a sob.

Kayla lifted the paring knife from Andrew's throat and wrinkled her nose at it. "This thing's getting kinda boring. Ooh, but I loved what you did when you fell! Now, where are...ah." She slammed the blade of the paring knife into the out-flung arm of a nearby corpse, then leaned to the side, fiddling with something. It took a good ten seconds for Andrew's fear-numbed brain to realize this might be his last chance to escape—and by then, it was already too late. Kayla loomed back over him, pressing his chest to the floor with one hand. The other waggled a long, sinisterly tapered stiletto pump in front of his face.

Kayla grinned. "Let's see how much damage I can do with this."

***

When the street-level door finally opened, Andrew wondered vaguely if it was morning or afternoon sunlight that spilled into the bowels of the club. He'd lost track of time after Kayla decided that if she wanted full access to his entrails, she'd need the knife after all. Kayla hissed and yanked the heel of the stiletto out of his stomach cavity; Andrew just winced, too tired to cry out. Kayla scuttled away under a nearby table, tossing the shoe to the side.

Footsteps clanged on the metal staircase, echoing harshly in the club's cavernous silence. From where he lay on the floor, Andrew could see several police officers making their way carefully down, guns drawn. They fanned out at the bottom of the stairs, speaking to each other softly as they covered the club. Andrew tried to listen, but he was too exhausted to concentrate. Under the table, Kayla drew in her legs and wrapped her arms around them protectively. She shot Andrew a quick wink before dropping her forehead to rest on her knees.

That was how the officers found her a short while later: blubbering, trembling, and terrified—the personification of the innocent victim. Andrew heard the police saying 'miracle' over and over, heard Kayla whimper out a tale of recreational drug use gone horribly wrong.

Apparently, he and Blake had drunk too many drinks, taken too many pills, and just lost it. Someone suggested roid rage, and she ran with that, spinning her story from massacre to betrayal as she related how the two of them finally turned on each other. And all the while she had stayed hidden, too scared she might draw attention to herself to even contemplate escape. As she turned over the bloodied knife she'd picked up for 'self-defense,' she shattered into sobs so convincing even Andrew almost believed her.

One of the officers knelt next to Andrew, gun trained on his head, as she checked his limp hands for weapons. Andrew tried to speak, but his voice had failed ages ago from screaming, and all that came out was a breathy rasp. The officer snapped a pair of cuffs on his wrists, sending a jolt of pain across his ravaged body, then moved off to join her team and check for other survivors.

A young policeman went to take Kayla in his arms. She buried her face in his shoulder, clasping her hands behind his neck— then glanced up furtively as her savior headed for the stairs. Apparently satisfied that no one was looking, she blew Andrew a kiss and flapped her hand in a cheerful little wave. Then she balled it into a fist and mimed stabbing the officer repeatedly in the neck. As she raised a finger to her lips, Andrew made another helpless rasping noise, hoping to God, he could attract someone's attention; but the policeman was already at the street-level door, carrying Kayla out into the sunshine.

Andrew closed his eyes and relaxed back against the floor. The pain was getting worse. Every breath, every tiny movement, seared his body with sparks of agony, but somehow, he couldn't hold back a smile. He was done—out. And whatever hell was set aside for semi-accidental black magic practitioners, it couldn't be worse than a world with Kayla alive in it. He shifted a little, almost relishing the pain that streaked across his lacerated abdomen. Kayla had more than paid him back for making her a monster. She was someone else's problem now.

Trap Set

Nate D. Burleigh

Inspired by The Surfaris' *Wipe Out*

"Sweet mother, please?" Kaz begged his computer. The bid on eBay held steady at two thousand dollars. He flipped his credit card between his fingers. Drops of sweat ran down his forehead, dripping off his nose. Then it happened, two thousand and five hundred.

"No!" he screamed. Only ten minutes remained before he lost the set forever.

"What the hell?" Kristina said, rolling onto her side in their queen-sized bed. She looked at him with tired, aggravated eyes.

"Sorry, babe. Didn't mean to wake you. I almost got it."

"Got what?"

"The drum set. I'm waiting until there's about two minutes left. I'm bidding three thousand."

"Three thousand? Are you out of your damn mind?" She bunched up her pillow and lifted herself into a seated position.

"That'll max out the card."

"I'm getting this kit."

"You know we can't afford it."

"Go back to sleep." He didn't look at her as he nervously tapped a drum solo on the desk.

She huffed, got out of bed, and stormed into the restroom. He couldn't help but catch a glimpse of her in her black-lace thong and half T-shirt. Her black, sleep-mussed hair drifted across her shoulders, and her ageless Asian skin glistened with the lotion she'd put on before bed.

"Once I get it, it'll open up a whole new world for my work."

"Whatever," she mumbled.

Kaz knew this was his only shot to own a true icon's drum set. The toilet flushed and, for a second, he heard running water. The bathroom door opened and Kristina walked back into the bedroom.

She'd pulled her hair into a ponytail. Which absolutely drove him crazy, and she knew it.

"We can get you a much nicer set at the music store for a quarter of that. I don't see what's so special about this particular one," she said, draping her arms over his shoulders and snuggling her cheek into his neck.

"I explained this to you before," he said, irritated. "It belonged to the drummer from Fatal Crush."

"They broke up, didn't they?" she asked.

"Only after their drummer disappeared off the face of the earth. Ricky Riddell had the fastest hands in the business."

She yawned. "I think I saw a bit about it on that Lifestyles show. They said he went mad before he disappeared."

"Right. You know that drum solo I'm always playing?"

"Yes." She flopped back onto the bed.

"They said he barricaded himself in his studio and would only play that one solo for days on end, without taking any breaks. Then, he simply disappeared. No one suspected foul play."

"What do you think happened to him?" she asked.

"Don't know. Some think he'll make a grand return sometime in the future. Some think they carted his ass off to an insane asylum. What I do know, is that they finally had an estate sale and I'm going to get those drums." His watch alarm went off. It meant only one minute remained before the end of the bidding. Kristina started to say something, but he ignored her and tapped in his final bid, three thousand dollars.

He hit enter.

"You didn't," she said, disgusted.

"Yes!" he cried out. His final bid edged out someone who bid twenty-seven hundred. He leapt out of his seat. "Holy shit! I got it!"

Kristina screamed into her pillow.

"Don't worry, babe. I'll pick up some extra shifts at the music store and hopefully land some new gigs." Kaz hadn't found a band that he really meshed with yet, so he'd been substituting for other drummers at local nightclubs and other venues.

"Whatever," she said, pulling the covers over her head.

"Turn off the light."

"Sure." He reached over and turned off the light on the bedside table. His bid still glowed triumphantly on the computer screen.

Using PayPal, he completed the transaction. The rest of the night he stared at the ceiling, auditory hallucinations of kick ass drumming blaring in his head. He'd paid an extra hundred and fifty for express shipping. The drums would arrive in two days.

Every couple of hours he checked the progress of his famous package on the FedEx website. Right up to the hour and minute it arrived at Sea-Tac Airport. The delivery truck came on time and, before long, Kaz had the trap set assembled and ready to rock.

"Triple-let, triple-let, boom, tom, crash." It was the most beautiful sound he'd ever heard. The acoustic value alone trounced his old set. The kit had been custom made. Although he searched it thoroughly, Kaz couldn't find the designer's initials, which he thought very odd. The drumhead of the snare had a disturbing inscription on it. The engraved name read, Ricky Riddell, but backwards, as if you were looking at the name in a mirror.

Kaz began playing. He ran through his favorite solos and riffs. Some of the riffs he'd never been able to play before, and he thought that this set had brought out the best in him. He knew that with these drums, he'd be unstoppable. He continued to play. Kristina peeked her head into the garage. "Are you coming in for dinner?"

He'd shed his shirt some three hours earlier. Sweat from his hard work glistened across the tattoo of two doves flying side-by-side on the right side of his chest with an inscription under each. The fluid trailed down his abdomen, soaking the front of his jeans.

"Yeah, give me a few more minutes."

"OK, but I'm not reheating it for you."

He ignored her and started playing again.

"Jeez, Kaz. Are you going to play anything else?"

"What are you talking about?"

"Seems kind of lame playing the same solo over and over." She lifted an eyebrow.

"I played a ton of different stuff. I think you've lost your mind."

She put her hands on her hips. "You've been playing the same song all day."

"What song?"

"The one you were playing earlier tonight on the computer desk. I know you like the solo but give it a rest."

"You're screwing with me, aren't you?" He shot her his wry smile that clearly stated: quit messing around.

"I'm not joking, Kaz. You've been playing it all day. It's kind of freaking me out. Just like that guy...uh..."

"Rickey Riddell," he finished her sentence.

"Yeah. Didn't you say that was the song he played before he disappeared."

"Yes. You're probably getting the drone of the beat confused. I swear I've been playing all kinds of different rhythms."

"Then do it now."

"Do what?"

"Play something else."

"Fine." He figured he'd just play a simple jazz riff and be done with it. Each tap of the cymbal rang out like millions of chimes ringing at the same time. He'd lost himself in the rhythm and blues and hadn't noticed Kristina tugging on his belt. He fell backwards onto the concrete, the drumsticks landing neatly on the snare.

"Holy shit, Kaz!" The look on her face horrified him. Streaks of mascara trailed beneath her eyes, and she looked at him as if she'd never seen him before.

"An hour," she sobbed. "I've been trying to get you to stop playing for an hour."

"What are you talking about?"

She backed out of the garage, her eyes darting back and forth between Kaz and the trap set.

He pulled himself off of the ground and followed her into the house. "I still don't know what you're talking about."

She sat on the sofa, staring at the blank screen of their forty-two-inch plasma television. "You wouldn't stop. It was like you were in some sort of trance. You even looked at me a couple of times, like you would hurt me if I tried to stop you. I finally had to pull you off of the stool."

He still couldn't wrap his mind around her words. The mini grandfather clock that sat on the hearth above their fake fireplace read seven o'clock at night. He'd played for nine hours.

Holy shit.

They ate their reheated supper in silence. After he helped clean up the dishes, Kristina went to bed, not saying a word.

A quick peek won't hurt anything.

He opened the garage door and stared at the trap set. Feeling the drumsticks whirling in his hands had been bliss and he wanted to recreate that euphoria. Time stood still, his eyes transfixed on the drums. They called to him, beckoning him to sit—play. It wasn't until he had to pee so bad that his bladder felt like it would burst, that he forced himself to stop playing.

He quietly snuck into the bathroom, finished his business, and took a long, lukewarm shower. He'd just started drying off when he heard a distinct *ting, ting, ta, ting, ting* coming from the garage. It sounded like someone tapping the cymbal. He threw on his boxers.

Ting, ting, ta, ting, ting, boom, boom.

Kristina slept soundly with her earplugs in. He picked up his Louisville Slugger from the closet and continued through the living room toward the garage. "If someone's fucking with my drums, I'll kill 'em."

Ting, ting, ta, ting, ting, boom, boom, CRASH! The cymbal rang throughout the house.

Kaz swallowed hard and slowly opened the door to the garage. The light was still out. He gently slipped his arm along the wall until he felt the light switch. A slow roll started on the snare. He flipped the switch.

The snare stopped with a deafening crash of the cymbal and when the light came on, the drums silenced. No one sat behind the set. Kaz eyed every corner of the room. Only one place someone could be hiding, behind a tool cabinet near the garage door. Kaz crept into the room, making sure he couldn't be seen by whoever hid behind the cabinet. Slinking his way over, his heart started pounding like a base drum deep within his chest. His mind instinctively added the hi-hat and a snare tap. He gripped the bat tighter and leapt around the corner.

Nothing.

His eyes flicked left, then right, searching for the phantom drummer. The room remained empty. He walked over to the trap set and realized his drumsticks were in the exact location he'd left them. Kaz scratched his head curiously. "I must have imagined the whole thing," he said and flicked the cymbal. When he did, the snare tapped. Kaz jumped back.

"What the..."

The hi-hat started. *Chip, chip, chip, chip.* Then the cymbal entered. *Ting, ting, ta, ting, ting. Base, BOOM, BOOM.* And ended with a loud *CRASH* from the cymbal.

Kaz stumbled backwards, tripped and landed flat on his back.

BOOM, BOOM, BOOM, BOOM, the base continued.

Kaz thought he saw the set move but couldn't be sure. Ice cold horror raced up his spine. The two connected cymbals that made up the hi-hat rose into the air, still connected to the metal rod. It chipped in rhythm with the snare as it headed right for him.

He shrieked and ran for the door. A swooshing sound startled him. As he turned, one of the drumsticks plunged deep into his right shoulder. The force threw him against the wall. Dazed, he tried to move, but realized the drumstick had gone completely through him, pinning him to the sheetrock. He tried to grab the end protruding from his shoulder, but the other drumstick drove itself through his left hand, pinning it to the wall.

Kaz screamed, squirming to get loose. The chipping of the hi-hat got louder. His favorite solo started playing on the tom. The hi-hat rose into the air by its stand, as if it were a long metal neck. The solo continued.

Kaz threw both feet against the wall behind him and pushed. His right shoulder slid off the drumstick, and he fell awkwardly to one side. The force from the drop tugged his left hand—pinned by the drumstick—so hard, the stick snapped in two. He slumped to the floor. Blood flowed down his right arm, pooling on the concrete in front of him. He sat up. Clenching his left hand under his right arm, he tried to stop the blood flow.

The chipping continued. When he looked up, the hi-hat lunged straight down. Kaz rolled out just in time and the connected cymbals crashed into the floor. Shards of concrete scattered across the room. He scrambled toward the door.

The solo sped up, echoing through the room.

Kaz reached for the doorknob and felt a sharp pain in his left leg. He looked down and the hi-hat had him by the ankle and foot. Like a dog playing tug-of-war with its master, the hi-hat pulled. It dragged Kaz back toward the set. He clawed the concrete, ripping off several of his fingernails, leaving a bloody trail that resembled a music staph. He turned and started kicking with his right foot. Each time he kicked, the grip of the hi-hat tightened. Bones snapped. Kaz wailed in pain.

The hi-hat lifted him in the air until he dangled above the snare. Blood from his hand and shoulder dripped onto the drumhead, slowly taking the shape of a five-sided star. Then it dissipated into the plastic. *No.* Now that he looked at it closely, it definitely wasn't plastic. Then he remembered. Ricky Riddell had been one of the cockiest musicians ever. So cocky, he'd tattooed his own name across his back.

Kaz wriggled back and forth, lifting himself, trying to break free of the brass crushing his ankle. His hand slid across the cold metal. Three of his fingers dropped onto the snare with a click. Kaz looked down. The fingers dissolved, becoming one with the set.

Kaz screamed. "Help! Help m—"

His sentence cut short as the glint from the cymbal flashed in front of him. Blood from the laceration across his throat flowed down his chin, pouring onto the snare. He gurgled one last time as it lowered his beaten and mangled body, dissolving it into the drumhead.

***

The sun beaming through the window pierced Kristina's eyelids. She rolled and threw her arm over where Kaz should have been. She thought it odd that he hadn't come to bed. Those damn drums, she thought. Then she shuffled out of bed, slipped into her silk bathrobe and wandered down the hall to the kitchen. She figured he had probably fallen asleep on the couch watching T.V. She hollered, "Kaz, I'm making coffee. You want some?"

No answer.

She finished filling the machine with fresh ground beans and walked into the living room. He wasn't sleeping on the couch. Then she heard the familiar beat of Kaz's favorite solo. Terror struck. It felt as if her stomach had decided to scale her throat. Holy shit, she thought. He's still in the garage?

She opened the door. Kaz wasn't anywhere to be seen. Goose flesh pranced up both arms, settling in the back of her neck when she saw the pool of blood on the cement in front of her.

"Kaz?" she whimpered.

The blood smeared into the finger streaks leading to the snare. She eased down the steps toward the trap set. The cymbal had drying blood across the front edge. Looming over the snare drum, she looked down. Except for the backwards name of the original owner scrawled on it, the drumhead looked clean.

BOOM! the base rang out.

Kristina jumped, screaming simultaneously.

Chip, chip, chip, chip, the hi-hat began.

Kristina stared in horror at the snare drum as an image etched itself into the drumhead. Two doves flying next to each other, under one, a small backward inscription appeared: zaK.

The Replacements

Claire L. Fishback

Inspired by Drowning Pool's *Bodies*

Morey Grigsby did not believe in body replacement. He did not believe a person needed a new body every five to ten years, nor did he believe that his would crap out on him. On his thirtieth birthday, however, he looked like he was ninety.

"Damn pollutants," he muttered, combing the thin white hair over his bald spot. "Stupid planet killers." He stuffed his partial denture into his mouth, clicking it into place. He showed his teeth at his reflection, leaned forward to examine a brown spot on his semitranslucent skin. "Damn stupid ignoramuses."

"Honey," his wife, Celia, now on her fourth body though she was only five years older than him, poked her head into the bathroom. "I think it's time." He knew by the look on her face that she despised him because he looked so old.

"No, never," Morey shook his head. "I refuse," he said. He believed diet and exercise would prolong his body's life, and though he was tired of hooking himself up to machines to live through the night, he did not want to trade in his body for someone else's. Because that's what the replacement was: someone else's body.

The replacement bodies were harvested by means of cloning aborted fetuses and genetically altering them so they would not grow brains. With no brain, there is no mind. With no mind, the person technically isn't a person. Just a body. They were hooked up to complicated machines to keep them alive so the organs would continue to function and the muscles wouldn't atrophy.

The brain of the person seeking a replacement was removed and implanted into the new body. The old bodies were recycled back into the system, the cells used once again to create clones of that body. Morey did not want someone else's mind floating around in his body, clone or not.

Celia looked at Morey with her large blue eyes filling with tears. He hated her large blue eyes. He missed his real wife. The wife he fell in love with. The dark-skinned beauty with big, round, dark chocolate eyes. He didn't like this blonde, tan skinned, perfect Celia. And though she claimed to be the same Celia, she just wasn't. "Why did you get a white woman's body?" he asked her, looking at her in the mirror. She shrugged and sighed when he glared at her.

"Hurry home after work," she said, not meeting his eyes. "I have a birthday surprise for you." She smiled at him but didn't meet his eyes, and the smile was gone as she turned and left the doorway. Morey got dressed for work and made his way to the office, daydreaming on the bus ride about his dark-skinned wife who was no more, while his eyes scanned the paper.

As usual, he ignored the disgusted looks from the other passengers. He was used to them pointing at him, whispering behind their hands. Judging him. He glanced sideways at a woman who was obviously staring. She looked a little green.

"Take a picture," Morey muttered. He turned his head slightly toward the woman. She leaned away from him, taken aback, then got up and moved to a different seat. Morey chuckled. Served her right for staring at him like that. He returned his gaze to the newspaper in his lap.

When the bus screeched to a stop, he looked up.

Out the front window, looking at the bus driver through the windshield, waving her arms and kicking the bus, was Celia. Not the blonde tan one, but the original dark beauty. Morey gasped. His heart fluttered and he feared it would go out on him. He pounded his chest and jumped to his feet, his knees protesting. The bus started to move after the woman, his real Celia, stomped across the street.

"Stop the bus!" Morey called. He gripped the handrail as the driver slammed on the brakes again and turned to look at him. "Thank you," Morey said. He shuffled down the aisle as fast as he could and made his way down the three steps onto the pavement. The bus took off, blasting pollutants in his face. He held his breath until the black cloud disappeared.

The woman was just entering the hotel across the street. He wanted to call out to her, but he knew her name likely wasn't Celia. Instead, he made his way across the street and followed her inside.

She stood at the counter at the coffee stand in the lobby.

The same body, the same woman, the same beautiful eyes. When she laughed, tossing her head back, flinging her long black hair behind her, he saw she had the same crooked front tooth, and her eyes crinkled in the exact same way his original Celia's had. His heart pounded and he clutched his chest.

"Don't give out on me now," he muttered to himself, tapping his breastbone.

She turned, her eyes widened, and she gasped. "I've never seen such an old body," she said, then demurely covered her mouth with her fingertips. "I'm so sorry," she said. "Sometimes I say things without thinking."

"That's okay," Morey said. He cleared his throat when his voice came out scratchy and old, but he knew it wouldn't do any good. His body was old. That was a fact. "I'm Morey," he said, holding out his hand.

"Tanya," the woman replied. She took his hand gently and stared at it as she shook it. "How old are you?"

"Thirty today," said Morey. "This is my original body."

"Wow," Tanya said. "Happy birthday." She still held his hand and turned it, examining the hair on his knuckles, the brown spots dappling his thin, loose skin. "Why haven't you gotten a replacement?"

Morey didn't know how to answer the question.

"I wanted to see how long this one would last," he said with a smile. His partial popped out and fell into his mouth, exposing his three missing teeth. He covered his mouth with his hand while he worked it back into place. He thought Tanya would be disgusted, but she laughed and moved his hand away.

"You have missing teeth!" she said. "That's so amazing. Let me see."

Morey pulled the partial out, cupping it in his palm, and smiled.

"How'd you lose them?" she asked.

"Boxing," he told her with a lisp. It was sort of true. Really, he got into a drunken fight when he was in his early twenties.

The barista behind the counter slid a cup of coffee to the middle of the counter. "Coffee's done," the girl said. "Ten ninety-five."

"Let me get that," Morey said. He fumbled in his back pocket for his wallet and pulled out a twenty. "Keep the change," he told the girl.

"Thanks, Morey," Tanya said, smiling her imperfect smile. Morey thought if he was a cartoon, his pupils would be hearts beating out of his eyeballs. She cleared her throat. "Are you busy right now?"

"Nope!" Morey said without thought. Of course he was busy. He was on his way to work, but he felt like she was going to ask him to have breakfast with her.

"Can you help me with something?" she asked.

"Yep!" Morey said, smiling uncontrollably.

Tanya took his hand and led him to the elevators. "I'm starting a business," she said as the car zoomed up five floors. "You seem like the perfect candidate to test my skills on."

"What kind of business?" Morey asked.

"You'll see," Tanya said with a coy chuckle. The doors opened with a ding, and she led him down the hall to the right. "This is my room," she said.

"I can wait in the hall, if you'd like." Morey said.

Tanya giggled. "No, please, come in," she said. She slipped the credit card key into the door and opened it.

The room was a standard hotel room. King size bed, smallish bathroom, a dresser with a television. A round table stood in a corner with a chair that didn't match. Tanya deposited her purse there and turned to face Morey.

"Take off your clothes," she said.

Morey choked on his own spit, flinging himself into a hacking and coughing fit. He pounded on his chest. Good God, she wanted him! This was way better than breakfast. To be with his Celia again? To ravage her like he had when they first got married just five years ago! Oh, to caress her round, firm butt. To gaze into her eyes and know the woman looking back at him loved him, maybe more than he loved her.

He could hardly contain himself, but he wasn't sure he heard her right. He coughed again, a long, phlegmy, face-reddening cough.

When he had himself under control, he looked at her with raised eyebrows. "What?"

"I said, take. Off. Your clothes." She raised an eyebrow and undid the top button of her blouse.

"What is your business?" Morey asked, reaching for his belt buckle.

"Sex," Tanya said.

Morey's heart fluttered again, and he cleared his throat several times. Was she serious? She unbuttoned the next button on her blouse, and the next.

How many men had she used Celia's body with? Morey's excitement faltered. But it wasn't really the real Celia, he reminded himself. Just a cloned version. He could pretend it was his real Celia. That would work. He would pretend.

As Tanya undid the last button, Morey glimpsed her beautiful breasts under a thin cotton bra. He fumbled with unbuckling his belt and untucking his shirt at the same time while slipping off his shoes. Tanya giggled again and moved closer. "Let me help," she said, dropping to her knees. She looked up at him as she pulled his belt free and unzipped his pants.

"Oh, my," she said with wide eyes. She smiled at him. When it was all over, they lay next to each other, silent save for Morey's wheezing. Disappointment filled him. It wasn't Celia. Of course, it wasn't Celia. It was just a clone of her body. Nothing felt the same, nothing even looked the same. She didn't do the things Celia used to do. She didn't move in unison with him; she didn't even look at him. In fact, the more he thought about it, he wasn't even sure she really looked anything like his original Celia. Was her skin that dark? Had her eyes had that slight upward slant? He stared at the ceiling, trying to calm his breathing. Tanya pulled him back to the moment with a breathy laugh.

"I can't believe you're still in your original body," she said. She rolled over onto her stomach and drew circles in his white chest hair. She fingered a withered, saggy nipple. "My body gave out when I was eighteen," she said. "This is my first replacement. It's only a year old, but I'm kind of getting tired of it already."

Morey wanted to tell her she looked like his wife, that he wished his wife had never changed bodies, but instead he asked her, "Were you black originally?"

Tanya nodded.

"My wife..." he started and mentally smacked himself.

"That's okay." Tanya smiled. "You're not the first married client I've had. Most of them are married, actually."

"Oh, right," Morey said. The disappointment flared again. Why did he ever think this imposter in his wife's body would be anything like his Celia? "How much do I owe you?" His voice was small and choked.

"Three thousand," she said, sitting up. "But I'll give you fifty percent off. Consider it a senior citizen discount." She giggled and held out her hand. "Fifteen hundred."

Morey swallowed hard. "Do you take a credit card?"

Tanya nodded.

After the transaction was complete and Morey had his clothing and belongings together, she walked him down to the lobby. "I'm always here," she said. "In case you get lonely." She brushed her lips across his and sauntered away. Morey sighed, then pounded on his chest again to get his heart beating. He watched her board the elevator.

"I'm an idiot," he whispered.

Later that day after work, Morey stepped into the house feeling heavy, like the day was smashing him into the ground. He thought of Tanya, of the sex. Disgust filled him, turning his stomach. His shoulders sagged and he closed his eyes.

In the designer kitchen, a martini sat on the granite counter. He smiled and took a sip. Perfect. She may not look like the woman he fell in love with, but Celia could make a mean martini. "Morey, is that you?" Celia called from the other room. Morey sighed and made his way to the living room. Celia lay on the black leather sofa in a white negligee embellished with marabou boas. "This is the first part of your surprise," she said with a wink and a smile full of perfect teeth.

"I'm not in the mood," Morey said. The guilt. He couldn't even look at her. He shuffled past her to the bathroom, martini in hand. Celia followed him.

"But it's your birthday," she said.

"Yeah, and I would like to be left alone." Morey told her, not meeting her eyes. Guilt mingled with disgust and disappointment.

Celia pouted, stomped her foot, and swirled away toward the bedroom. He heard her slamming dresser drawers and throwing things. He shook his head and went to calm her.

"I'm sorry, Cel," he said. She was halfway out of her lingerie, sitting on the edge of the bed.

"You don't love me anymore," she said, crossing her arms.

She wiped at a tear.

"Yes, I do," Morey said. He sat next to her and put his arms around her. "I don't love your new body, but I still love you."

She pulled away.

"It's the mind that matters," he told her, trying to convince himself of this. "It's you in there, just not out here."

"Is that why you slept with her?" Celia asked, her voice clipped.

Morey coughed and hacked. He pounded on his chest. "What?"

"You know what I said, and you know what I mean," her voice was all venom. Her eyes cut into him when she looked at him through her lashes. She stood and stomped to the dresser, jerked open the top drawer, and pulled out a piece of paper. It was an email. "The credit card company sent me an email about a suspicious charge," she said. "Hookers Anonymous? Really, Morey?"

"I-I'm sorry?" He didn't know what else to say. His whole body flushed, heating him. He felt hot and sticky and slightly tingly.

"I knew it was true. How could you?" Celia shrieked. "Fifteen hundred dollars?" She threw the paper at him, but it drifted to the floor. She turned away. Morey sat still, feeling stupid and horrible. Her shoulders trembled. He thought she must be crying, but a wicked laugh cackled from her throat. When she turned around, she was smiling.

"Drink up, Morey," she said. He looked at the martini, nearly gone, the olives not even covered by the clear liquid. "Your other surprise is waiting." The smile disappeared. Her eyes tightened and took on a malicious gleam.

Morey dropped the glass. Not on purpose. His hand stopped working. His arm dropped to his side. A numb tingling spread up his arm and across his chest. His heart, oh, God, his heart was finally going out. But no, it was still beating. He could feel it in his pulse points. He fell backward onto the bed, then slid off when his legs gave out. He crumbled onto the floor, frozen in place. Only his eyes could move. He looked up at Celia standing over him. Her cell phone was at her ear.

"Come and get him," she said. "Bring the ambulance; I'll pay extra for expedited service." She left the room.

"Celia!" he cried. "What did you do to me?"

Celia came back in and crouched next to his head. "I'm getting you a new body for your birthday," she said, petting his hair. "You see, I don't love this old disgusting thing anymore," she stuck her lips out, cocked her head. "But that shouldn't matter, right?" She patted his head and stood up. "It's all about the mind, not the body."

"No," he croaked. "No, I don't want a new body, this one is fine!"

The doorbell rang. Celia bent and kissed his forehead and ran to get it, tossing on a silk robe on her way out of the bedroom door. She returned with two men carrying a stretcher.

"His body just gave out, but his mind is still good," she said. "Let's get him to the hospital."

"No, I'm fine!" Morey shouted. "She drugged me! There's nothing wrong with me! I'm drugged!"

"There, there, sweetheart," she said.

Morey cried and shouted; he struggled hard, but his body would not move.

"You have to believe me," he yelled. "She drugged me! There's nothing wrong with me!"

"Don't listen to him. His body is old. It's affecting his mind; he's out of it!" Celia shouted. Her perfect brows were low and brooding.

"We'll get him into a new body as soon as we can," one of them said. As they wheeled Morey out to the ambulance, he overheard Celia say, "No, that won't be necessary," before the doors slammed shut.

What did she mean: 'it won't be necessary'? She said she was getting him a new body, had she not? He tried to scream, but his vocal cords broke. He called out to Celia, to anyone who would listen, but no sound came from his throat.

At the hospital, Morey was wheeled into a room. The doctors gave him a sedative. He fought with all his might to stay awake, but they pumped more into him and finally he passed out.

When he came to, he was staring at their four-poster bed. Celia lay asleep. Everything was very quiet. Silent. She rolled over and sat up. No sound. No rustling of sheets. Good Lord, was he deaf? He tried to move an arm to wiggle a finger in his ear, but he couldn't move. Perhaps the drug hadn't worn off yet. He wondered what his new body looked like and wanted to cry. There was nothing wrong with his old body.

Then it hit him. If he was staring at their bed, was he sitting on the dresser? He tried to look around to figure out where he was, but again, nothing came of it.

Celia got up and stretched. He tried to speak, but no sound came out. In fact, he couldn't feel his lips. She approached the dresser, her mouth moved but no sound came out. She laughed. He knew it was that fake, high-pitched laugh she did because she held her hand against her chest. She bent over slightly, her eyes on whatever her hands were doing. Morey could see down her nightgown into her cleavage.

When she stood up, she held a note up to his eyes.

"I hope you slept well," it read. She reached toward him and he started to move, his vision jostled about. She was taking him somewhere, but...how? She wasn't strong enough to carry him. She stopped and walked around behind him. His line of sight turned ever so slowly. The edge of the bathroom came into view. The doorway, the towels, the mirror.

If Morey had a throat and new vocal cords, he would have screamed. Celia wasn't carrying him. Oh, no, she wasn't. She was pushing him on a cart. All that remained of Morey was a square container with a brain and eyes. The eyes were held steady with hooks attached to the mouth of the container, which sat in the center of a cart inside fluids to keep it supple. Positioned around the jar were machines pumping oxygen and blood into and out of his brain. Celia held up another note. "I thought about cutting off your dick," it said. "But decided this was a much better alternative." She tossed her head back and laughed.

Morey heard silence.

Window to The Soul

Robert Essig

Inspired by Billy Idol's *Eyes Without a Face*

Sin City, USA. How Trisha found herself back in Las Vegas, a place she wholeheartedly referred to as The Land of Rape and Scummy, she could only guess, because she really had no clue. Even as she politely refused assistance whenever a good samaritan or flight attendant offered help after noticing her cane tapping as she begrudgingly trudged her way onto a plane that would take her to the very place where she lost her eyesight, she couldn't shake the feeling that she was putting herself in a trap.

Don't fool yourself, honey. You know why you're going back to The Land of Rape and Scummy. You actually think you can find the bastard who fucked up your life, and...

It was true. There were news stories local to Las Vegas that she heard on the Internet dealing with a string of murders that left the victims without eyes. Listening to the Vegas news had been an obsession for Trisha ever since the little escapade that cost her her eyes. It appeared that the bastard was at it again.

***

The strip club was called Glamour Girls, or Glitz Girls, something like that, but the man in the black leather trench coat never looked at the sign as he walked in. There may not have even been a name outside, only censored plasma images of fake breasted women taking their tops off, enticing lonely men, perverts and tourists into a seedy world of two-drink minimums, dollar tips, and a series of rooms for 'private' lap dances.

The man in the leather trench coat paid his two-drink minimum and took a seat in one of the booths where he had a good view of the catwalk that stretched the length of the building, lined with stools where men, and even a few women, gripping fistfuls of one dollar bills tilted their heads upward at the strippers.

After half an hour, he drained both of his drinks. When the ditzy cocktail waitress asked if he would like another, he requested a lap dance.

Giggling, she said, "I don't do those. I just serve the drinks."

"*J'ai besoin de tes yeux,*" said Mr. Trench Coat.

The cocktail waitress smiled. "What's that mean?"

"It's French for: 'Your beauty knows no bounds.'"

She smiled, placed a hand on his shoulder and leaned in close to whisper in his ear. "I can give you a private dance after my shift. Meet me in the back of the building at two."

As she pulled her face away from his, he admired her beautiful eyes. They had caught his attention as he walked into the strip club, and he knew everyone was looking to make a buck. They all turned tricks on the outside, and sometimes using the language of love flattered them into confidence. Although, what he said should have terrified her; a reminder of the murder wave that had recently struck Vegas. *J'ai besoin de tes yeux. I need your eyes.*

At two a.m., Mr. Trench Coat was waiting at the rear of the club. He walked with the waitress down Fremont Street to the east side past the El Cortez casino where Mr. Trench Coat had a hotel room.

The cocktail waitress didn't make it out of the room alive.

***

Trisha took a cab to Fremont Street. Her stomach was beginning to tighten with anticipation. It was hard to believe that she lived here once upon a time, and even harder to believe that she actually returned. After her stay at the hospital recovering from the crude extraction of her eyes, she moved to Massachusetts to be as far away from Vegas as possible, vowing never to return.

But something strange happened as her obsession resonated, her specialty voice-activated computer constantly tuned into the Las Vegas news. The murders began, and something inside told her to return. It was an urge like the pull of a wondrous fragrance, and she couldn't resist, even at the admonition of her friends and family. She had to return.

Based on smells and sounds, Fremont Street hadn't changed.

People drank more there, more openly at least, and, if you wandered off the strip in any direction, you would quickly find yourself in a less than comfortable part of town littered with junkies, bums, and the seedier tourists who took refuge in the hostels and roach motels.

Trisha booked a room in a motel just off the strip, but not too far down Desolation Boulevard. There were only two bums and one prostitute greeting her with weary spite-filled eyes at the door, and she only knew of their presence from the wheezy breathing and foul odor.

Once inside, she was directed to her room, counting steps so she wouldn't attempt an ill-fated break-in to someone else's room by mistake. A blind woman must know her numbers and keep them tucked away in her mind without confusing them if she wanted to remain free.

The room was cozy, and she couldn't hear telltale scurrying and creeping of bugs and mice. The place smelt of stale cigarettes though it was a non-smoking room, but that was to be expected. Rules were flimsy in dive motels, particularly ones used for prostitution, and that was a question the desk clerk wouldn't have answered honestly had Trisha asked.

After turning the air conditioner on and opening her suitcase on the floor in the corner, Trisha lay on the bed contemplating what she had done, why she had returned to the very location of the worst night of her life. And most importantly: what was her next move? *J'ai besoin de tes yeux.* Trisha shivered as the words came to her and a voice, ageless yet smooth that wasn't hers at all, whispered in her mind.

***

The man in the trench coat snuck the cocktail waitress's body out of the motel through a rear door to avoid passing the front clerk. She was a tiny woman, easily concealed in a large suitcase. He was meticulous about cleanliness and blood, which allowed him to reuse the suitcase for all his victims.

After placing her body in a gutter, he returned to his motel room where her eyes waited for his attempt to reach what he liked to call Divine Enlightenment, though his search for such divinity had become more of an obsession, or perhaps an addiction, rather than simply a search.

The eyes are the windows for the Soul. The Soul is the window to the afterlife, and Mr. Trench Coat peered into that window as often as he could, bearing witness to something that was never meant to be seen with human eyes.

In a dish sitting atop his bed were the waitress's eyes. They were pale blue when she lived and had since clouded over. He considered that perhaps he should have chilled them in an ice bath or in the mini fridge to retain their vibrant color.

Grabbing the eyes, Mr. Trench Coat breathed deeply and began to chant. Old leather-bound texts lay ignored on the bed as he focused on his breathing instead. He didn't need the books anymore; every word, every syllable the ancients wrote centuries ago were etched into his brain. It was a ritual he had done many times before in his quest for the secrets; secrets that only the eyes of the dead could answer.

The first time he performed the ritual, it had hurt terribly and Mr. Trench Coat wasn't sure he had the balls to journey with the human soul. But now it was second nature, as if he had learned how to gouge his own eyes out at an early age from his parents.

His voice remained steady, constantly speaking the ancient words as his fingers pushed between his own eyes and skull, hooking the back of the fleshy bulbs and pulling them out. Once removed, both eyes rested on his cheeks, the optic nerves dangling from inside his skull like the tails of giant sperm. Mr. Trench Coat then brought the cocktail waitress's cloudy eyes close to his face. His chanting increased and the optic nerves came to life, his words reaching out to their freshly dead tissue. Mr. Trench Coat filled his empty cavities with the woman's eyes, the nerves reaching into his sockets and connecting to his thalamus in a way that nature never intended.

Electricity surged through Mr. Trench Coat's body. He stopped chanting and breathed deeply. His new eyes draped his vision with a gray fog, but as he blinked the blood and tears away, color returned and he could see...

Everything the cocktail waitress's soul could see as it journeyed far away from her cold dead body. Space and time swirled around him and his body was filled with an overwhelming sense of bliss.

He shook in orgasmic pleasure as her soul floated through the planes of existence, and he watched the journey while remaining rooted in the motel room. The ancients described it as a form of astral projection, but it was unlike anything Mr. Trench Coat had ever read about in so-called philosophy books.

Almost there, he thought, feeling that he was about to break through the haze that hid the answers to the afterlife, the true destination of the human soul and further knowledge that would serve to make him even more powerful than he'd already become through his previous journeys. Every trip had taken him to slightly different planes, but patterns were starting to emerge. He had ideas of what it all meant, but he needed just a little more before he was sure he had it figured out. He also needed a little more because the thrill, the body high he felt during his soul rides, was quite addicting.

"No!" he cried out as the connection was suddenly cut. The vision vanished and the woman's eyes fell from his skull. The high was drawn away as if some switch had been tripped.

Mr. Trench Coat breathed heavily, his head woozy from the rush. He carefully replaced his own eyes and lay down on the bed to revel in the blissful state his journey had taken him on.

He had been searching for the secrets of the afterlife for at least a decade now. He had patience and even though he had fallen just short again, the ritual was still rewarding and served to satisfy the urge within that now wanted the high more than the answers. It wasn't as if he had forgotten about what the texts had shown him, what he was searching for. The high was intense and pleasurable, but his heart was still tied to the words of the ancient ones, and he knew Sin City was the very place where he would find the eyes that would finally show him the complete journey.

He would just have to search out another set of eyes and hope...

***

The demons of Trisha's past were everywhere. Vegas was full of them. Having turned her life around after the loss of her eyes, finding Jesus and becoming born again, she could hardly relate to the wild woman she had once been in those reckless lost years living near Fremont Street.

She had been a stripper back then, turning tricks in the rooms above the strip club. The proprietor of the joint pimped his strippers out, claiming that he was doing them a favor by keeping them in the club and off the streets. So much for that shit. It was one of the Johns that cut out her eyes. Fortunately, she kicked him in the balls and flew out the door and into the strip club screaming bloody murder. The asshole got away, and the rest is history.

She knew she was going to have to return to the strip club. It wasn't likely that any of the girls she worked with were still there. In Vegas there was always fresh meat, and strippers tended to become addicted to drugs and alcohol, eventually becoming useless and haggard or just disappearing, seeking help outside the invisible walls of Sin City or worse. Trisha still didn't understand why she was sitting in a stagnant motel in Las Vegas, why she was going to return to the very place where her life changed forever. Everything in her flashed warning signs in bright red, but something prevented her from seeing them. Perhaps she was blind mentally as well and physically.

J'ai besoin de tes yeux.

Trisha gasped as the phrase entered her mind again. The voice was something sinister, and, if she wasn't comfortable with her blindness, she would have thought there was someone in her room whispering into her ear.

He had said that, the man who changed her life by attempting to kill her. It had stuck with her so deeply that she had written the phrase in her mind a thousand times as she laid in her hospital bed recovering. It was the phrase she used to learn the ways of her mind, the mental dry erase boards she was going to have to use were she going to allow herself to return to civilized life without having to depend on others. Blind or not, she didn't want to depend on anyone to open a door, help her across a street—not even a seeing-eye dog. He had told her that the phrase meant: 'you are very beautiful.' It did nothing to flatter her being that he was paying to fuck her, but it stuck in her mind like a scar, and when she finally settled down in Massachusetts, she did some research and discovered that the phrase translated to: 'I need your eyes.'

That was when her obsession with her attempted killer began.

You know where to go, said the ageless voice.

Shivers ran up Trisha's back and arms, creating a landscape of goose bumps. The voice frightened her, yet she knew it intimately, as if it had been communicating with her in dreams...or nightmares.

And it was right.

She knew where to go.

***

"But I don't understand," said the hostess at the door of the strip club. "If you can't see, then why come here. There's a two-drink minimum, you know."

Trisha was becoming increasingly irritated with the ditz at the front entrance to the club. "I'm meeting someone here. I'll pay for the two drinks and wait in a booth. Is that alright with you?" The last part came out with some attitude.

"If that's what you want."

After the hostess seated her, a waitress came along, and after another ridiculous battle, Trisha paid for her two drinks and sat with the sounds of "Closer" by Nine Inch Nails, laughter and cat calls, and women asking miscellaneous men, "Would you like a private lap dance?"

Trisha remembered those days. The catwalk, the poles, the faces looking up at her, the dollar bills and how some guys would try and slip a finger in her G-string as they tipped her. Then there were the drugs and alcohol. Sustaining a state of mood altered suspension was the only way she could degrade herself in such a manner, particularly when it came to the lap dances and the tricks.

Her stomach rolled, and when her cocktails arrived, she downed half a vodka and tonic in one gulp. It wasn't a good feeling being back in the very place that was such a detrimental memory in her mind.

J'ai besoin de tes yeux.

Trisha gasped as the words came into her ear, but not of the ageless voice she had heard before. This time the voice was familiar in a whole new way. This time she was damned sure it was the voice of the man who attempted to kill her.

Her body tightened up as if he had slid into the booth with her, but she would have felt the shift of his body weight had he done so. The voice was in her mind.

Through dark shades she saw nothing yet tried to attain the appearance of a seeing person, and then something extraordinary happened. It was something she never could have imagined, something that defined what her life had become after the bastard—whom she knew was at the strip club as well as she knew her own name—took her eyesight. For the first time in years, she could see a light.

Two lights, in fact—orbs.

The music and raucous crowd began to swell in her brain as she focused on the glowing orbs that danced in the darkness. By their location to one another and the slight oval shape of them, she ventured a guess that they were representative of eyes.

J'ai besoin de tes yeux. This time it was her own voice dancing in her mind as she realized what the glowing orbs were: his eyes!

He *was* there.

Panic gripped Trisha's nerves and shook them violently; she became transfixed, as if the orbs were putting her under a trance. They were brilliant, like two miniature stars, lacking a pupil and iris, but otherwise like a regular set of eyes, and, though she could only guess where they were directed, to *whom* they were directed, there was a moment when they grew wide and seemed to stare into her very soul. She had no eyes for them to connect with, never mind the dark shades, yet they seemed to lock their gaze upon her as if noticing something of immense beauty in a room of horrors.

Trisha wanted to look away, not to draw attention to herself, but she couldn't. Like the very drive to get her on the plane and back to Vegas, she was powerless to the eyes' wiles. She would have closed her eyes had she the ability to do so, but...well, her eyes *were* closed, not that she actually *had* eyes. The loose skin of her eyelids remained closed, perhaps even sealed after all these years. The fiery eyes locked on her as they crossed the room, only hiding themselves behind invisible lids for just a moment at a time. Her breath held tight as the eyes danced before her. She could now see blue irises burning deeper than the fire around them. There was a shifting on the booth as he slid in, welcoming himself to her company.

"You look lonely," the man in the black leather trench coat said.

"Yes," replied Trisha. She hoped he didn't pick up on the fear that quivered slightly in her voice.

A pregnant pause, the eyes narrowing as Mr. Trench Coat carefully regarded his prey. Trisha never felt so naked, so compromised, so... helpless. Yet she knew there was something between them, and she also knew that he didn't recognize her.

"Why the dark shades here in a dark booth? I'm sure your eyes are beautiful."

Trisha gasped. She tried to keep her fear under control, but it was all too familiar; the man sitting next to her, the voice, the eyes. "I prefer the dark," she said. It was cryptic and true. Her whole life was dark after what he had done to her.

Mr. Trench Coat chuckled. A sick, wet wheezing came from his throat as he did so. "I like the dark, too. Would you like to go somewhere more private? Somewhere dark?"

My whole fucking life is dark!

Trisha could have screamed and scratched his eyes out right there in the strip club, but she knew better, and deep inside there was something nameless that helped retrain her anger and fear. This trip to Fremont Street wasn't about revenge as she had convinced herself back in Massachusetts. It was about something fathomless that Trisha didn't understand.

What she did know was that it was all about the man sitting with her, the man who bore eyes of fire like she had never seen before.

"We can go to my place," she said. As the words left her mouth she regretted them. She had no choice. In her mind, as she stared into the eyes of fire, the ageless voice mimicked her very words, using her as a marionette.

"That will do just fine," said Mr. Trench Coat.

***

Something happened on the way to her motel, which wasn't but a ten-minute walk from the strip club. Trisha's body began to feel fuzzy, as if she had been soaked in anesthesia. They spoke not a word to one another as they merged through the onslaught of drunken vacationers and dead-broke local louses, weaving this way and that, Mr. Trench Coat following closely behind.

The fuzzy feeling was almost like being blind now to other senses Trisha had learned to rely on, yet she walked faster, her cane hardly being used to guide her way. Something else guided her. The ageless voice guided her.

You do not need to worry, my dear.

She struggled with her own mind, trying desperately to banish the ageless voice and regain control of her faculties, but the voice was also power, and, by the time she reached the motel, Trisha was no longer herself.

"You get around pretty good for a blind woman," said Mr. Trench Coat. In the strip club he had no idea she was blind. There was worry in his eyes now as they walked down the hallway to her room.

"I can see just fine," Trisha replied. "The cane deters the...bad people."

Mr. Trench Coat smiled as she unlocked her door. "How do you know I'm not bad?"

"I'm not worried about that."

They entered her room. Immediately, he grabbed and threw her on the floor, pinning her. Expecting a struggle, Mr. Trench Coat looked surprised as she lay there submissively.

Mr. Trench Coat muttered, "This won't take long."

Still restricting her movement, he began to chant. Trisha had no clue what language he was speaking, but she could clearly hear the words he spoke. The repetitive language began to make her head swirl, and soon enough the ageless voice that had coaxed her to this desperate moment recited the words in unison.

Mr. Trench Coat wrapped his hands around Trisha's neck. In doing so, he knocked the dark shades from her face. The maniacal smile he proudly displayed earlier turned sour in an instant. "No eyes," he whispered in disbelief, his grip loosening, the cryptic chant breaking.

Behind her dark glasses were ugly folds of flesh that had sealed over in the years since Mr. Trench Coat defiled Trisha's life.

Before Mr. Trench Coat could process the shock, Trisha's hands freed themselves from his grip with adrenaline-fueled strength. Her fingernails were long and dug into Trench Coat's face quite easily, removing the fleshy orbs that he had removed so many times before in his addiction to the experience of riding souls.

Mr. Trench Coat struggled as pain shocked his system. Never before had he felt this way after removing his eyes, but now they were in the hands of someone he had created all those years ago when Trisha lived through his handiwork. He clutched his bleeding face, his screams so agonizing that they were above natural pitch. His last thought before he died was that he would know first-hand what happened to the soul. It was a shame he wouldn't be coming back from this final journey to relish in his discovery.

Trisha stood, her mind still reeling from the start of the ritual, his eyes still clutched in her hands. Her mouth opened, almost as if possessed, and she began reproducing the strange words Mr. Trench Coat had spoken earlier, the words the ageless voice seemed to be familiar with.

A part of her was scared, but another part enjoyed the sensation brought on as she chanted. Dark voices spoke inside her head with the Ageless One. Faster and louder, as if pushed on by the ancients themselves and their dark magic, Trisha chanted with the dark voices and placed the eyes to her face. The folds of flesh bit like toothless mouths, tears like strings of drool running down her face, and suddenly the once dead eyes were inside her skull. With the placement of the eyes, Trisha suddenly regained her consciousness as bright light flooded her brain like piercing daggers causing jolts of pain.

She stopped chanting and screamed. Hands to her face, she touched the eyes in disbelief. It took several minutes and even after the eyes began to focus, her vision was clouded. She could see the hotel room and the form of Mr. Trench Coat, dead on the floor. Yet at the same time, she could see something else: flashes of light and the sensation of travelling at amazing speeds.

What have I done? she thought.

She knew the fact that she was able to see anything was wrong. And she knew what she was experiencing, although mildly hypnotic, was wrong.

Whatever he was chanting, whatever I continued, unleashed...is wrong.

She had no idea how right she was. Her newfound vision flashed between the journey of Mr. Trench Coat's soul and the room before her. Her untrained mind was unable to focus and hone the ritual in the manner it deserved. She staggered around the room, the effect more nauseating than intoxicating.

She closed her eyes, but could still see the colors swirling and experience the...

Oh, my God!

Screaming filled her mind—screams of pain and agony of tortured souls. Her sight traveled over scorched rocks and burning desert sand. Entities filled the barren lands. Sensations of malice and hate filled her senses like some wicked intoxicant.

As much as the visions assaulted her, she became entranced by the soul's journey. Dark voices once again begged her to chant, to finish the ritual. She had already gone further than Mr. Trench Coat, a feat that he had tried for years. Ironically, it was done with his eyes, and the place of his soul's resting, the place his eyes guided her to, was not a pleasant one.

As hypnotized by the malice as she was, Trisha realized this was wrong. Whatever she was feeling, whatever Mr. Trench Coat had started with the ritual was wrong. These places that the soul went when it died were not meant for human eyes. They were meant only for the soul who had reaped it. The voices called out to her, pleading as if she could save them from damnation, but she ignored them.

Trisha screamed in pain as well as triumph as she jammed her fingers in the flesh around her new eyes and pulled them out. Her new vision was gone along with the journey, leaving her exhausted. "He can suffer his fate alone," she whispered, squishing the eyes underfoot.

She breathed deeply and left the room, hurting physically yet happy that her whole life lay ahead of her. Whatever she chose to do in life, she knew her final journey would be one of peace rather than the burning desert that had awaited Mr. Trench Coat.

The Invitation

Nathan Crowder

Inspired by David Bowie's *Rock 'n' Roll Suicide*

Chaz Hedlund took a drag on his cigarette and tried to block out the sound from the other room. He had buried the phone in the front part of the hotel suite beneath sofa cushions, but he had been avoiding the bedroom since returning to the hotel. He could still hear the phone next to the bed ringing. There had been no respite since Billboard's tracking numbers came out that morning. Chaz couldn't bring himself to answer the phone and couldn't be bothered to just take it off the hook. Not with the corpse with the convertible head staring at him from across the room.

"Eventually, you might just want to answer that, Chaz," the famous corpse said.

"Shut up." Chaz took two pulls off the tumbler of bourbon in his left hand and chased it with more cigarettes. He avoided looking at his visitor.

The corpse tilted what remained of his head back in exasperation. There was a wet sound as something slid from the ruined skull and landed on the floor behind the chair. The sound drew Chaz's attention, and for a mercifully brief moment, he could see the back wall through the shotgun entry wound.

His guest's head tilted back down. "Fine. Would you rather talk about sports? I hear the Mariners went to shit this season."

Chaz stared at his visitor through a blue haze of tobacco smoke. He couldn't remember seeing photos of the rock star's body. The death was high-profile. A nation of disenfranchised youth mourned. Was he wearing that same red & white striped shirt when he put the barrel under his chin and pulled the trigger with his toe? Maybe. It seemed impolite to ask.

The phone stopped ringing. The sudden silence was almost worse.

"I understand that this is a difficult thing for you to accept," the corpse said. "Success is a hideous bitch-goddess. At first, you think it's giving you all these things, all these opportunities. Big contracts, heavy rotation on the radio, everyone knowing your name, your face, your favorite band. Women want to fuck you, just to be famous for doing it.

Name a vice, and in every city you hit on tour, someone is offering you a buffet of sin. But nothing is really free. You just don't pay attention to the cost. Then, one day, you look in the mirror and don't recognize that poor, sad sack of shit staring back at you."

"I never asked to be famous," Chaz said. He stubbed out what remained of his Camel filter and lit another one. "I just wanted to play my music."

"And you wanted people to hear it."

Chaz nodded, only half-realizing he was doing it. "Yeah, I wanted people to hear it."

"A lot of people."

"As many as would listen," Chaz said. His voice trailed off. He shuddered lightly. He swallowed the rest of his bourbon and shuddered again. The urge to refill it was almost overpowering. Chaz stared at the bottle on the floor, willing it to raise and fill his empty tumbler. His glass remained dry.

"You know what that is, don't you?" the corpse said. The ghost of a smile crept onto his pale face.

"What?"

"That's fame."

Chaz filled his lungs with Turkish tobacco smoke. "Fuck."

"Exactly."

The phone started ringing again. Chaz rolled his eyes towards it, then back at the corpse. "Are you going to get that?"

His guest smiled coyly, the effect somewhat sullied by the blood on his teeth. "I don't think they're calling for me."

"You could check."

"Answer the phone, Chaz." It was not a request, but an order. Chaz wasn't good with orders. He leaned forward in his chair but reached for the bottle of expensive bourbon instead of the phone. He poured himself half a glass. Tucking the bottle between his thigh and the side of the chair, he leaned back. The ringing continued, unabated.

"It could be good news," the corpse said.

"We both know why they're calling," Chaz grumbled.

"It could be people calling to support you. It's not like you're all alone."

Chaz stared at his uninvited guest again. He wrestled with the possibility that this was more than mere hallucination, more than a complete psychotic break. Why would his subconscious summon up one of rock & roll's more famous suicides unless it was trying to tell him something? And what would that be? Did his traitorous brain summon this specter as a cautionary tale or a guide?

"I'm not alone?" he felt like laughing. "Mike and Gordo were too busy to take my calls. How not alone am I if my own bandmates can't be bothered to talk with me?"

The corpse leaned forward in the chair. His expression read as concerned. The fact that a dead man looked concerned on his behalf was a chilling thought. "Maybe Mike or Gordo are trying to call you now. Have you thought of that?"

"It's not them." Chaz said. He remembered how he had seen them last—passed out in the VIP room of the Fairfax. He pouted and refused to look at the phone.

"It could be."

Chaz hurled the half-full tumbler at the wall near the corpse's head. It shattered and sent high-octane liquor and shards of glass everywhere. "It's not them!"

The corpse licked at a drop of bourbon rolling down his face. He raised an eyebrow in apparent approval of the quality. He laced his fingers in front of him. "Feel better?"

"What the fuck is wrong with you?" Chaz shouted. "No, I don't feel better! What the hell are you thinking? For that matter, why in the green hell are you even here?"

"I'm here because you need someone," the corpse said. "I'm here to let you know that you're not alone."

With his drink hand now empty, Chaz began to regret having thrown the tumbler. He retrieved the bottle at his side and took a draw on that. He put the cap back on the bottle—the phone stopped ringing again. He thought back to earlier, stumbling home from the after-gig party. The squeal of brakes filled his memory and brought a sour expression to his face. "I wasn't trying to kill myself. I was just careless."

"I never said you were trying to kill yourself," the corpse said. "Why would you think that?"

"It was an accident. And the car missed me by more than a foot."

The corpse waved away the thought with a thin, calloused hand. "I believe you."

Chaz went to take a drag on the cigarette. It had burned down to the filter, and he sucked air for a second before he figured it out. He pondered lighting another one while words whirled in his mind. "I don't know. Maybe I wasn't trying to kill myself, but I would have been fine if it had happened."

"And I didn't ask," the dead rocker said.

It was early morning when Chaz had reached an intersection a few blocks from his hotel. He had been drinking for hours; to say nothing about the pills some blonde girl had given him. Chaz had been on autopilot and stepped off the curb without looking. It wasn't that he wanted to die. He just didn't particularly care at that moment if he lived or not.

The squeal of brakes was the first sign, the first thing that cut through the fog to let him know someone else was on the road that time of morning. Rather than cause a scene or get stuck answering questions for the police or press, he hurried the rest of the way back to the safety of the room.

The dead legend was waiting for him.

He still couldn't comprehend why the corpse's grim visage didn't terrify him.

"You know that you're dead, right?" Chaz asked.

"It's come up," his guest said. "You know your album..."

"Don't say it."

Chaz's stare bored holes in his guest, but the dead can't be intimidated.

"It's a huge hit," the corpse said. "Could be the album of the year. You should have a drink and celebrate."

"The album is crap," Chaz said. "We had four songs on there that were worth a damn, and they're never going to be released as singles. The rest were forced on us by the label."

"You'll get more control over the next few albums." His guest didn't sound so certain.

Chaz fixed the corpse with a critical eye. "Yeah? Way I see it, we're a cash cow for the label. They insisted on certain songs, a certain look, a whole, manufactured rock package, and it paid off for them. It paid off like fucking gangbusters. And they have us for a four-record deal. Why would they want to mess with that success?" He had had misgivings about the four-record deal at the time. That was a lifetime for most bands. But they promised distribution and radio play. And the amount of money involved was intoxicating. Two years ago, the band had toured in the stereotypical conversion van, sleeping on couches and living on ramen. None of them had been prepared for that many zeroes at the end of a number.

"Maybe they want to keep the band happy," the corpse suggested.

There was a beat, then both men laughed.

"Shit," Chaz said when he finally regained his breath. "Maybe I would be better off dead."

The corpse turned serious faster than Chaz could blink. “Maybe you would. I mean, look at me—I hung it up when our band was at our peak. No embarrassing slide into irrelevance, no sad bankruptcy or rehab. If Elvis or MJ had been given a rifle and a magic looking glass to see their future, do you really think they wouldn’t be here talking to you now instead of me?”

Chaz felt his blood chill. There was a pistol in the bedroom, left by a friend who “wasn’t comfortable with him traveling without some kind of protection.” He’d never left a gun with Chaz before, but there it was in the bottom of his kit bag next to a box of ammo. “I thought you said you were here for me, to tell me I’m not alone.”

“Remember, you aren’t all alone,” the corpse said. It wasn’t as reassuring as it had sounded earlier. The phone started ringing again. The corpse rolled his eyes towards it. “Answer the phone.”

Chaz heard his voice shake. “No.”

“Answer the mother-fucking phone!”

The phone was in his hand before Chaz felt his arm move to answer it. He watched the corpse, cautious for any sudden moves. He raised the receiver to his head slowly, as if he were afraid it would bite. “Hello?”

“Chaz? Chaz Hedlund?” He recognized the voice, but his brain was slow to process it. In the background, he could hear a too familiar guitar riff. “Hey, man, we’ve been listening to the album. Some tight licks. I particularly love your cover of Axis, Bold as Love.”

“Jimi?” Chaz’s voice caught in his throat.

The rich, baritone laugh on the other side of the line told him he was right. “Just wanted to call and congratulate you. I hear tell you might be joining us at the after-party.”

His entire body started to feel numb. His mind turned to the gun in the bedroom. He couldn’t shake the image. And he couldn’t move the phone from his ear. “What after-party?”

“Hold on,” Jimi said, “someone else here wants to talk to you.”

The phone was passed. A woman picked up, her voice thick with whiskey, raspy with cigarettes. “Hey baby, it’s Janis. Hurry your cute ass over here. There’s a bottle of the good stuff with your name on it.”

The corpse with the flip-top skull pushed himself up from his chair. He ambled his way towards the bedroom.

“I don’t know what you’re talking about,” Chaz said, his protest sounded hollow in his own ears.

“He didn’t tell you?” Janis shrieked with laughter. He could hear her shouting to the rest of the room. “Hey guys, get this! He doesn’t know about the after-party!" She returned her attention to the phone. "You're invited, of course."

Chaz felt his stomach tighten. He could hear his kit bag being opened – the pistol being loaded one chamber at a time. His voice was weak. "Invited?"

The corpse came back to the front room. He set the pistol on the table in front of Chaz. After he gave it a casual spin, he sat back down in his original seat.

"The after-party..." Chaz repeated into the phone. He could sense her curly locks being shaken in disbelief on the other side of the phone, her eyes twinkling behind round glasses. "He'll show you. Don't take too long." The line went dead.

Chaz stared at the pistol.

He left the phone off the cradle.

"It was Sid who came to visit me," the corpse said. "I think I would have preferred Morrison, but he was a nice enough guy.

Compelling. But not as compelling as history."

"So, you want me to kill myself?"

The corpse lowered his head. It was a horrible sight. He looked back up at Chaz, his face expressionless. "Chaz, it isn't really about what I want. I'm just here to give you the invite. Take the invite and come with me to the party. You'll be famous, hell, iconic, as long as the rock & roll plays. If you don't take the invite, you'll never see me again. You won't see any of us ever again. The invite comes once. That's it."

Chaz retrieved the bottle of bourbon and took a long draw on it. The smoky alcohol burned like holy fire going down. "And if I don't take the invite now...?"

"Then you get to be famous for a while. You'll even enjoy some of it. But the tastes are going to move on. They always do. You'll be culturally irrelevant in five years or less. You'll be a joke in ten."

He thought back to the guitar riff he heard on the phone earlier. A room full of rock legends had been rocking out to his music. Not the ones the label had forced onto the album—his music.

The barrel of the pistol was colder against his temple than he expected. He tried not to think about it and focused on the sound of distant guitars and drunken revelry. The temperature of the barrel would only matter for a few seconds. And anyway, he had a party to get to.

The City

S.C. Mendes

Inspired by Guns and Roses' *Welcome to the Jungle*

Max paused briefly at the fork in the cobblestone road, trying to gather his bearings. He blocked out the cries of the street vendors barking from their carts at the milling crowds and focused on remembering. A child of ten, clothed in filthy rags, detected his hesitation and quickly swooped in offering guide services. Max waved the child off and headed toward the left junction. Left felt like the correct choice, but it'd been a long time since he'd navigated the labyrinth of streets, and memories were often unreliable. Within a few steps though, *déjà vu* invaded his body and Max knew he was heading the right way.

Guess you never forget some places, he mused. *No matter how hard you try.*

The ancient metropolis, which had no use for a name, was enclosed by twenty-foot walls bordering its circumference and allowed for only one way in...or out. The flatlands surrounding the brick barrier were deserted for miles in every direction, adding to its isolation. No communities dared to settle within eyesight of the blackened walls, and the only reason anyone traveled to the infamous city was if they were in need of something special. Something that couldn't be acquired anywhere except for within the lawless boundaries of the walls.

It'd been nearly two decades since Max himself had stepped foot inside the walled city and yet, now that he was back amidst the hustle and bustle, old cravings didn't just stir inside him, they felt like they never left. The sights of the city, the smells, the sins, none of them had changed, and suddenly, twenty years felt like yesterday.

The city doesn't change, he reminded himself. *Only we do.*

Max followed his distant memories through an alley of tall, moldy brick buildings. He was pleased to see the salesmen and crowds thinning out—another indication that he was heading in the right direction.

The vendors were entertaining and peddled quality goods, but in the overall landscape, they were child's play. For Max to find what he was looking for, he had to head for the heart of the rotten city. Its poisonous center was home to the most wretched creatures ever to walk the earth, creatures who sold everything for a price. And, if Max wanted to find Stephanie Holt, that was where he'd have to go.

Likely, it would require an Other's assistance.

Their presence no longer made him uneasy the way it had when he first visited the walled city. Back then, Max hadn't even wanted to conduct business with the strange creatures. Though it only took a few days for him to change his mind and realize that the Others made the city what it was. They were the blood that fueled everything inside the walls and the reason people traveled from distant lands just to step foot into the legendary metropolis.

Nearing the end of the alley, Max side-stepped past a dead body. Blood and urine pooled under the lifeless heap. Two feeders, the city's equivalent to sewer rats, squirmed over the body, gnawing at the warm meat it provided.

Finally, he recognized a tall brick structure and stopped in front of the windowless brothel. He'd been there before and it was a good place to start. Besides, wherever women were for sale, there was a good chance a butcher would be nearby. And Stephanie needed a butcher.

A series of screams rang out somewhere down the street, but Max ignored the sounds and took a wallet-sized photo from his jacket pocket. He studied the picture one last time, committing every line of the girl's face to his memory. He crammed the photo back into the pocket and looked up at the unwelcoming building, reminding himself why he had taken the job.

"How long has it been?" Max had asked the parents.

"She ran off yesterday," the father explained. "I know she went to that...that place," he struggled with emotions. "I told the police, but they won't touch the city. No authorities will."

Of course not, Max had thought. *Cops got better things to do than get killed.*

Police were the only people not welcomed in the city, unless of course, their visit was strictly for personal recreation. Badges meant nothing; chaos was law inside the walls.

"But you will, won't you?" the mother had pleaded with tears in her eyes. "Please bring her back."

"I'll try," Max said.

The father had handed Max an envelope of cash. "The rest when you bring her back."

The mother continued crying as she handed him the photo.

"Why'd she choose the city?" Max asked.

"She's pregnant," the father stated dryly.

Max nodded again and let the conversation end. Because of its isolation, no one accidentally wandered into the city. There was always a reason. Either hopelessness, curiosity, or some devious craving, but always a reason. And now Max knew Stephanie's. A pregnant teen had two choices: have the baby or visit the city. Several women had made the same choice in hopes of a quick fix and monetary gain. Unfortunately, most realized too late that the walled city offered nothing for free and the price tag was always higher than they had anticipated.

Max took a deep breath, then entered the building, anxious to finish the job as quickly as possible. His uneasiness wasn't the result of the city itself, or even the inhabitants, human or otherwise. But rather the old feelings that continued to stir inside him. The city offered a sense of unstoppable freedom that couldn't be matched anywhere in the world. Few could resist its calls and temptations, and once within the walls, no one survived long without changing. The last thing Max wanted was to revert back to the man he used to be.

Stale smoke and alcohol greeted Max inside the dim brothel. It took a few moments for his eyes to adjust to the darkness. Ladies whistled and called softly to him from the furniture. Max ignored them and approached the bar at the back of the room and the inhuman creature behind it.

The Other held up a hand when Max attempted to speak. His eyes closed as he inhaled Max's scent, then grinned, revealing rows of glistening fangs. "You're not here for ladies, are you?" He sniffed again. "No. You're looking for meat."

Damn, Max thought. Others could smell sin a mile away. Twenty years and the stench of past mistakes still lingered.

"That's impressive," Max said. "I figured where there's a brothel, there's usually a butcher in back."

The human-like creature cackled and sniffed again, processing the information his scaly nostrils provided. "Been a long time. You're not sick, but perhaps you're in need of a little pick me up. Energize yourself with that old youthful zest. Or perhaps you're just craving the taste. Nothing quite like it, is there?"

Max's mouth suddenly filled with the coppery taste of the forbidden meat. His heart raced as he recalled the experience after its consumption. He closed his eyes, trying to push away the sensations and regain composure.

I'm not that person anymore.

"I'm craving a different taste today," he countered with confidence. Just as his memory of the streets returned, so did his ability to deal with its shifty citizens. There was a verbal game you had to play and he knew the rules. "She's about five-four, brown hair, green eyes." His face remained stoic. "She's definitely not from around here. I saw her on the outskirts; had a feeling she was looking for a butcher. I want her and I'm willing to pay."

He waited as the Other tilted his head and studied Max with vertical pupils. Its response could be the difference between finding Stephanie and losing a lead.

"You're lucky," he said. "I know the one. Real young girl, fresh fetus. Came in last night. I have the delicacy. I can have it prepared anyway you like, or you can take it fresh."

"I appreciate the offer, but I just want the girl. For her, I'll pay." The commonplace tone of his own voice made Max's stomach knot. But that was the city and that was how he needed to talk. On any given day, a thousand people negotiated and bought items that were just as vile without showing any emotion other than greed and lust.

"Why waste your time on that girl? I have plenty of women, not currently suffering from the knife," the creature tried to seal a deal.

"Other sixteen-year-olds? I doubt it. I like them as young as possible. That's why I'm here. No meat. Just the girl. I was hoping to snag her before she made it to a butcher, but she's still acceptable."

The creature nodded, believing Max's farce, and came out from around the bar. "You humans and your love of young twat. Follow me."

The creature took him up a rickety staircase, and down a hallway. Blood stained floorboards lined the hall and muffled moans of pain and pleasure escaped through the paper-thin doors on either side. They stopped at the last door, and the Other retrieved a key. Max could hear faint crying from inside the room.

The door swung open revealing Stephanie, sprawled out on a sheet-less mattress supported by a steel frame. A bloody towel filled with ice was nestled between her legs. The creature leaned over and whispered a price in Max's ear. He nodded and handed over some of the money he received from Stephanie's father.

"Enjoy," the thing smiled and retreated down the hall.

"Who are you?" Stephanie stammered through tears.

"Not a word. I'm taking you home." The girl, who only two days ago had been so eager to leave home, made no argument.

Max checked her sutures. The bleeding had stopped, but she'd have to see a real doctor as soon as possible. He hadn't been in time to save her unborn child, but at least he had Stephanie. He wondered if she knew why abortions were so valued inside the walled city. Few people did. Leave it to the Others to figure it out and then make a business of it.

Together they struggled down the stairs and past the bar.

The exit beckoned, but before they reached it an Other's voice called out.

"Max Elliot. I thought I smelt you. Welcome back."

Still supporting Stephanie over his shoulder, Max turned slightly. The butcher, an Other that had sold to Max years ago, had come from the kitchen and joined the bartender. A blood smeared apron was pulled tightly across his obese belly and sweat dripped down his grinning face.

"Just wanted the girl, huh?"

"Yeah," Max responded coldly.

"Sure I can't offer her a taste?" the fiendish butcher asked. "She'll be healed in no time. Won't even have the scars. But you know all about that, Max."

The teen looked up at him through confused eyes. She really didn't understand.

"No thanks," Max said.

"How about you, then? How many years you think you got left, Max?" The creature didn't give him a chance to respond, "You'll have a hell of a lot more once you eat again."

Max said nothing. He was too busy swallowing the rising bile that burned his esophagus. Remembering his past always made him sick. Back then, Max had made several trips to the butcher, eagerly accepting the embryonic delicacies, and reaping their rejuvenating rewards. Yet he hadn't stopped there. In addition to the butcher, Max had engaged in a wide array of other services offered by the city. All of which he now regretted.

But that's the past, and I aim to keep it that way.

"Huh. Well, I bet you'll be back soon enough."

"I doubt it," Max muttered. Stephanie buried her tear-soaked face into his coat and the two headed out to begin the arduous journey home.

Max was thankful when the crumbling archway finally rose into view over the boisterous crowds. As Max and Stephanie crossed under the only way out, two young girls passed by them, chatting excitedly. He stopped and stared at them. Their faces were smooth and vibrant, completely devoid of the hard, cracked lines that were almost customary of the city women. Their voices, too, were healthy and full of life. Neither looked pregnant, and Max couldn't fathom what reason the two could have for visiting the walled city. What poison could they possibly be searching for that would lead them to such a depraved place?

For a split second, Max thought about grabbing the girls and telling them to run. To run far away because all the city does is take. It lies through smiling lips, promising the fulfillment of untold desires. But in the end, it sucks a person dry and spits them out as nothing more than a faded shell of their former self. And that only described those who were lucky enough to get away from the city's stranglehold of doom.

But Max said nothing. He simply watched as the bright-eyed girls wandered deeper into the maze of streets, eventually being swallowed up by the sea of faded souls and creatures.

About the Authors

Ben A. Bell was born in Boston, MA, but now lives overseas and works as a freelance writer. His short story "Le Collier Diabolique" is available on Smashwords. His works have appeared in: Niteblade, Emerald Tales, Pill Hill Press - 365 Days of Flash Fiction, Farspace 2, Literal Translations, Pill Hill Press - Rotting Tales, and Whortleberry Press - Peace on all the Earths. He blogs at: http://www.bellshadow.blogspot.com/

Nate D. Burleigh lives in Vancouver WA with his wife and three children. He's been writing pros for nearly three years and has a baker's dozen short stories published in various venues to include ezines and print anthologies. His thinking is that he has finally found something he really enjoys doing. His debut novel "Sustenance" has been published by Panic Press and his second novel "Origin" is now in the editing stages. Please drop by his blog at http://natedburleigh.blogspot.com or his Facebook page and let him know how you liked the story.

Aaron Polson currently lives in Lawrence, Kansas with his wife, two sons, and a tattooed rabbit. During the day, Aaron works as a mild-mannered high school English teacher. His stories have been reprinted in The Best of Every Day Fiction 2009 and 2010, listed as a recommended read by Tangent Online, received honorable mention in the South Million Writers Award and Ellen Datlow's Best Horror of the Year. Aaron prefers ketchup with his beans. You can visit him online at www.aaronpolson.net.

Natalie L. Sin is a horror writer living in the Midwest. Her stories have appeared in various print and online publications including "Necrotic Tissue," "The New Bedlam Project", and "The Red Penny Papers." When not writing, Sin enjoys strong coffee, Japanese rock, and dreams of tuna.

Monique Bos is author of The Dark Jests of Lost Ghosts: An Urban Gothic Tale and Subversions: Short Stories and Poems. She collects gargoyles, loves bad creature movies, regularly visits the zoo (where she recently was bitten by a giraffe), and moonlights as a book scout.
During the day, she teaches writing classes at a community college. She, her dog, and her three cats live in Colorado.

Jenna M. Pitman is a writer from the Pacific Northwest. Her work has appeared in a variety of locations both online and off. To learn more please visit http://rejectedrefuse.livejournal.com.

Nathan Crowder is a Seattle-area author and HWA member with strong ties to his southwest roots. He is primarily known for his short and long superhero fiction, as well as darker pieces in such collections as Cthulhurotica, Rigor Amortis, and Close Encounters of the Urban Kind. He has a particular love of music and keeps a constant soundtrack going while he works. This is his third musically inspired story. He can be found online at www.nathancrowder.com

G. Winston Hyatt remembers well a time that came one day in the Year of the Fox. His work has appeared in Criminal Class Review, Necrotic Tissue, Night Terrors: An Anthology of Horror, and other places.

David Renfrow is a part time fiction writer living in Harrisburg, PA. David splits his time between learning to be a children/family therapist during the day, and using his free time to explore the darkest recesses of the human psyche. David mostly writes horror and dark fantasy. Previous work has appeared in numerous anthologies from Living Dead Press, Pill Hill Press, and Static Movement. He can be reached at zombiedave09@gmail.com.

Mark Taylor comes from the southeast of England and writes horror and SF. His love of horror spawned at an early age, and he's never stopped following it. He continues to work towards his novels, all the whilst maintaining his first love - shorts. You can usually find him or contact him through his blog: www.filingwords.blogspot. com.

Neil Willis won his first short story competition at the tender age of 8 years old – a ripping yarn about pirates and giant frogs. Sadly this promising start was put on hold while he pursued other interests: girls, basketball, exams, several careers, one wife and two offspring.
Neil (now a little over 40) has finally found the time to return to writing, focusing mainly on Flash Fiction and the occasional poem. Neil lives in rural Oxfordshire with the same one wife and their two extraordinary children.

Claire L. Fishback has been writing horror, thriller and suspense since she was eleven years old. She has written four novel length pieces and hundreds of short stories. She lives in Morrison, CO with her amazing husband, Tim, and dog, Belle.

Chris Samson lives north of Boston. He grew up in the 1980s wanting to become a teacher (specifically an archeologist), writer (specifically for the Daily Planet), or ninja (the kind that ate pizza and lived in the sewer). He has pursued all three careers with varying degrees of success. His stories also appear in LL Dreamspell's ebooks, Dreamspell Haunts Vol. 2, and Dreamspell Steampunk Vol. 1. Follow him on Twitter at Strangeverse, or drop him a line at Mr.Chris.Samson@Gmail.com. Rock on, readers.

Marc Sorondo lives with his wife and daughter in New York. He's had other work published by Pill Hill Press, Post Mortem Press, Wicked East Press, and UnEarthed Press.

Joleen Kuyper likes to write dark stories of all genres, in which terrible things happen to her characters. In real life though she is actually quite a nice person. She likes reading, cooking, eating and going for walks - on the rare occasions she can be torn away from her laptop, home to her writing and her internet addiction.

A resident of the Tongass Forest where the average annual rainfall is approximately 13 feet, **Bryan Oftedahl** tends to find plenty of spare time to burning. Since watching a late night horror fest on television at the age of seven he has preferred the darker end of the literary spectrum. Writing since early teens, literature has thus far proven to be his favored means of staying occupied during free time either writing or reading, doesn't really matter. Only recently has he been seeking publication but even at the foot of that path it's more of a hobby than a career move.

Quentin Pittman is a practicing attorney, amateur magician, and teller of tall tales. He lives with his wife and four children in Wichita, Kansas.

KV Taylor hails from the foothills of West Virginia, but currently lives in the DC Metro area with her husband and mutant cat. Her short fiction can be found at kvtaylor.com, and her first novel, Scripped, is forthcoming from Belfire Press in June 2011. She edits for Morrigan Books and collects *The Red Penny Papers* in her dining room.

Belen Lopez is a student. She lives in California.

Morgan Dambergs is a big speculative fiction fan, and she's been writing fantasy, horror and science fiction stories for almost as long as she can remember. Her short story "Reflections" won first place in the FenCon VI Short Story Competition in 2009, and has been accepted for publication in the charity anthology Amaterasu. You can find her writing and publishing blog at invitingghosts.blogspot.com.

Somewhere in southern California lurks a creature by the name of **Robert Essig**. This beast is known to have a macabre fascination with horror and is fortunate to implore an imp of whom whispers dark delicacies to him in the night. Robert's fiction has been in over 30 publications including Necrotic Tissue, Bards and Sages Quarterly, The Zombist (Library of the Living Dead), and Tales of the Talisman. He is the editor of the anthologies Through the Eyes of the Undead (Library of the Living Dead) and Malicious Deviance (Library of Horror). Visit him at:
robertessig.blogspot.com.

www.ingramcontent.com/pod-product-compliance
Lightning Source LLC
LaVergne TN
LVHW091149080826
845145LV00008B/2310

* 9 7 8 0 9 8 4 5 4 0 8 4 6 *